THE BIRD TABLE

Also by this author

GIVEN IN EVIDENCE
UNDISCLOSED MATERIAL
ON APPEAL

THE BIRD TABLE

Jonathan Davies

A *Little, Brown* Book

First published in Great Britain in 2002
by Little, Brown

Copyright © 2002 Jonathan Davies

The moral right of the author has been asserted.

A CIP catalogue record for this book
is available from the British Library.

HARDBACK ISBN 0 316 85947 8

Typeset by Hewer Text Ltd, Edinburgh
Printed and bound in Great Britain by
Clays Ltd, St Ives plc

Little, Brown
An imprint of
Time Warner Books UK
Brettenham House
Lancaster Place
London WC2E 7EN

www.TimeWarnerBooks.co.uk

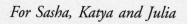

For Sasha, Katya and Julia

THE BIRD TABLE

Prologue

He stamped his boot hard into the embankment, but couldn't get a proper foothold. Each step needed two or three kicks into the sodden earth to prevent him from sliding down the steep slope. Who would have thought it would be so difficult? The bank was only about twenty feet high, but the whole way down he was forced to cling to the wet grass just to stop himself from going straight into the water. Mud began to cake his tunic trousers, and water began to seep into his boots. Then his foot slipped, his back arched, a tuft of grass gave way in his hand and he slid the last few feet towards the drainage ditch. The only thing that prevented him from going right in was the body. He tried to get to his feet but the narrow bank wasn't firm enough, he could feel it giving way beneath him. Eventually he leaned back against the steep earth behind him, gasping for breath. A large lorry, high enough to spill light down from the motorway above, swept past and at last he saw close up what he had glimpsed earlier. It was a man, half in and half out of the water.

The policeman couldn't see the face. Indeed it didn't seem very likely he had one, since the back of the head had been blown out.

Part One:
Cross-examination
for the Crown

1

Very early morning. The road was still, pale white in the moonlight, and frost shone on the long clipped beech hedge standing guard in front of the house. Sally, stepping carefully to protect her heels from the gravel, was still partly asleep, detached, hearing the sound of the wind. Tall skeletal outlines of last summer's cow parsley, too big surely to be just a year's growth, swayed gently in the sharp, cold air. Across the dark fields, moonlit shadows rippled softly over the winter plough, moving slowly down towards her as she walked to the garage. This was the time when everything paused. Life was still, so still you wondered whether it might never start up again.

The garage was heated, so getting into her car no longer involved scraping the windows, leaning over the bonnet awkwardly trying to keep her coat clean; instead the leather inside was soft, warm to the touch – she could feel it giving way beneath her leg when she twisted to drop her coat on to the back seat. Dim lights illuminated the interior and then faded away as she settled herself. When she turned the ignition key the engine fired so quietly that she could hardly hear it; almost the only sign that the motor was turning was the sudden spurt of the rev counter. The dials on the dashboard glowed green, adjusting themselves automatically to the level of light.

She pushed a button and the garage door lifted slowly, letting in the morning air. She edged the car down the drive, gravel crunching gently, up to the wide gates. The road was clear, she picked up speed as the gate clicked tight shut behind her.

She punched the radio. It took a moment to adjust itself and it wasn't until the corner of the road that a voice said, 'Welcome to *Farming Today*.' It was twenty to six. She turned the corner, sweeping up the Topham Cross slip road and on to the motorway, accelerating as the voice on the radio described the price of potatoes in different places.

The road was almost completely deserted, so she was right on time. She moved the car into the outside lane and effortlessly doubled her speed, then dropped it down a little. As long as she didn't go much faster the police wouldn't bother her. She knew that, she had checked it once, chatting to a senior traffic policeman at the back of a court. The quiet ease of the motor car soothed her. The tension of trying to get out of the house unnoticed dropped away.

The children hadn't stirred as she had showered and dressed – her room was far enough away for them not to hear her – but later she risked creeping in to run her hand over their heads. She pulled the covers around them and smoothed their hair back; her hand came away slightly damp. Bargee, the younger's teddy bear, had fallen between the bed and the side table. Sally picked it up and slid it beneath the sheet. The child accepted it immediately and turned over into a deeper sleep, her finger going automatically to her mouth.

Going into their room was tricky: one of them might wake up. One morning she had been completely delayed, late for court, flustered – the whole day had been ruined, and she had left a crying child calling behind her. But she found it just as hard to leave without going in to see them.

She had to leave before they woke: she thought about it, and told herself again that it was better. If she was out of the house when they awoke, then they didn't seem to mind, certainly they didn't show it. She smiled. How happy they were with Anne, the nanny. Sally clicked a fingernail on the steering wheel. She was fooling herself, of course they minded. But what was she expected to do? Throw it all away? Become a housewife?

Her attention was attracted back to the road. Headlights began to close up on her, and, whoever it was, he was doing at least a hundred, maybe more. She watched as the lights came nearer; she pulled over to her left and the car shot past. She stayed in the middle lane for a moment and then swung back in time to sweep past a Norbert Dentressangle lorry lumbering northward.

As she passed she glimpsed the driver looking down at her, a young woman in a powerful car. When she drove this road on summer evenings truck-drivers leaned out of their windows to call to her. She drifted away from the present and remembered the sweet, dark smell of the diesel in cabs of trucks when she was a student hitching rides. Once climbing in out of the night she had heard an old song,

With the windshield wipers slapping time,
As Bobby sang the blues,
Nothing ain't worth nothing, but it's free.

What the song said wasn't true, she was freer now than she ever had been. What she wanted to do, she did. Had it all come too easily?

The car swept on into London. The dark shadow of the Sun in Sands roundabout loomed above her, Blackheath to her left, then the long left and right sweep, down to the Blackwall Tunnel. Dawn was breaking to her right, reeking over Greenwich bay – *Here and here did England help me, how can I help England?*

Scraps of poetry and images from her past jostled her in the dark of the car. For a moment she luxuriated in thinking about nothing, or at least anything that happened to swim up into her consciousness, and then, with an act of decision exactly like that with which she had swung her legs out of bed that morning, she put her mind in order and focused on the problems that the day was going to bring.

Roger Nichols, accused of rape.

She had to cross-examine him straight away, and then, since it was unlikely he had any witnesses, make the closing speech for the Crown. With luck the whole thing would be finished by lunch time, or at least her part would be, and she would be able to start on another piece of work. They might even start the next case for her immediately in the court next door; it had been waiting for her to get free all the previous day. But that would depend on how the list office felt – after all, they ran the place.

She pulled off the Embankment just before Blackfriars,

turned past the palm trees, completely out of place here, cut in to the left under the building to avoid the traffic lights and seeing that the next lights were green outside Blackfriars station put her foot down hard. The car leapt forward, for the first time that morning giving a real demonstration of the speed of which it was capable, and she shot on to the roundabout at the north of the bridge. She pulled over to the right past Unilever and then turned sharp left. As she took the right-hand turn towards Tudor Street she glanced upwards at the gold statue of the housewife goddess over Unilever's back entrance. The one doing the dance of Siva with the soap packet.

She might have been that. Her mother had been, until she refused to do it any more and disappeared.

The barrier at the Temple entrance swung upwards.

'Good morning, Miss Donne.'

Sally stopped the car. 'How are you, Bert?'

'Well enough, Miss Donne,' Bert said, but his eyes shone. He knew what was coming and she knew the role that she was going to have to play.

'And how is that daughter of yours?' she said.

Bert beamed, hardly able to say anything, pleasure constricting his throat.

Sally acted out what was expected of her. From the very first the men with whom she worked had only ever wanted her to play a small number of roles, and as long as she did so, they hardly noticed her.

'In her last year now, Miss Donne, and she's working hard.'

'Well, you tell her from me, I expect a first-class degree. And then I expect her to present herself at my chambers, and we'll teach her how to work. You tell her that, Bert.'

She moved the car forward and stopped again, 'And Bert . . .' Bert stopped with the barrier raised in his hand. 'You tell her to come and see me whatever happens. Christ Church, indeed. In my day Somerville was good enough.'

This was the mixture as required, grande dame and friend. It would make Bert's day. She parked her car just inside the entrance, right in front of her chambers, collected her case and the flat bag of papers from the boot of the car and made her way up the steps. As she did so she heard a clock striking and the door ahead of her swung open. 'Seven o'clock, Miss Donne,' said the junior clerk as she went inside.

From outside you could see lights begin to spread out over the building, first vertically as she climbed the old staircase, then across the front as the huge Georgian windows, delicately criss-crossed with thin beading, lit up and shone down on to the great square. Inside, in the warm room, decorated like a country house save for the discarded wig and gown lying where one would normally expect a sewing basket, the junior clerk put her bags down and said, 'I'll get you some coffee, Miss Donne.'

Chambers slowly filled up. First the next junior clerk arrived, then a young member of chambers to collect papers which had come too late for him the night before. 'Could you get me a cab?' he asked the second clerk. There was a pause, and the barrister added, 'Not on the chambers account, of course.' The second clerk relaxed and said, 'Of course, Mr Pierce, sir. To Euston?' He knew where the barrister was going. He had booked the brief himself.

Sally worked on.

At half past nine the senior clerk arrived, and hanging

his cashmere coat on a bentwood peg he said, 'Has Miss Donne gone yet?' When he was told No, he said, 'Well, start organising her, please, William.'

William picked up the phone and dialled a number. 'Miss Donne is just leaving, could you make sure there is a place, please.' He waited for a reply, put the phone down, went upstairs and said, 'Miss Donne, you had better be getting over to the Bailey, I've confirmed a place in the car park behind for you. And Paul said to tell you that there is another matter you have to look at today.'

Sally acknowledged the clerk's call and continued writing for a moment, then she put down her pen and closed the papers. 'I'll go now,' she said.

They arrived at the car. The clerk opened the door and held it. It had started raining. Sally got in and then, just before it was too late, she rewarded him with a flashing smile, 'Thanks, William, I'll see you later.' He stood watching as the tail of the sports car whipped round the corner and out of sight.

2

'Come, come, Mr Nichols. You don't mean that, do you?'

'That is what happened.'

'You say, do you, that moments after making love to her, she was suddenly in a flaming temper?'

Sally Donne stood glistening in the well of the court. The black of her suit contrasted with her embroidered white collar and silk shirt. There was no decoration on the suit save the piping on the waist of her jacket and, just inside the flare of her cuff, a flash of a rich, coloured lining. 'You are saying that she was behaving irrationally, apparently not knowing from one moment to the next what she wanted of you?'

'It seemed so, yes.'

Roger Nichols was accustomed to dealing with strong opponents in business, and on occasion had bargained with tough women negotiators, but this was different. This lawyer had a way of asking a question that made any answer seem ridiculous. And what was worse, she was describing out loud things that he didn't even speak of with his close friends. Asking why he had done what he had done. You just do things, you don't think about it.

This was something for which he had no language. He looked down at his own counsel. He had warned him, but not even in Roger Nichols's nightmares had he imagined it could be like this. 'It seemed so?' Sally repeated what he was saying, giving him the opportunity to add a remark, and instead of staying silent he said something extra.

'This woman presented herself to me,' he said. 'Why should I refuse her?'

He wanted to say that he was perfectly capable of finding women more than willing to sleep with him, but he stopped himself. He had been specifically told to avoid saying that. But she was uncannily quick; it was as though she knew what he was thinking. 'You mean you can get a woman any time, so why should you bother to rape this one?' The question was so precise, so accurate, that his face instantly gave her the answer, and, when he tried to deny it, he did so a heartbeat late. Even if the jury had not noticed what had happened, he knew that she had. He felt even more defeated.

'Oh. So that's it, Mr Nichols, is it? You're an attractive man. You have no trouble with women. So why should you bother with taking this one by force? Is that what you're saying?'

'No, no.' Roger Nichols was discovering that it's not only facts that betray you, but your feelings as well. Lying about either infects what you say.

'I'll suggest a reason then, and you tell me if it's true. This woman worked in a nightclub and because of that you assumed she was sexually available. Isn't that what you thought?'

13

Again this was so exactly what he had thought that he couldn't deny it, although why should thinking a woman was available mean he was going to rape her? He had to try to say that. Normally he would have been able to do so but it was becoming increasingly difficult: the lawyer was identifying attitudes in him which, when she described them, seemed shameful, though he hadn't at the time thought them shameful. He still didn't think so, but nevertheless he seemed to confirm that they were with every answer he gave. It was all coming out back to front. He couldn't understand it.

'No. It wasn't like that,' he said. She was even beginning to convince him that he was guilty.

'You offered her money to keep her quiet.'

Again it was twisted. He had offered the woman money because he thought she expected it. Perhaps that was what had made her angry, suddenly realising he thought she was a prostitute.

'Now you say that's why she became angry. But why should she become angry if she agreed to have sex with you?'

'I can't say what she thought . . .'

'But you are doing so, Mr Nichols. You're saying that you thought she agreed to what happened.'

'I didn't think she agreed. I know she did.' He felt a bit stronger.

'You mean she is lying now?'

'Of course she is.'

'But if she was going to your room for money, then all she had to do was take it when it was offered.'

'I thought she was doing it for money. I was obviously wrong. She must have felt insulted.' There. He had managed to get it out, but by then it sounded so weak.

14

'You haven't said that before.'

'I've never been asked that.' The moment the words left his mouth he realised it was a catastrophic remark.

'Nothing else, Mr Nichols.' Sally took her time. 'You've been asked nothing else. In the police station, in this court. That's all that this whole investigation has been about.'

He could say nothing.

'But you want the jury to accept your word for it when you say you thought she agreed?'

He looked at her, momentarily confused by the change of subject. She repeated the question. Again he felt he had let himself down, as though failing to understand the question would seem to the jury like an attempt to avoid it.

'You said you were wrong about offering her money. If you were wrong about such a simple thing as that, how then can the jury accept your word upon whether she agreed?'

'I'm sorry.' By now he felt it was more important to explain that he hadn't heard her, not that he was trying to avoid the question. 'I didn't hear you,' he said, then he realised he was making it worse.

'All right, Mr Nichols. I understand that. But what is the answer, now you have heard the question?'

'Could you repeat it?' he said.

'If you were wrong about the money, why should the jury think you are right about her consenting?'

He listened and replied, 'But it's not the same thing.' The two ideas were entirely different, yet in the atmosphere of the court they had become fused together.

'It is the same. You want the jury to accept that you

15

made an unfortunate mistake over her being a prostitute, but that you were right about her consenting to your doing what you did.'

Roger Nichols looked at Sally Donne. He knew that his whole life was turning on how he dealt with these questions, but he could see no way to combat her manner, so confident was she, so assured. Every time she touched a question, any normal response was turned inside out. He sensed it was merely a technique, but in the few moments he had to react, he couldn't counter it.

He tried. 'The way you are putting it – you are running things together, things that don't go together.'

'Am I, Mr Nichols? Well, we shall have to let the jury decide upon that, won't we?'

Jeremy Scott wanted to put his head in his hands, but he controlled himself and sat, staring ahead, not looking at his client.

Sally's perfume, very slight, but just noticeable, lingered in counsel's row, overcoming the rather dank smell of the law books piled on to the seat next to him. The books smelled slightly because they were still wet. They had got wet when he was caught in the rain on the way to court that morning. He had only avoided a complete soaking by jumping on a bus. The bus had stopped conveniently, stuck in the traffic on Fleet Street, and he had sunk gratefully on to the long seat by the open door. He settled and looked around him. Inside it was warm and damp; the few passengers sat clutching their bags on their knees and for a moment Scott felt he was part of an ordinary life, not like the one he was heading for at the Old Bailey up the hill. Life there was cut through and through with tension

16

and anger. But then, who knows? He couldn't know what fears lay behind those detached faces opposite him.

He liked buses, especially the old ones, small public meetings on wheels. His father had driven a bus when a medical student, and had told him about the skid pans, and that judge on the south coast, he had been a bus conductor. Scott sat quietly. Then the bus became caught up in the traffic again, just before Ludgate Circus, and he watched, doing the thing people on buses do best: doing nothing.

A smart black sports car pulled up behind them with a slight sigh of brakes on the damp road. Scott looked down at the windscreen and through the reflections on the glass he could see Sally Donne. She was tapping her finger to a rhythm, staring straight ahead of her. He was able to watch her unnoticed.

She was sitting in the car slightly sideways, her skirt tucked up at the knee, completely relaxed, deep in thought. He was affected by her sudden presence, as if walking in the country he had glimpsed a bright bird all colour and dash, intense and live, and out of reach. She looked up at him, but obviously couldn't see him through the glass of the bus. He watched her looking towards him. She had an air of complete self-possession. He had noticed that about her before, and like anything of which you would like to be part, but which exists on its own in complete disregard of you, it was tantalising.

It didn't take much to make him feel cut off, but nothing did it with quite this intensity. Here was a person completely in control of her life, successful, and completely indifferent to him. How absurd the feeling was. He noticed his mood and judged it. He and Sally

17

hardly knew each other, but then that was the point, wasn't it?

A gap opened up in the inside lane and Sally's car surged forward, weaving neatly around the back of a van stuck in the middle of Ludgate Circus. She flew up the hill out of Scott's sight, gone. She was getting to court her way, he in his. Her way didn't involve getting wet.

'If you thought she was a prostitute why did you not say that to the police officer who was called to the hotel?'

'I was embarrassed. There were so many people in the room.'

'The police officer warned you, didn't he, that you should say anything that mattered there and then?'

'It was difficult. I was shocked.'

'But you're a man of the world. You've been about a bit. Why not just speak up?'

'It's different.'

'It's meant to be different, Mr Nichols. That's why you were told you should say anything that needed saying.'

'I couldn't believe what was happening. I didn't under-stand it.' Roger Nichols wanted to say it seemed so absurd.

'Are you saying you didn't understand what the officer was saying?'

'Well, not like that.'

'Because you didn't say so at the time. The officer who arrested you says he asked specifically if you understood what he was arresting you for. That's right?'

'Yes.'

'And now you are saying you didn't understand?'

'No, no. I meant at the time I was confused. The sudden arrival of the police.'

18

'They took half an hour to arrive at the hotel, Mr Nichols.'

'I didn't mean that.'

'What do you mean, Mr Nichols?'

The judge interrupted. It was like a referee at a boxing match intervening to prevent further punishment.

'If you could pause there for a moment, Miss Donne.' The judge beckoned to where the court clerk sat on a seat below her. Scott turned his face up to the domed roof of the court. It looked as though Mr Nichols was going down like a lead balloon. Five years at least, maybe more.

Five years' imprisonment. He reflected upon it. You would have to steal a million in the City to get five years' imprisonment. Even then you might not get five years. It always surprised him when the newspapers said that the courts didn't take rape seriously: there were very few offences where the sentence was five years for a first offence.

He looked up to where the judge was sitting, only to discover her looking straight back at him. He kept his gaze steady and she turned away. The judge was wearing a ruff, at least that's what Scott thought it was called, an explosion of lace at her throat. Scott knew her. She was everything a modern judge should be: educated at a local high school, her father a policeman . . .

'We shall rise now,' the judge said, 'and sit again in an hour. Unfortunately I have other matters with which I must deal immediately.' Scott could hear the prepositions being marched into their proper places. The judge glanced at Scott, as if checking that he was not reacting in a way that needed correction, turned and left the court.

* * *

'You're being a bit heavy on him, aren't you?' Scott had bought Sally Donne a cup of coffee and stood pouring one out for himself.

Sally was amused. 'What do you mean?'

'Well, anything anybody says in a witness box can be made to look absurd – if you ask the question in the right way.'

Sally said nothing.

'Yes?' Scott said and looked at her for an answer. He was forcing her to reply, so she did.

'This isn't a game, Jeremy.'

'That's exactly what I mean. It isn't a game, but when you cross-examine you make it just that. Running ideas together, for instance. Just because a question is capable of being asked that doesn't mean it's capable of a sensible answer.' He stopped. Even his incompetent grasp of relationships enabled him to realise he was being too aggressive. They took their coffees over to a group sitting in the deep armchairs at the other end of the large, light room. Sally immediately became the centre of attention. Scott sat on the edge of the group and looked out of the window.

He could see Big Ben above the buildings – those buildings had to be the south side of the Strand – and in the far distance he could make out a green canopy of trees. They must be in a park. Where would that be? Surely not Richmond, that was much too far away. Above the city a jet glistened in the sky.

Looking down from planes coming back from holiday Scott had often seen London laid out below, vast, yet at the same time a tiny plan of itself. He used to pick out the various courts dotted through the capital; he supposed if he were a doctor he would do the same for the hospitals. Snaresbrook Crown Court was almost the first landmark you saw in London beneath the flight path of the planes wheeling in over the Essex marshes. It was easy to identify because of the lake beside it.

He remembered picking out Fleet Street, looking like a narrow canyon from above. The people in the jet would be looking down on him now. They might even see the glint of the light on the statue of Justice on the top of the Bailey.

'You don't, do you, Jeremy?'

'Don't what?' He was taken aback. Sally was speaking to him.

'You don't care.'

'About what?'

The group with which she was sitting laughed at his confusion.

'See what I mean? He's not with us.' She turned back to him. 'About getting ahead, Jeremy.' She was explaining.

'What are you talking about?'

One of the men said, 'Sally was saying that there were those people who wanted to get ahead, and there were those for whom it wasn't important, who don't care. She said she was one of the first and that you were one of the second.'

They continued looking at him, expecting a response.

'That's wrong,' said Scott. 'I do care. It's just that I'm not much good at it. Don't imagine I wouldn't like to, just like Sally.'

They laughed.

'Well, at least I don't pretend I'm not ambitious,' she said. 'Do you think I enjoy inviting judges to supper?'

A young man appeared at Sally's shoulder; he was

carrying a freshly prepared bundle of papers tied in red tape, a defence brief. 'Here's the papers for tomorrow, miss.'

Sally took the papers from him and got up in one movement, 'Thank you, William.' She unfolded the papers. 'What is this William? Why am I being asked to do this? This is defence work.'

'Paul said to give it to you, miss,' the young man answered.

'But I won't be free. The thing I'm doing now will go into tomorrow.'

'That's arranged. Your court isn't sitting before lunch. This judge has other work in her list.'

'How long will it take?'

'Not long, Paul says.'

'OK . . .' Sally was doubtful.

'Who's this?' she said as she sat down again.

'Defence solicitors,' said one. 'Isn't that Monty Bach? Jeremy, you'd know. Isn't that the firm Monty Bach works for?'

Scott looked up. 'Yes. Why?'

'Sally asked.'

'You're not going to work for Monty, are you?' Scott said. 'You're a prosecutor.'

'We'll see,' Sally said, getting up. 'Look at the time, Jeremy. We have to get on with it or I won't finish cross-examining today.'

'You're married?'

'Yes.'

'But separated?'

'Yes. Sadly.'

'Not your fault then?'

'No.'

'Is it never your fault?'

Scott stirred in his seat. Sally was obviously going to go all out now. He knew he would have to intervene sooner or later, though one look at the judge's face told him he was not going to get anywhere.

'What do you mean?'

'Is it never your fault, Mr Nichols?'

'I don't know what you mean.'

'Perhaps that's the point. You take what you want, don't you?'

'How?'

'You did here.'

'I did not.'

'What about the mark on her arm?'

'That was nothing to do with me.'

'She said you grabbed her arm.'

'I didn't hit her.'

'I'm not suggesting you did. Why do you want to deny that, when it has not been suggested?'

Roger Nichols had no reply.

'Of course grabbing is exactly what somebody taking what they want does, isn't it?'

Scott said, 'How can he answer that?'

'Are you objecting, Mr Scott?' the judge said icily.

'I am pointing out he can't answer that. It's an invitation to argument, not a question.'

The judge said, 'Well, let's see, shall we, before we interrupt?'

Scott looked at the ceiling.

'These marks, let's consider them again.'

'They were nothing to do with me. I didn't touch her that way.'

'So you've said.'

Roger Nichols wanted to say, 'Women bruise easily sometimes,' but he was learning, and he said nothing. Though it was true, of course: his wife used to show him bruises on her thigh where she had only bumped against the kitchen table. Bumping against a table had never bruised his leg. But if you said that sort of thing in this company you would merely be accused of making excuses for violence against women.

'No doubt you would say women bruise easily?'

He didn't reply.

'You would say most women on the jury probably have bruises like this?'

'I didn't hit her.'

'Yes, but you were quite prepared to have sex half-dressed?'

For a moment Scott reeled. What on earth did that have to do with it? Sally promptly provided the answer.

'This wasn't exactly a loving moment, was it?'

'No,' said Nichols.

'And it involved violence?'

'No.'

'You didn't even bother to get undressed.'

'No.'

'You just wanted your satisfaction?'

'This was a paid transaction in a hotel bedroom. At least I thought it was.'

'Luckily for her a member of the hotel staff came in.'

'I did not rape her.'

24

'When that happened, you didn't say, "Wait a minute," or "Hang on," you just ran for the bathroom.'

'I went to the bathroom, I didn't run. Anyway, what was I meant to say?'

'You could have shown some consideration for her.'

'I don't see how.'

'She burst into tears.'

Nichols said nothing.

'Why do you think she did that?'

'That's not a question he can answer,' Scott said, risking it again.

The judge said nothing, and Sally began again. 'Why do you think—'

'This is an improper question. I invite the court to intervene.'

'I don't think I need do so,' said the judge. 'I think Miss Donne is moving on.'

'I'll put it another way.' Sally turned to the defendant. 'You say, of course, that moments before she was quite happy?'

'Yes.'

'And promptly, the moment someone else arrived, she was in tears, shouting at you.'

'Is that a question?' said Scott. This was getting nasty.

'Mr Scott, be quiet.'

Scott sat and watched as Sally kept going at Roger Nichols. This was the kind of cross-examination the Old Bailey used to revel in, and now that rape had been elevated into a special sort of sin it seemed to be coming back.

Sally said, 'Something must have made her cry. Something must have caused the bruise. But none of that was your fault, Mr Nichols?'

25

'No.'
'It never is your fault?'
No reply.
'Oh well . . .' Sally said, sitting down.

The court rose, clattering in the dust. 'You did all right,' Scott said to his client. It wasn't true, but he had to say something.

'No. I was awful,' said Roger Nichols. 'I kept saying the stupid thing, when I should have kept my mouth shut.'

'You were OK, Mr Nichols. It's not easy to stand up to that sort of cross-examination. The jury will realise that.'

'No, they won't.'

Of course Scott's client was right. The jury, unless they were unusual, wouldn't bother with the difference between a fair question and an unfair one. Roger Nichols was depressed. He said, 'You know what I won't be able to stand? I can cope with going to prison, but people looking at me and saying, "He's a rapist," I won't be able to deal with that.'

Scott wasn't anxious to go on talking, and there was nothing much to be said. He stood still as his client left the court.

It had been awful. The cross-examination had become a rout. Sally had been able to ask any question and make the defendant seem evasive. Of course those questions had proved very little, save that she was better at asking questions than the defendant was at answering them. Nothing to do with the case: they were all designed to make him seem unattractive. By asking them she had managed to turn a weak case against him into a strong one. It was not a cross-examination designed to find out new facts, and it was made worse by the defendant's confusion in the face of it, confusion which seemed like a guilty reaction. Scott had done it to witnesses himself, and afterwards had always felt slightly sick, as though he had been cruel to something helpless. And even helplessness seemed to tell against the defendant, as though an innocent man would be armed against this sort of attack. But Scott knew that innocence was not the best defence in a criminal court; in fact innocence in these circumstances was a handicap.

He came to himself standing between the double doors leading into the court. Behind him the courtroom was being cleared, glasses and water being gathered up, and the jury papers put away. The room was resuming its profound indifference to the little tragedies played out in its gloomy interior. Scott set off across the central hall, his steps ringing on the tiles. He looked up at the painting on the ceiling where a beefy nurse perpetually rescued an injured man from a bombed building while, in the background, the Old Bailey burned. It wasn't a good picture, painted just after the war, but maybe its quality was that it was entirely lacking in self-consciousness; perhaps the last time that was possible. Scott took the lift and found himself standing in it with Sally.

He knew that he ought to be able to drop straight out of what was going on in court and become indifferent, but this time he needed a little longer. Sally looked at him and laughed. 'Say something to me, Jeremy, even if it's only that you think I'm being unfair. Because you obviously do.'

'Well, there is that.'

Sally said, 'It looks to me as if you're in danger of believing your client. I'm told that's a great mistake for a defence lawyer to make.'

'Well, it's certainly the mistake you're making.'

'Oh no. I'm just testing his story.'

'That wasn't testing.'

Sally could see he was angry. She paused and then she said, 'Jeremy, I said it before – this is the real world, it's not a game,' and when the lift doors opened she walked straight away from him into the women's robing room.

He changed and went downstairs, distracted by what had happened. She was right of course. When you got to this court fairness wasn't relevant. If you prosecuted at the Old Bailey, you did so to get the defendant convicted and that was that, fairness didn't enter into it. Scott had spent too long doing second-rate work, where there wasn't any real pressure, cases where it didn't very much matter if a man got off wrongly. In those cases one could indulge in the luxury of excessive fairness. But here, if a guilty man got off, it might enable him to bomb or murder again, so understandably the atmosphere was a little different. He knew that his reaction only showed he wasn't at home in the hard world. Sally reacted like that because she was, she was a proper prosecutor. He shut his mind to it; it was a bit late now to worry about that. In fact even thinking about it was an illustration of the same weakness.

Ways of beginning his closing speech were starting to run through his head, and as he left the building he stood for a moment in the security doors, trying out an opening sentence. Eventually he pushed his way out and discovered it was still raining. The world had continued turning.

He stood considering the case. The problem was that it was so easy to picture Roger Nichols as a rapist, not only because the cross-examination had been designed to make him look like one, but also because the image of violent

28

men had become part of the currency of ideas – all men take what they want, all men are rapists. But then it wasn't long ago that the very idea of a woman consenting with pleasure to sex had been indecent, so maybe it was only a necessary shift in the balance of things: the disapproval had to light upon something, it couldn't just disappear. And of course it was ironic that women had then been the guardians and creators of that original disapproval as well.

There was a slight overhang at the main door of the court and Scott stood for a moment in the shelter trying to cover the bundle of papers he was carrying. He realised he was standing next to Terry Davies, the officer in charge of the case. Scott knew him well and, warily, they liked each other. The policeman turned and spoke to him, almost as though he had been waiting for the opportunity. 'It's an odd one, this one, Mr Scott.'

'Why do you say that, Terry?'

'She didn't fit.'

'Oh? What are you saying?'

'Well.' Terry Davies paused, then he said, 'You know that what I think of the case isn't relevant, Mr Scott?'

Scott was non-committal. 'Not out here,' he said.

'It's not that I think he's innocent, Mr Scott, it's that I think there's something that doesn't fit. He's guilty? OK, but it still doesn't fit.' Scott said nothing, waiting, then it came: 'I just wonder whether she would have reported it at all if that maid had not wandered in.'

'The maid,' Scott said.

'It's the first complaint that tells you most. As well as the injuries, of course, if there are any. But how the woman gets the story out to begin with, that's what matters. And this one was odd.'

29

'Did you question that chambermaid properly?'

'Mr Scott, we had her there for six hours.'

'Why?'

'To find out what she was doing there.'

They stared gloomily at the fake Irish pub across the road, where the Rumboe had been. A man in a cape unlocked a bicycle from the railings and a taxi swished past. 'But there you are, Mr Scott, we've got Miss Donne on our side, haven't we? She makes up for any small holes in our case.'

'That's just what's worrying me, Terry,' Scott said. He stood there, but Terry wasn't going to say any more, and Scott set off through the rain down towards Blackfriars station.

The woman who had accused Roger Nichols of rape was a nightclub hostess. She had willingly gone to his hotel room and had helped him drink most of a bottle of champagne. One thing that struck Scott was that it was she who had ordered the wine. To Scott that meant she was familiar with the place, maybe even had an interest in the cost of a bottle, but when he asked her about it, all she would say was that she had stayed there before. What for? Scott hadn't got anywhere on that at all.

Well, she hadn't been invited upstairs for polite conversation, she must have known that. The notion, as she claimed, that she hadn't even contemplated the idea of sex was frankly ridiculous, but she insisted that she had not. 'Just because I go to someone's room, it doesn't mean I am agreeing to have sex,' she said, and she had the whole weight of political correctness on her side. Then a maid had blundered into the room, just as she started screaming. Or was it just before she started? That was the crux.

Roger Nichols had sworn that the screaming had started after the maid arrived. He said it was the maid's arrival that had started the whole thing off. For a moment it looked as though they would be able to show that the maid was in on it, a classic set-up. But that possibility had dissolved when they discovered she had only started work at the hotel that morning. Her arrival was, as the Crown said, mere chance. But to Scott it hadn't felt right either.

He walked down the hill to Blackfriars station, bought a ticket, queued and climbed on to the packed train without even noticing what he was doing. He drifted off again.

Americans see relationships in terms of power. In the States you can't *be* racist if you don't have power over the other person. Maybe they see sexual power the same way? But she had ordered the champagne, she was in control, that made it odd. And she didn't seem the type that Roger Nichols could overwhelm. That wasn't a physical judgement, but an emotional one. The woman just didn't seem like someone to be pushed around.

Scott wondered how he could include all this in his speech. It wasn't possible. There was no rule against a woman ordering champagne.

He read the newspaper over the shoulder of the girl standing in front of him. She turned the page and Scott never discovered whether the vicar had actually slept with his parishioner or not. 'Bonking vicars', 'call girls', 'sexy romps': it was odd how newspaper images were generally about twenty years behind the times. Perhaps it was the same with juries. Were they thinking of this case in the same way?

Half an hour later Scott found himself at home. The speech had developed a little, though he still hadn't worked it out. It wasn't coming easily, but he had all night to get it. He started opening cupboards looking for a drink. It was this half-state that was the best for developing speeches. He wandered around his flat picking things up as he tried out various phrases.

Much later the telephone rang.

'Jeremy?'

'Yes?'

'It's Stephen here. Something's come up. Would you be able to come over and advise us?'

Stephen was the solicitor in this very trial.

'Now?'

'Yes.'

'About this case?'

'Yes, but I don't know the detail. Vic rang us and said someone had got through to him on the emergency line. He had something to tell us.'

'What?'

'We're not exactly sure. But it was about some sort of set-up. If it's what I think it is, then we want to treat it with kid gloves.'

'Where are you now?'

'I'm heading for the office. I'll be there in forty-five minutes. The witness is coming now.'

'The Brixton office?'

'Yes.'

'I don't want to talk to anyone who might be a witness.'

'No, I just want you to be there to tell us what else we have to do.'

'OK. I'll be there in about forty minutes.'

The top of Brixton Hill is not a cosy place. Traffic roars across the South Circular, joining the stream coming up the hill from Brixton, turning the pavements into a wasteland. Scott pulled up outside the solicitor's office. There were no lights on. He had got there first. He sat outside in the car. Occasionally people passed by. Mostly they were heading for the Portuguese restaurant fifty yards down the road. A car drew up behind him and parked. No one got out. Scott sat feeling the presence of the other man. After a while he switched the radio on to block the feeling out. He listened to the antics of a journalist pursuing a victim up to his front door, asking awkward questions about the franchising company he ran. Scott paid half attention. The whole basis of the programme was a complete and uncritical assumption of the man's guilt. How many of the listeners would not just assume that the person who was being pursued was guilty, simply because he was being pursued? How many of the jury would have listened critically to the attack on Roger Nichols that afternoon?

Stephen arrived. Both Scott and the man from the car behind got out on to the pavement.

Later Scott started ringing round to find Sally's home number, and eventually they faxed through the statement that had just been taken from the witness.

'We have to send it to the Crown,' Scott had said. 'If this is the truth, then the sooner we do it the better, and at this stage we have to act as though it's true.'

Stephen looked unconvinced.

Scott said, 'It doesn't sound like fearless defending, but it'll make everything else much easier. After all, we're going to have to ask for time tomorrow, and then we're going to have to apply for the prosecution witness to be recalled, so we can put the allegation to her. We'll have to tell the court what it's all about then. And if we do it, it means we've been open with the prosecution. That's always worth a lot with the jury.'

'OK. Send it.'

'And Stephen, we have to tell the witness what we're doing.'

Stephen got up and went to the office next door. Scott could see the outline of a figure who must be the witness through the frosted glass. There was a conversation which he couldn't quite hear. He had to sit in another room, because of course barristers are not allowed to meet witnesses.

The conversation in the lift with Scott had annoyed Sally. She knew it was nonsense, but she couldn't get it out of her mind. Her job was straightforward. If the evidence was there she should use it to convict the defendant. It was simple: everyone she worked with played the same rules. There was no argument; whether the rules were right wasn't anything she ever thought about, it wasn't normally something that was ever discussed with the people who shared her chambers. But today she said, 'And then I was accused of bullying the defendant.'

'That's the nature of cross-examination, isn't it? I know that Scott, he's a wanker.'

'Of course,' she agreed to both comments.

'That's how the truth comes out. That's what cross-examination does.'

But still there was something in what Scott had said that had jarred. She was trying to identify what it was. She knew this conversation was merely the repetition of shared assumptions and wasn't going to answer what was un-settling her. Maybe she had gone too far?

'What bullying I see is always on the other side, the defence bullying the Crown. The defence gets away with everything, the judges have to let them.'

This was exactly what Sally thought, but she hesitated a moment before agreeing, though the hesitation made no difference.

'All we do is present evidence. It's not for us to say whether it's fair or not.' The subject was dealt with.

It was the detachment that sometimes troubled her, the exact application of the rules in disregard of everything else, even common sense. But you had to be hard, and hard with yourself. The points in a case were clear, and it ought to be possible to list them one by one, and having done that you had done the case. There was nothing left to talk about.

Her first years at the bar had been spent teasing out those questions, reading sets of papers, gutting them and producing a summary on which someone standing up before a court could rely, perhaps without even reading the documents. It was her chambers' rule that anybody should be able to pick up any set of papers on any desk and immediately present them to a jury. Doing that didn't allow time for worrying about the fairness of anything. Not only was there no time for it, it didn't arise. What the rules allowed you to do was, by definition, fair. Perhaps that was what Scott had been complaining about.

'Sally, I have to change the subject. We have to talk. Now if you're appointed, you know you're not going to be able to do that case with me.'

Sally was talking to Mickey Michaels, the senior silk in

chambers. He had been in practice so long that he embodied her chambers' standards, he didn't just set them.

Sally began to protest that they wouldn't appoint her. 'No, no,' he said. He wasn't interested in her over-modest reaction. 'What I want to know is this. If you can't do the case, can Sharma do it? Is she up to it?'

'No problem,' Sally said immediately, 'perfectly good.' She was going to say more, but Mickey shambled away; he had got his answer.

Sally could see Sharma standing outside the kitchen on the staircase holding a document. She was conservatively, almost dowdily, dressed, but what was immediately striking about her was her quiet determination. The document she held stood no chance. That was it: Sharma was committed to doing what Sally had done – she was exactly what Sally had been. There was no future in doubting things, no point in it. Doubt wasn't just weakness, it was worse: it laid the ground for incompetence. It allowed soft thinking, and that led nowhere at all. Sally started to pack her things to leave.

By the time she got home, the children were in bed. Her husband had arrived before her, and when she had come down from changing and looking in on the children he had almost finished eating. She stood by the cooker and watched him.

'Are you going to have anything?' he said.

'Maybe later. There's some pâté.' Pâté was high-energy food. He grunted, he was used to this.

'Do you have problems with fairness?' she said.

'Only when someone is watching me eat.'

'You can't complain. I trained myself not to eat. I gave

up cigarettes. Then black coffee. Now food,' she said, 'so go on eating if you want to. It's your choice.'

'I will,' he said. He was not in a good mood.

'Do you ever have problems with fairness?' she repeated.

'No,' he said, 'that's what the rules are for. That's what the judges and the rules committees are for.'

'What? Do you really think that Judge Teflin sitting on the Crown Court Rules Committee is worried about fairness?'

'No. You've got a point there. But don't worry, he doesn't have to think about it. With him fairness just wells up, unbidden.' He washed a plate. 'What's all this about, anyway? Has someone been treating you unfairly?'

'No, it's the other way round apparently.'

'You've not got it in you to be unfair,' he said. She thought he was going to touch her, but he did not – he only made a kissing motion towards her cheek, and as an afterthought put his hand momentarily on her waist. She felt her back thrill. That would take her mind off things, that, here and now in the kitchen, with the danger that the nanny might walk in right in the middle.

'Enough of this,' he said, 'let's leave life to the rules committees. I've got work to do.' Sex on the kitchen table was the last thing on his mind.

She leaned back against the warm surface of the stove, and the bar pressed her where his hand had been, pulling the white silk shirt down tight over her breasts. The image of Sharma, still young, still untouched by anything, standing with the document in her hand, drifted before her. Maybe it was a waste of life after all.

37

She followed her husband to their study and opened the brief William had brought her that morning.

She began to take in the story, and the two of them sat in silence, as they did every night, working. Then she said, 'This is astonishing,' looking up. Her husband didn't respond to her remark. He was reading in front of the fire, crouched over a thick book with a pencil poised over the page. Occasionally he made a darting mark in the text. His knees were pressed together, his heels were pointing outwards. He resembled a Charleston dancer, frozen in a moment of reflection.

She watched him, disturbingly aware of a feeling of distaste. The way he sat looked as uncomfortable as it looked ridiculous. But he had always sat like that; she had noticed it occasionally before their marriage, but now she noticed it all the time. What was it people said about marriages breaking up because of the way people ate their breakfast? Of course that was nonsense in itself. What it meant was that those reactions were an indication of other, deeper feelings. She consciously retreated from the idea.

She repeated what she had said and her husband responded. 'Yes?' he said, slowly stretching the word out, eventually looking up from what he was doing, as though to emphasise the distance from which he was returning. Sally knew she was going to have to go through the effort of finding out what he was annoyed about, but for the moment she pressed on. 'It's amazing,' she said, 'this girl I'm appearing for tomorrow – to all intents and purposes she doesn't exist.'

'What do you mean?'

'She seems to have created a complete identity in order to commit the crime, and then disappeared, so when she went they discovered that she had no past, no history, nothing, no records, no family, no proper address. Not one piece of her was true.'

'Why did she disappear?'

'I was coming to that.'

'Go on then, tell me.'

'She stole twenty million dollars.'

'What?'

'A day's take at a group of casinos in Las Vegas.'

'Good God.'

'The complete pick-up for a Tuesday night.' Somehow, that it was a Tuesday, the immediacy of it, gave poignancy to the image, though she wondered how they knew it was night-time. 'I didn't think they had day and night in Las Vegas,' she said.

'Did she do it?'

'Nevada State Police say she did.'

'I mean, was the money taken?'

'Yes. Someone took it, there's no argument there.'

'How big is it?'

'What do you mean?'

'I mean how big is twenty million dollars? Do you need to carry it away with a fork-lift truck, or what?'

'Three big sacks. Laundry-bag size, it says here.'

'Good Lord.'

They lapsed into silence. Then Brian said, 'Has she still got it?'

'The money?'

'Yes.'

'I don't know. We'll see if she's on legal aid.' Sally turned the papers over. 'No, it doesn't say. I don't know who's paying.'

'So were the Maxwells.'

'What?'

'The Maxwells were on legal aid.'

'I don't think she's got the money, she's in Holloway.' There was more silence. 'I don't suppose she'd be allowed to keep it in there with her.'

'Ha, ha,' he said slowly.

This was her chance. 'What's the matter?'

'What do you mean, what's the matter?'

'You're upset about something.'

'Who says?'

'Brian, what do you think happens when people live together? They get to know each other. I know when you're upset.'

'I'm not upset.'

She tried a different tack. 'What did you do today?'

'Oh, nothing.'

She waited. He wouldn't be able to keep it in now – in a moment he would start talking. How could he be so unaware of himself? Maybe it was a necessary qualification for a politician.

Eventually it came. 'Those damn customs people.'

'Oh?' she said.

'They're still annoying us.'

'Is this in the House, or some other work?' Sometimes she couldn't remember from which part of his complicated life his problems came.

'I told you about it. It's from committee.'

'Oh yes. I couldn't remember whether it was from the committee, or the staff side.' This was meaningless enough to prevent him getting more upset. If she admitted she had forgotten what he had been talking about, it would have given him another opportunity to be annoyed and sulk. 'You take no interest,' he would say. It was beginning to be true.

'That damn committee. On one side people are pressing for a hearing, and on the other there's the possibility of criminal proceedings. That's what I'm trying to work out here.' He lifted the book to show her what he was reading.

'Well, I'm going back to my twenty-million-dollar girl,' Sally said, 'and the next time you're angry with your fellow members, don't take it out on me.'

She turned back to the brief. It wasn't in any form that she was used to and she had to pick up the story slowly from a number of different documents. The central events were set out in the report from the sheriff's office to the federal authorities, copied on to Nevada State writing paper. The state had its own writing paper. For a moment she wondered if there was United Kingdom writing paper. Who would be entitled to use it? The Queen?

The report was written in a curious mixture of old-fashioned language – 'felony fugitive' – and modern slang – 'took off like a butt fly' – but the story was crystal clear. Her client was accused of stealing twenty-four million, three hundred and thirty-eight thousand dollars. She had taken the money in three canvas sacks from the armoured van she was using to collect cash from the casinos. She had last been seen loading the bags into a small plane at an airport outside Las Vegas. After that, nothing, until she was arrested in London – at least that's if the woman arrested in London was the same person. The woman who took the money had called herself Frechette Wallace, and the name of her client in Holloway prison was Gaynor Honey Beeline. Hardly a name you would invent.

41

A movement made Sally look up from her papers. Her husband was scratching his ankle above his sock.

At least, you wouldn't choose that name if you were living in a large old house in Kent, with an MP for a husband. Then you would be Ms Sally Donne or Mrs Sarah Murray, like she was, and not about to run away anywhere. Not even if she wanted to. In the moment of quiet Sally thought she could hear the distant tapping of a CD player. That would be Anne's stereo. Sally thought she was out. Perhaps she had left it on; she often did, so that her end of the house seemed continuously full of activity. For a moment Sally's concentration flickered away. The children nowadays were as glad to see Anne as they were to see her, maybe more. She had noticed last Sunday when Anne had come back from seeing her boyfriend in Topham that the children were instantly all over her. It was difficult to get used to, this sharing of the children so completely; she had not felt this about previous nannies. But she supposed it was a good thing.

Sally returned to the papers spread in the pool of light in front of her. It wasn't clear why Gaynor had been arrested. But what was clear was that the Nevada authorities wanted her back home in the maximum security women's jail, where, most days apparently, she would be sexually assaulted – for the rest of her life. The solicitor had let himself go in his description of what might happen to the client when she got to prison. In extradition cases of course that could be relevant. Sally pressed on with the story.

The sheriff's department were claiming that Gaynor was the woman who had worked for the security company in Las Vegas. She had joined as a secretary, the perfect employee. Slowly she had worked her way up through the company until she qualified for proper security work, then, they said, she took her opportunity and disappeared with a delivery load. Sally checked the dates. It hadn't taken her long – she had only been in the company for a couple of years – so clearly getting promoted hadn't been very difficult, but the idea of her getting the job and working away, concealing her intentions, creating a complete, disposable identity was riveting.

The woman had joined in all the social activities, was friendly with everyone who worked there, though she hadn't dated any of the men. She had put 'unmarried' on her form and had given a home address where the firm could contact her. But the address was false. When they tried to find out who she was, or where she came from, there was nothing there at all. The papers set out the efforts they had made. Her home address was an empty flat, unused for four years. Her references were all false, the schools she had given in her background history either didn't exist, or if they did there was no trace of her, nor of anyone fitting her description. Her social security number belonged to a woman who had died of Aids in Los Angeles a couple of years earlier.

There were pages of interviews with staff, undertaken in an attempt to find out anything they might remember which helped. Each had talked of ordinary conversations about life outside the office, though no one could remember meeting her anywhere but the depot, or at company events. Some thought they had, but when asked to recall clearly what had happened, had realised that they were only remembering her vivid descriptions of a party, or a place she had gone to.

'I remember a barbecue she described at her condo once. Someone fell into the pool. She was laughing, I can almost hear the noises of the party still. But now we know there was no party, no pool.'

That wasn't necessarily so, Sally thought, it could just mean that the party had been transposed from one place to another, that was a common trick in the courts. But the next statement took it much further. Frechette had apparently taken a week's holiday in a hotel, in the mountains. There were postcards, chatty letters and gifts. But no one faintly resembling her had been to the hotel at the time, and for the second week the hotel had not even been open. She had invented a whole life.

The centrepiece was a long interview with Frechette's male colleague, her co-driver on the armoured truck. That day the truck had made all its usual stops, with all the usual breaks, even an unauthorised break to collect do-nuts. At this point there was a footnote, 'See 5.6' – Sally turned to it. There were interviews with the donut shop staff. The investigation had certainly been meticulous.

The interview with the co-driver had gone on for many hours. It had to, since he was a suspect himself. Sally had seen this before, when a partner by running off had cast suspicion on the other. Often suspicion was unintention-ally increased by a note intended to exonerate the other. That at least showed some sympathy for the person left behind. Here nothing had been left. Frechette Wallace was obviously totally in control of her feelings.

Sally sorted through additional documents. Checks had been made throughout the company premises, through all the firm's paperwork. There were no marks, no finger-prints, no clothing, nothing personal left in her locker. It was obvious that the missing woman had been aware of the nature of the search that would be made. She had changed her locker often, so it wasn't entirely clear which was the last one she had used, and when she had a locker she washed it regularly. Other members of staff had not seen that done before, although, when they saw it happening, it had seemed perfectly natural. Of course there were no fingerprints.

The registration details they had stored in the company computer had disappeared, along with her formal identification documents. It was only by luck that they had kept microfiches of her job application separately. Not only were her main files gone, but a substantial number of files where there were cross-references back to hers had been deleted as well. The investigators realised that because of this anyone discovering their absence casually would only have concluded that there was a fault in the filing system, rather than anything suspicious. The company was still searching in the hope that it was a filing mistake, but knew it was not.

Sally turned back to the statement of the man working with Frechette on the day of the theft. He had said, 'Nothing seemed different. She was as calm, or as tense, however you want it, as she always was. She was never really friendly, she didn't start conversations, but if you talked to her she talked back. Once she mentioned a man. I remember thinking, So she does go with someone, but then later when she mentioned him again I realised she was talking about someone else's friend. Nothing. I knew nothing about her, but until you asked me, I didn't know I knew nothing. I just thought she wasn't a great talker. She seemed very centred. She must have been strong, to give nothing away. Never to talk, two years, that's lonely time.'

Sally's mind wandered. This girl was a 'sleeper'. In the old spy stories there were always references to sleepers, left in post for years before they were 'activated'. Was there someone else behind it, helping? A secret sharer. Or was it possible to cut yourself off from everyone in that way? Sally had drifted away from what she was reading when the ringing of the phone jerked her back to the room. She leaned over and picked it up. 'Hallo?' she said.

'Is that you, Sally?'

'Yes.'

'Jeremy Scott here.'

Sally reorganised her mind.

'I got your number from your clerk. I hope you don't mind my phoning you.'

'No, of course not. What's the matter?'

'Look, something has come up. A witness has appeared. Do you have a fax?'

'Yes.'

'Can I fax you something? I know we're not sitting till late tomorrow but I don't want to spring this on you. You must have some time to consider it.'

'What is it?'

'A witness. A new witness has appeared. He came forward this afternoon after the court rose. He went to the solicitor's office. I want to send you his statement.'

'Why?'

'So you can decide whether you want to investigate it. It's extraordinary.'

'OK, send it down. The fax is on.' She gave him the number.

She put the phone down and sat looking at the fax machine which, a few seconds later, rang and then, after a lazy pause, began to click and whirr.

She read the statement as it appeared on the machine. 'Another extraordinary thing,' she said to no one in particular, certainly not to her husband, as she took the paper from the machine.

Scott rang back. 'What do you say, Sally?'

'Who is he?'

'I don't know.'

'Is he a friend of your client?'

'Of course not. Our client doesn't even know he has come forward.'

'You mean you don't know whether your client knows that he has come forward, and your client's not about to tell you if he does.'

'Come on, Sally, stop being so hard-boiled. We've sent it so you can check it.'

'What can I do tonight?'

'Nothing of course. But you can get a copy of it to the officer tomorrow morning. I know he's worried about the case.'

'He hasn't said so to me.'

'Well, he wouldn't, would he?'

'What does that mean?'

'Policemen don't tell their counsel they think there's something wrong with their case.'

'Nor do they tell defence counsel.'

'They do, Sally.' Scott nearly tried to explain that he and Terry Davies would always talk to each other, but he stopped himself. In the mood Sally was in she would just

47

see it as a male thing. He said, 'At least tell him. Or allow me to speak to him tomorrow morning before you get to court.'

There was silence at the other end.

'You won't help?'

'How can I help?'

'Well, it's what I said – you can ask your policeman to do some background checking.' Scott waited. There was silence. He said, 'It might be the truth, Sally. After all, everyone who stands in the dock at the Old Bailey isn't necessarily guilty.' More silence. Scott became exasperated. 'Despite what your head of chambers says.'

'Good night, Jeremy.'

He'd offended her.

'OK, Sally.' He put the phone down.

Scott looked at the wall of the office where there was a calendar with a blonde woman holding a law book. She had nothing on, save a wing collar, bands and a white horsehair wig.

'What on earth's that?' he said.

'It's a legal calendar,' said Stephen. 'We got it to cheer the girls up.'

'Sally's not interested. I misjudged her – she didn't seem to respond. I don't know what's the matter, she's not normally like that. She's not even going to ask Terry Davies to do any checking. She'll just attack it as a lie invented to get the client off.'

'She has no evidence of that.'

'She doesn't need evidence. If you're prosecuting you don't need evidence to allege the defendant or his witnesses are lying. He's the one accused, so naturally it follows that he'll do anything to get acquitted, and therefore anyone who speaks up for him is lying. The Crown is free to make any allegations it likes, and, if one allegation fails, then all they need do is shrug and move on to the next.'

While she was talking on the telephone Sally had thought she could hear a noise in the distance. It seemed to come from upstairs but she couldn't be sure. There were many sounds around the house – animals, particularly foxes at night – but it wasn't that. She put the fax down and looked up. Her husband hadn't moved; he was still sitting in his wing chair reading, for God's sake, a copy of Hansard. She listened for a moment, but heard nothing.

The door to her room was open and she knew that the children's door was open as well. If they were calling she would hear. The telephone rang again.

'What do you say, Sally?'

'Who is he?' she said.

Scott was suggesting that the Crown should do some checking. After all, he had faxed her the statement in advance, which was open of him. But her mind was only half on what he was saying. He seemed to think that Terry Davies was worried about the case. The policeman hadn't said anything to her.

Scott said, 'Policemen don't tell their counsel they think there's something wrong with their case.'

That annoyed her. How did he know whether she did or didn't get on with the case officer? She picked up a hint of male collusion. At that moment there was another cry from upstairs. She was certain of it this time, it was Jenny.

'Nor do they tell defence counsel,' she said.

Scott said something in reply but she didn't hear it.

'How can I help?' she said, listening both to him and for another sound from upstairs. He said something about her head of chambers. He was becoming offensive. Then, 'Goodnight, Jeremy.' Her husband hadn't moved at all. She put the phone down and ran upstairs.

Was Anne there? Then she remembered again that Anne had gone into Topham to see her boyfriend. Sally thought she had heard her stereo a little earlier, but maybe she wasn't back yet. The children's door was at the end of the passage. The night light was on. Harriet was fast asleep but Jenny, Jenny was pushing herself hard up against the bed head, forcing herself backwards as though trying to get away from something. Her eyes were wide open, and her mouth was drawn back. She was whimpering. In a stride Sally was across the room, picking up the child. But Jenny did not relax at her touch, she was stiff and unforgiving. She tried to twist away from her. She continued to whimper. Her head was covered in perspiration and the collar of her pyjama top was soaking wet. Sally tried to squeeze her close, but she resisted, staring over her shoulder, not responding to her or to what was happening at all. Then she began to scream, short, sharp, incoherent noises. Her body jerked in Sally's arms as though she was trying to get away. It was terrifying.

Sally tried to soothe her, running her hand over her hair, whispering in her ear. It had no effect. This was a full-blooded night terror, but even knowing what it was didn't help. She couldn't be reached, she was separated from her.

There was a movement behind her and Anne came in making a gentle cooing noise. 'It's all right, baby, it's all right,' she said. Anne put her hand on the child's head, smoothing her hair just as Sally had done, and Jenny immediately relaxed and softened. She became a child again and hung in her mother's arms. Her eyes closed and she fell asleep, relaxing and softening in Sally's grasp as though nothing had happened.

Sally stood and held her for a moment, swept by a feeling of uselessness. 'Let's change her top,' Sally said. 'Feel it, it's soaking.'

Anne went to a drawer and pulled out another pyjama top, and they changed the small, unresisting child, who allowed her arms to be bent backwards out of the sleeve, while her head flopped down against Sally's shoulder. She slept peacefully through it all. Sally rubbed her hair and neck with a warm towel from the rail, turned her pillow, gave her the teddy and straightened the cover. Through all of this the other child hadn't stirred.

'Thank you, Anne.'

'That's all right, Miss Donne,' Anne said.

Anne was picking up the clothes where they had fallen and was packing them into the laundry basket.

'Terrors never last long. But it's frightening, there's no doubting that.'

Sally watched the young woman, capable and aware far beyond her age. She seemed to know about children viscerally – just as some people are musical, or others can dance. But then she had six brothers and sisters.

Over her shoulder Anne said, 'Our little Victor was the same. There was nothing no one could do. He just had to scream it out.'

She was as certain of what she was saying as if she had been directing Sally to the nearest bus stop. Sally listened. She was shaken by the experience. She had been able to do

51

nothing to help her own child, a stranger had to do it. Was Anne reassuring her, or apologising even? Jenny had stopped crying the moment Anne had walked in the door, doing in an instant what she herself could not do for her own child. She repeated it to herself again. Her daughter had not been crying for her mother, but for someone else.

Sally wondered whether Anne was patronising her. Probably not. But then if you're good at something, you know perfectly well that you are, and you also know if somebody else is not. That was what she was saying, wasn't it, that she, Sally, wasn't any good with her own child?

'Is everything all right at home, Anne?' she asked. As she spoke Sally realised that she was hitting back at her. She had started to protect herself against a young, uneducated, inoffensive girl.

'Well, I'd say it is, Miss Donne. But I'm not sure.' Anne picked up the laundry basket and straightened up to look Sally in the face. 'But I'm not sure at all. Because I don't think my Darren really knows what he wants.' Darren was Anne's long-time boyfriend, utterly feckless, always on the edge of trouble with the police. Sally watched this young immature face and wondered, Is she a threat to me? She said, 'Oh, I'm sorry, Anne, what is it now?'

'Driving,' Anne said, 'always driving. It's a wonder anything else gets done. The police found him with a motor car, but they couldn't show he'd driven it. He's so cocky, Miss Donne, I'm frightened.' They stood and looked at each other, each unable to control the world in her own way, each assuming the other could.

Anne changed the subject. 'Will you be leaving early again tomorrow?'

52

Sally said, 'I don't know,' and then, because she did know, 'Well, yes, I am. I have to go early again.' It was as though she was being forced to admit something discreditable. Did she have to? Of course she did. 'You'll manage all right?' Stupid question.

'No problem. The children are no problem at all, Miss Donne.' Anne turned the light off and they paused next to each other in the passage, Anne holding the laundry basket, the old-fashioned image of a servant and a mistress. Anne said, 'It's the big children like Darren who are the really difficult ones,' and she set off down the passage to the back stairs to go to the laundry room. 'They think they know what they want, but so often they don't at all.'

Sally watched her walk past the polished oak chest. On the top there were some silver animals and Meissen china, along with pictures of the children. A brass lamp with a deep red shade cast a shadow on the shining carpet. A rug shimmered near the top of the stairs, where the girl picked her way down, her spare hand holding on to the turned balustrade.

Was Anne attacking her? This was becoming close to paranoia. How could she feel so threatened? It meant nothing. Naturally the children were close to Anne, that was in the way of things. She herself had become close to the woman who had taken over from her mother. That had been Millie who used to come in on weekday afternoons, but then, when her mother had left, Sally had been on her own. Millie in a way was all she had.

But there was something else going on here, something inside her. She was being supplanted, and yet at the same time she thought perhaps she deserved it. How could she deserve it? That was complete nonsense. She stood at the top of the stairs, silent in the night. What she was doing was no more than what thousands of women like her did. She was going to have to fight. What a ridiculous way to speak about her relationship with a young girl! This was a challenge, and it was happening in a place where a good university degree was no help at all. Was it the place where all women lived, once, before – what was it called – emancipation?

Sally went to her room without even going downstairs to see her husband. What use was he?

3

The next day Sally Donne went to Holloway women's prison to meet Monty Bach's client. She turned out to be a most unlikely looking bank robber, dressed in the bottom half of a shell suit and a T-shirt which said, 'I don't like being in here either', and underneath, in smaller letters, 'but *I've* got no choice'. She was carrying a thick, folded wallet with pieces of paper spilling from it. She put it down on the formica table in front of her and said, 'You're Sally Donne.' Her voice was light, with an American accent, though Sally couldn't trace from which part of America it came.

'Yes,' Sally said. 'I'm sorry we're meeting this way.'

'If we hadn't met this way then we would probably never have met at all,' she said. 'But nevertheless, now we have, I'm pleased we did.' She stretched her hand out, obviously intending to detract from the sharpness of her reply. Her grip was assured.

'I'm a barrister.'

'I expected you to be wearing a wig.'

'No. Not all the time, only when I'm in court.'

'That's a shame. I'd been looking forward to seeing that wig. But you're still a lawyer?'

'Yes, I'm a lawyer.'

'Good. I told Monty I wanted a woman lawyer.'

'Well, I'm that too.'

'He said it would be difficult.'

'I wonder why he said that? It's not difficult at all. The place is running with women lawyers now.'

'I love the way you say that. "Running with lawyers" . . . what does "running with" mean right here?'

Sally thought for a moment, then she said, 'Running with. Don't fish run in rivers at certain times? Don't you say that in America?'

'Crawling. Crawling with lawyers.'

'I suppose that's a rather different attitude to them. You don't like lawyers in America?'

'You could say that.'

'Well, they're better than the alternative.'

'What's the alternative?'

'Your being put on the next plane to Nevada perhaps.'

'You got me there. I need a lawyer.'

There was a noise at the door.

'Thank you, my dear, thank you.' Monty Bach appeared, beaming at the young woman prison officer who let him in. He entered the room sideways, lifting his bulging briefcase up to his chest so he could squeeze past the table's edge. In his other hand he was carrying a plastic cup of tea. He wore a black homburg pushed back on his head. His black, fur-collared overcoat was being dragged open by the table top, revealing a green, stained, moleskin jacket. A biro stuck out of one of the pockets, a khaki handkerchief trailed from his wrist.

56

'Well then, ladies, here I am, here I am. Enough of this chatting.'

Sally stiffened. She had heard about Monty Bach, had seen him in court but had never dealt with him. God, what a mess. He squeezed himself between the table and the wall, and was forced to pull down his jacket and waistcoat from where they had ridden up over his stomach.

'Why, oh why do they always have to make us so uncomfortable? Look where they're all sitting.' Monty paused while pushing his shirt back into his trousers and looking out through the glass door to the large open space where the prison staff were sitting, also drinking out of plastic cups. 'It's a bias against the defence, of course. Unconscious, I dare say, not that they're very bright even when they're conscious.' He remained half-standing, tugging at his waistcoat, getting himself comfortable. Sally watched him, almost expecting him to undo his trousers and hold them up by spreading his knees apart to tuck his shirt tails in. It was something she had seen her husband do.

Monty went on, 'But definitely it's there, the unconscious bias is there. Talk to any prison officer. For them, providing facilities for prisoners to see lawyers is about as low on their list of priorities as it can be, whereas it should of course be at the top.' He subsided on to one of the plastic chairs. 'But then, that's the nature of our society, instinctively secretive and authoritarian, and all the time pretending not to be.' He peered into the briefcase on the table in front of him, pulling out and stuffing back bundles of papers. He found what he needed. Then he beamed at the two women. 'You've met then?' he said.

Sally felt impatience welling up in her. What was this,

57

some sort of mothers' meeting? But her response was cut short by Honey's reaction.

'Hi, Mr Bach. How's your wife?'

'Intolerable, my dear. Intolerable.' Monty leaned forward and put his hand on hers. 'But there we are, there we are, I can always get out to see you.' He turned and included Sally in his smile. 'I get out here most days if I can. At present Miss Beeline is the light of my life.'

His client smiled back at him. Sally was struck by the simplicity of it.

He leaned back. 'Well, Miss Donne, it's good to meet you. You've prosecuted me before, but we've never met. Monty Bach. I'm Monty Bach.' He held out his hand.

Sally kept her reactions steady, showing none of her feelings. She was used to a more professional approach.

'Good to meet you, Mr Bach.' She could tell that he knew what she was thinking. His eyes twinkled.

Monty Bach was an old man, probably well over seventy, and it was said that he had started working in the courts when he was fourteen – that was during the Second World War, for heaven's sake.

'Miss Donne knows very little about extradition law, Gaynor,' Monty said, turning away. Sally's mouth nearly dropped open, but she controlled herself and sat still. 'But that's not the point. She knows how a court works. And anyway I know enough about this to get us going. Today I just wanted you to visit with each other – as you say in America.'

Gaynor smiled at Sally in response, as though she had just been introduced to an expert who would save her life, rather than being informed that her lawyer knew nothing about the law. She said, 'Well, that's Monty all over. He

58

gets me a lawyer and then he tells me she knows nothing at all about what she's doing.' For a moment Sally thought she heard a slight southern inflection in the last words. 'But no matter, I'm sure we'll get along just fine.' Monty smiled in support and suddenly Sally felt in a minority. Whatever else he did, Monty was obviously good at keeping his clients happy. Why was she feeling left out? She realised that things were going on that she wasn't very good at. Sally wondered for a moment whether she was as much in control as she thought.

They looked at her expectantly, wanting her to start. In the silence Monty started to unpack his snuff tin.

Jeremy Scott was in no hurry. That morning Sally was involved somewhere else and the court was sitting late. He picked his way slowly down Fleet Street watching people pass by. He paused outside Henley's thinking of buying himself a cup of coffee, moved on to the Prêt shop, but didn't go in. He crossed over to the Seattle Coffee Company. It looked very full, so he walked on down to Madison's. Across the road was Coffee State and a little further down the French Coffee Company with a Turkish coffee shop next to it. If Fleet Street was anything to go by, then central London must have literally thousands of new coffee shops. He looked back and counted. There were eight of them in about a hundred yards. No wonder Joe's Café, the greasy spoon next to the old Telegraph building, had closed.

He realised he was still standing outside the window of Madison's and, recognising the thinning hair and cigarette, he saw a face he knew looking back at him. Scott grinned and moved on. It was an old friend, an expert in bankruptcy, but they had drifted apart now; they didn't even bother to chat.

Scott met Stephen in the Costa Coffee in Blackfriars station, opposite Old Bailey, and they discussed how to deal with the new witness.

Stephen said, 'I talked some more to our witness after you left. He confirmed that he hadn't seen the woman since then, and that all he did was make the payments.' Stephen examined the bowl of multi-coloured sugars and selected a purple tube. 'He was very meticulous about it. He drew the money from a bank account which he had set up specially, and he got a record of some sort every time he went to the hotel to leave the cash, a receipt for a newspaper or something. The mechanics of the payment were a used envelope which was addressed to the hotel, and he was told to leave it in the mail box to make it look like ordinary overnight mail. Obviously they wanted to watch him deliver it.

'He couldn't find anything on the envelope to mark it out, but anybody keeping a lookout must have had a method of spotting it. The bag went round the hotel to the various desks, so presumably only the mail boy there could have identified who actually received it.

'But our witness photocopied everything, even the money, date-stamped the photocopies and then had them countersigned. Amazing, and everything pre-dates this case. It's cast iron.'

'It sounds too good to be true,' Scott said.

'These things happen. Remember the man on the bus in the Bodkin–Adams case who overheard the nurses discussing their story? Who'd have thought that could have happened?'

Scott took another sip of coffee and watched the man behind the counter reading an electrical engineering manual.

Stephen said, 'They were clever, they didn't ask too much. That's the mistake blackmailers normally make, they get greedy. They gave him four envelopes and asked for fifteen hundred pounds in each. Now that's less than his legal costs would have been if he'd been accused of indecent assault, let alone rape, *and* he was guaranteed a result, whereas trials can go wrong. As you know. Who wouldn't pay? That was it. He never heard any more. Blackmail on easy terms.

'I asked him more about how he came to us. He said he was trying to forget all about it until he read this case. He recognised the hotel, and what made him realise that it had to be the same people was the maid. The maid coming in.'

Scott said, 'There was always something odd about that maid.'

They sat looking at each other, thinking of all the angles. Scott said, 'If the maid was part of the blackmail, why did they go ahead with the rape charge? Why not just blackmail as usual?'

'We talked about that. We decided that the maid coming in *was* a mistake, she wasn't the one who was meant to come in. Someone else was meant to, and the irony was that by setting up the situation so well, the allegation followed on quite naturally.'

'There's the difficulty. The prosecution will say no-body's blackmailed anybody here.'

'They can't say that if he identifies her as the same woman.'

'Yes. It's the end of it whatever else happens.' Scott paused and said, 'Have you worked out how to do the identification?'

'Well, I've got his description of the woman on a timed tape recording,' Stephen put a cassette on the table, 'and Vic said he'd stand with him at the top of the main staircase to see if he can spot her coming in. It's what he used to do when he was in the police.'

'What if she doesn't come?'

'She'll come. She's been every day so far.'

'Vic'll do that?'

'Yes. Vic doesn't know what the woman looks like either. That was how he used to do it when he was in the police. They're going to get there in about half an hour.' Stephen looked at his watch.

'I'd better not be anywhere near.'

'No,' Stephen said.

'Does Roger Nichols know anything about this yet?'

'I haven't told him, like you said.'

'It's better.'

'Shame though,' said Stephen, 'it might have cheered him up. When I saw him last he looked pretty depressed.'

'Yes,' said Scott, 'for him this is real. For us it's only an elaborate game.'

At lunch when she got to court, Sally saw Scott in the bar mess eating on his own. She wondered whether to join him. The trouble was he was so prickly, one day perfectly friendly, the next acting as though – she tried to identify what it was – as though he was surprised that anyone should even want to talk to him. And of course that was just what happened, no one did – she had often seen him sitting alone in the mess.

But today Sally needed a change. She picked up her apple and threaded her way through the tables towards him. At least she knew if she sat with him he wasn't going to go on about who was who, who had what case, or even – she swerved away from Johnny Marriott who specialised in that kind of thing – who had and who hadn't been at Covent Garden the night before. She didn't want to gossip, rather she wanted to tell Scott about Monty Bach. She was still feeling off balance after the conference that morning.

'You don't do defence work, do you?' Scott said.

'Not any more.'

'It's different.'

'Of course. But how?'

'I'm trying to tell you. A lot of it is allowing yourself to think sloppily and yet accurately at the same time.'

'What do you mean?'

Scott pondered on it, and Sally wondered if he was going to reply at all. Then he said, 'Well. Look at you. You're not going to approve of Monty Bach, I don't imagine. He's all over the place. If he can lose a document he will, and he's got no clue about the law. But he's the perfect buffer between people like you and the client. He makes them feel real. He doesn't challenge them. Lots of barristers make defendants feel they have to apologise for not being clever enough. Because it's difficult for clever people not to let cleverness show, even if they try to hide it.'

Sally listened. He was describing exactly what had happened that morning.

'Let yourself go a bit. You have to think like the client. After years of thinking like a lawyer, you've got to start responding like a human being again. Make logical mistakes. Get angry occasionally.'

Sally watched a group of Treasury counsel at the far table laughing. Normally she would be with them, but today she was glad she wasn't. Thinking like a lawyer, straitjacketing human nature, never responding to ordinary feelings. That's what was happening. It was true.

'After all, that's what good lawyers, especially prosecutors, don't do. Get angry. You too, Sally.'

She was silent.

'You weren't very helpful on the phone last night,' Scott said.

'No. Look, Jeremy, I'm sorry, I'll read your witness statement again. But all the time you were talking, there was a child crying upstairs. Not a very good excuse, I suppose.'

'There, that's what I mean, Sally. What better excuse could there be? Why didn't you say so at the time?'

He was interrupted by a shout from someone standing by the telephone: 'Call for Jeremy Scott?' He got up and took the phone. He heard Stephen say, 'We got it, Jeremy. He spotted her before I even noticed that she had come in. It's solid. Come on down, we'll be outside the court.'

Scott put the phone down and went back to where he had been sitting. 'Sally, I've got to go. Please think about that statement,' he said. 'I'll see you later. You know the court's not sitting till quarter past?'

Sally watched him disappear through the double doors, unwinding his robes which he had bundled into one of the lockers. He was odd. He could be a good lawyer if he wanted to be. But it was almost as though he didn't want to be, or even disliked himself for being one at all, as though he had to pretend. She thought about it. Normally that wasn't the kind of thing that interested her, but today things seemed different.

'Hallo, Sally.' A face appeared in front of her. It was Noel, carrying a coffee. 'Can I get you one?'

Sally glanced at the clock. 'Hallo, Noel, you here on one of your interminable customs cases? Yes, coffee. Yes, lovely. Decaffeinated, please.'

'Sugar?' Noel said. Then when he saw her face, he said, 'Of course, no sugar.' His eyes took in Sally's embroidered waistcoat, and her thin waist. On the plate in front of her was a single apple core. 'Now that's what I call discipline.'

'Bloody discipline,' she said, as he went over to the counter. He carried a cup back to her.

'Do you think I should help the defence?' Sally told Noel about the statement Scott had given her.

'Of course not, it's his defence. Why should you get involved?'

'But if it's true?'

'Come on,' Noel said, 'there's good evidence against the defendant. It's for the jury to judge. Not for you, nor anyone. Just the jury.'

'I'm worried.'

'You've nothing to be worried about. I'm surprised at you, Sally.' He laughed. 'You're growing soft in your old age.'

'Maybe that's what happens,' Sally said.

'Well, stave it off as long as possible. You should be able to cross-examine him into a cocked hat without even looking at him. Especially without looking at him.'

65

'All parties in the case of Nichols,' the tannoy said. Sally got up feeling better. What was she doing? After all this time she ought to know what to do, she was here to prosecute, not faff around.

'He's not here. He hasn't turned up yet. It's the first time he's been late.'

When Sally got to court Scott told her that Roger Nichols hadn't come. 'We're phoning now. He's not at home, but then he was going to see his wife last night, so he may have got held up on the line back from Maidstone.'

'Can't we just carry on? It's only speeches left. All we need say is that he has been held up.'

'No,' said Scott. 'I want to reopen my case.'

'Of course. I forgot.'

'I have to speak to him first to confirm with him that he wants to call the evidence.'

'You still think he doesn't know about it?'

'I do, yes. And I advised he shouldn't be told.'

'He doesn't even know a witness has come forward?'

'No. My solicitor is a bit suspicious of everyone, I'm afraid, and wasn't going to allow any hostages to fortune.'

'When you say suspicious, you mean suspicious of me?'

'I suppose that's right.' Scott laughed.

'And when you say "my solicitor" is suspicious, you mean *you* are suspicious.'

'Sally! Why should you think such a thing? After all, I showed you the statement.'

'But you're not going to give me a chance to ask Mr Nichols questions about the manner in which evidence appeared?'

66

'No, Sally. At least, I'm going to make it more difficult for you. If you want to suggest it was he who organised this then you're going to have to do it cold. And I reckon you're going to have to, because I've got these.'

Scott showed her the photocopies of the payments the witness had made, and the receipts with the name of the hotel on them. 'Look, he kept a complete note of all his dealings. Bank accounts, withdrawals, till receipt for a purchase he made at the hotel every time he went in to make a payment. Exactly the time he said, copies of the envelopes and copies of the money. Thirty fifty-pound notes each time. And all this was done months and months before Mr Nichols even knew your victim, black-mailer, or whatever she is existed, and certainly before any allegation of rape was made against him.'

'How do we know it's the same woman?'

'We know.'

Sally looked at the documents and she thought of what Noel had said. 'No,' she said. 'It's my job to prosecute this man. It's yours to defend him. When he turns up let's get on with it. Call your witness and we'll see how he deals with cross-examination.'

They sat in the empty court waiting for something to happen. Roger Nichols still hadn't arrived. The judge sent a message saying they would go on waiting for a while, but that she would come into court shortly. Occasionally a journalist poked his head in to see if he was missing something, and other court clerks used the court as a passage to get to the judges' corridors and administrative areas.

Scott knew that at the back, where the judges' rooms were, there was a profound feeling of gloom. In the long corridor there would be a guard nodding gently on a chair and no other activity at all. The rest of the courts were busy. Dust slowly settled in the building. Suddenly Stephen's phone rang, a curious, questioning noise. He searched for a moment in his briefcase and then took the case and the phone, still ringing, outside into the main hall.

The door clunked shut and the silence resumed its grip. The bailiff sitting on a wooden chair by the double doors opened a novel and almost immediately fell asleep. After a while Stephen beckoned Scott from the door. His face was very white.

Scott came back into the court and said, 'He shot himself.'

Sally jerked her head up.

'What?' she said.

'He went down to his wife's house in Kent, got his shotgun from the study, went outside and shot himself. He's dead.'

'When?'

'Last night. His wife thought he had gone back to London. They found him in a drainage ditch beneath an embankment on the M2.'

'Dead?' Sally found herself repeating it.

'He had very little skull left.' Scott was feeling upset and it was beginning to translate itself into anger. 'We'd better tell the judge.'

Scott went to speak to the clerk. Then he sat in his place in counsel's benches at the far end of the row from where Sally was sitting. She looked at him and they sat separated. After a few minutes the judge came in. Sally looked at Scott, who stood up to address her.

'I have the most unfortunate news,' he said. Unfortunate seemed the right word. Scott doubted whether the judge would find what he had to tell her 'distressing', the other word that went through his mind.

'Most disturbing,' the judge replied, choosing a response that Scott had not begun to forecast. The judge turned to Sally. 'Has this been confirmed?'

Sally stood up. 'My officer has been in touch with Kent police. It is confirmed.'

'Then we had better tell the jury, who can then be discharged, can they not?'

Scott knew that this was not a question so he did not move. The judge went on, 'Tomorrow, evidence can be given of the identity of the body and the indictment can also be discharged.'

The matter was over as far as she was concerned. And of course she was right. The jury filed in. Scott noticed that one or two of them immediately sensed that something had happened.

'Ladies and gentlemen, I have just received some unusual news.' Again the judge's choice of words was unerring. 'The defendant . . .' The judge paused and turned over the cover of her notebook where Roger Nichols's name must have been written. '. . . Nichols,' she said, after reminding herself of his name, 'was found earlier today. He had taken his own life.' Two or three of the jurors let out a gasp, and some of the women covered their mouths. After a while one began to weep. The judge continued, 'You therefore have no further function to perform in this matter and are discharged from coming to a verdict. I offer you the City of London's thanks.'

The judge looked to her left where an usher called out

in a sing-song voice that the court would sit the next day at ten-thirty o'clock in the forenoon. 'God save the Queen,' the usher suggested. The judge rose and left. The usher followed, leaving Scott looking at the jury. They stared back at him. There was nothing to be said or done. After a while they were invited to file out, which they did, now not looking at him any more.

Outside Scott saw the police officer talking to the woman who had made the complaint against Roger Nichols. With them was a man whom Scott recognised as Vic, the ex-policeman who worked for his solicitors. Another man stood a little further back, the witness who had come forward last night. Occasionally the woman glanced at this man. She looked frightened. As Scott passed, Vic turned and told him that Stephen had gone. He'd ring.

Scott followed Sally to the lift. It was filled with another group of jurors who were heading home, so they couldn't speak. It stopped at the second floor. Sally got out. As she turned to nod goodbye, Scott said, 'They're going to arrest her, you know.'

'I know,' said Sally.

4

Sally didn't feel like going home, nor did she want to go back to work. She left her car at court and set off down the street towards Blackfriars.

Part of her mind was still occupied with the jury speech she would have been making at just about this time, if the guy had not blown his head off. The speech had come to her easily; she had almost not had to prepare it at all. It was based on a repetition of the central questions in her cross-examination, the ones that had really thrown Roger Nichols. The questions that had killed him.

She looked up. Coming towards her was the reassuring shape of a London taxi, and without thinking, perhaps in order to feel she was doing something positive, she hailed it. It wasn't until she was sitting inside and the cabbie turned round expectantly that she realised she had not said where she wanted to go – nor had she even decided.

'Albemarle Street,' she said, the first street name that came into her head.

The taxi rocked its way back up Fleet Street, down the Strand and across Trafalgar Square. She gazed, distracted,

71

through the window. London passed by, pigeons wheeling in the winter air. She suddenly realised that the taxi had stopped. 'Here you are, miss.'

She searched her handbag, trying to find some money, feeling the cabbie's eyes upon her. She handed him the money and waited while he counted out the change. 'Keep a pound,' she said.

He thanked her. Then he said, 'It's a horrible place all right.'

'What is?'

'That Old Bailey. It's a horrible place. I saw you coming out, and what with you being so low like . . .'

She smiled and said, 'I work there.'

'Oh, that's not as bad then. But it's still a horrible place, whatever you do there.' He drove away.

The day wasn't cold yet, although it was already growing dark. The street was busy with people carrying parcels and stopping to look in the glowing shop windows. The light silhouetted the shoppers like a fantasy on a Christmas card.

Albemarle Street is packed with art galleries. She walked slowly past the shopfronts, staring at the paintings. There seemed to be a predominant style, the luxurious recreations of an ideal nineteenth-century life. Here was one. A stout country gentleman in a tight Pickwickian waistcoat was being entertained with punch, while in the background a young man played blind man's buff with young women in Regency dresses. The whole scene was covered with a golden sheen. These were pictures designed to go with staggeringly expensive wallpaper and freshly bought gilt furniture.

Sally turned and crossed the road, past the House of

Gold where a couple were leaning over the counter examining a bracelet exhibited across the wrist of the bony shop assistant. Behind the group stood a security guard. Sally watched them through a steel mesh grille.

In the next shop the richness of colour had spread from the pictures to the very shop itself, which glowed in the light of a row of chandeliers. As Sally looked through the window a messenger arrived, pressed the bell and the door was automatically opened to him. She stepped in behind him and stood in front of the shop's central display. It was a huge canvas of a fjord or a loch. Mountains towered in the distance. A small boat was making for the near shore. The paint had been laid on thickly, sometimes a quarter of an inch deep. Close up, it broke into arbitrary patterns, but when she stood back it resolved itself into a gleaming, varnished image of the still cliffs lit by the setting sun. Moving back another step she realised that the shop owner was standing behind her.

'When was it painted?' she asked, feeling a need to acknowledge his presence.

'Turn of the century. He died in 1910, relatively young.'

The man was looking expectantly at her. Did he think she was thinking of buying it? For a moment she imagined the picture in their large study at home, and then depressingly realised that her husband might well like just such a monstrosity bearing down on him.

'How much is it?'

'Thirty-six thousand pounds, madam.'

'More money than I have, I'm afraid,' she said, smiling, and she turned to the door. At least it was something to be mistaken for a person who could spend that amount of money on a picture. She walked up the street, back towards Piccadilly, and turned to venture into another gallery where the door was open. The large, deep interior was painted white with no relief at all, save the twenty or so pictures on the walls.

Immediately she recognised the artists, a Matisse with soft petal-like lines of colour, and on the wall opposite it, a dark writhing Vlaminck. At the end of the room there was an Andy Warhol painting of a woman's head. She stood in front of it. The head looked back at her, indifferent.

On her right she saw a narrow passage which must lead to a back room. A notice confirmed that more pictures were being displayed there. She went through the narrow space and found, immediately in front of her, a man struggling with a trestle table. He pulled at it, got it straight and then started backwards, moving towards Sally. He suddenly saw her and had to stop.

'I'm sorry. I got in your way,' she said, standing back for him.

'You couldn't have known,' he said genially.

'Am I allowed in here?' she said.

'Yes, yes. Yes. Please carry on.' He disappeared around the corner, pulling at the table.

Once left alone Sally experienced the childish pleasure of being in a small hidden area, separated from, yet at the same time close to, ordinary life. Nearby she could hear conversation and a clinking of bottles. The privacy gave an added glow to the pictures as she walked round the walls.

To the side of the room, there was a framed water-colour, much smaller than the rest of the pictures. In it a naked woman was sitting on an unmade white iron bed, staring at the artist. She looked utterly self-contained, quite unperturbed by the artist's enquiring eye, happy

74

merely to sit still, content in her own being. Sally was attracted to the picture and stared at the round face and ample body. Who was she? Was she a chambermaid? The room had the atmosphere of a hotel. Sally wondered why. Perhaps it was the metal bed and the emptiness of the room. Obviously it was in the south of France: the whole picture rang with the light of the south.

After a while she felt her attempts to trace a story or pin the picture down with categories were pointless. The girl's self-contained presence made any need to label her irrelevant. Sally stepped back. The detachment of the woman sitting on the bed made the whole farrago of dressing up and going about trying to be somebody seem quite unnecessary. She was just a person, she needed nothing more.

Then Sally became aware of a man standing by her shoulder. He said, 'Henri LeBasque. He was a friend of Renoir's. For a while, they all lived together in the south of France.'

Sally said, 'Yes, she looks like the kind of woman Renoir painted.'

'A little tubby for modern taste, I think. But then so was Marilyn Monroe. She is very beautiful, isn't she?' The man leaned forward and gestured at the swell of the woman's apple cheeks. 'Now that's skilful. Look how the shadow on the face is created by nothing more than the intensity of the wash.'

Sally could see the man's profile and caught a fugitive wisp of scent. He studied the picture carefully. His eyes glittered. The ease with which he was addressing her, completely certain that she would respond, made her feel she had to say something in reply.

'The pencil lines, were they put in first or later?'

'At first I should think,' he said, and then he added, 'No, that's not a silly question. You were thinking of ink and wash where the ink lines can be added later.' He turned and faced her. 'It's probably a study for a larger painting. There is a LeBasque very like it. I saw it in a catalogue once, a private collection, a *collection particulier*. But perhaps this is not a study for something else, maybe it's just a picture he wanted to make.'

Sally looked at him.

'It would be a good buy,' he said, 'he's much underrated.'

Sally realised she must be talking to the owner of the gallery.

'I say it's worth it though I'm not selling it, I'm just a visitor like yourself,' he said. 'You'd have to ask Anthony Brown the price.' He smiled and moved away from her towards the next picture.

Sally found that she did not feel in the least put out by the sudden appearance and disappearance of this companion. It was almost as though they were part of the same club, or school, knowing each other by membership and consequently needing neither an introduction nor an excuse to speak together.

She thought, and was interested by, the length of time it had taken her to get round to the idea, was he trying to pick her up? It was rather exciting, something that had not happened to her for some time. Certainly if he was, he seemed to have given up now. He stood with his back to her.

Sally turned and looked down the passage. There was a little cubby hole which she hadn't noticed before and in it a girl was using a computer. She decided to enquire about the price of the picture.

'Could you tell me the cost of one of the pictures?' Cost was an odd word. But it seemed a better word. Later it was a word she remembered.

The girl said, 'One moment, please,' and leaned back. 'Anthony,' she called, and then addressed Sally again, 'Mr Brown will be with you now.'

Sally turned back to the watercolour; the man who had spoken to her had disappeared. She couldn't see where he had gone. There didn't seem to be a door.

The owner told her the price and Sally thought about it. It was a lot, but then she earned more than that most weeks.

'Will you accept a cheque?' she said.

There wasn't a flicker on the owner's face. But he wasn't going to let her walk out the door with the picture under her arm. 'Of course, madam. And where would you like it delivered?'

She took her cheque book out and, as he noticed the name of the bank and she gave her address, she felt him relax. He wrote the address down in a strong italic script.

'I'll be just one moment,' he said, and then he paused. 'Might I invite you perhaps to join us? We are having a small gathering.' He held his hand out and guided her down the passage back to the small room where the picture hung. 'Just here,' he said. He opened a door in the wall, apparently out of nothing – the join was quite impossible to see. This must be where the other man had gone. Inside she saw a trestle table, covered with a tablecloth. On it there was a series of bottles, and at each end a spittoon. Around the table stood a group of people swilling wine around in glasses.

'We're having a tasting,' said the gallery owner, 'but of course, if you wish, just take something to drink. Michael,' he said, speaking to the man who had struggled with the table earlier, 'another guest. Miss Donne. Michael Jarvis,' he said, turning to Sally, introducing her. 'Every year at about this time he gives us a treat. I'll leave you with Michael and arrange your picture.'

Michael Jarvis was wearing a dark, pinstriped suit with a V-neck blue sweater, the uniform of the upper middle classes who work, but not at the kind of work people normally do.

'I'm a private shipper,' the man confided. 'It gives me a chance to go to France a lot.' Clearly it didn't matter much to Michael whether he sold what he went to France to buy. 'Now look at this,' he said. 'No, don't bother with the whites, what's the point of white wine for heaven's sake? Try this. From Provence.'

He poured out a small amount of red wine and handed it to her. 'Syrah Grenache. Keats would probably have drunk pure Grenache. Perhaps that's why he had a head-ache. Keats.'

She tasted the wine. As it flooded her mouth, she remembered she had eaten nothing that day save the apple at lunch. She swallowed the wine, realising she shouldn't.

'Now this one. Let's move north up through France. A spot of old Pinot, old Pinot? Yes.'

They moved along the table. Occasionally Sally spat the wine out, but more often she took a mouthful.

'Michael, Michael!'

Her host stopped talking and looked in the direction of the voice. 'Oh, there's old Mrs Rucker. I have to go. Have some more. Have some more.' He continued to repeat everything twice. 'More of the Provence. It's quite the best. Quite the best.' He walked quickly away holding his hands up in front of him, ready to greet another acquaintance.

'He's right, it is the best.' The man who had previously told her about the picture was standing next to her holding the bottle. 'Go on, have a proper drink,' he said, and he poured her a full glass of wine.

'I shouldn't. I'm driving,' she said. It sounded like a line from a television soap opera.

'Don't drive then. Why go anywhere?'

'You keep telling me what to do,' she said.

'Yes.' He drank from his glass, looking at her over the edge. He was a good head taller than she was, slim and beautifully dressed. He wasn't young, yet he was obviously very fit and his clothes hung on him as though he was wearing them in spite of himself. She stood her ground. He said, 'I'm sorry if I seem to do that. I don't mean to. Did you buy the picture?'

'Yes.'

'I thought you would. You obviously liked it. You noticed the difference between yourself and the woman on the bed.'

Sally could think of nothing to say to that. Was it an offensive remark or not? Certainly it made her feel very vulnerable.

'What will you do with it?'

Sally hadn't thought about that. 'Do with it? I don't know. Hang it up, I suppose.'

'I thought you might be giving it to your husband or something.'

She laughed; the wine was affecting her. 'No, no. Not his taste at all.' He smiled and she carried on. 'Stags at bay, that sort of thing is his idea of a good painting.' It occurred to her she was being very disloyal at a moment's notice with a man she did not know at all. But she went on. 'Like that extraordinary painting that used to be in the Tate.' She dimly remembered a visit they had made many years ago.

'I remember it,' he said, 'straight ahead as you go down the left-hand corridor. Glencoe or something. Huge, about twenty feet tall.'

'That's the one.' Everything he said was exact.

'There's a gallery that sells what you call "that sort of thing" just up the road.'

'I know. Thirty-six thousand pounds a picture,' she said. 'They tried to sell one to me.'

'You didn't buy it for him?'

'Golf clubs would be more the point.'

'Are you a collector?'

'No.'

'You bought the LeBasque on a whim?'

'No. I bought it because I liked it.'

'You bought it because of the difference from or the similarity to yourself?'

She didn't reply to that. For a moment she felt that she might be blushing. What an odd idea.

'When you got out of bed this morning you weren't going to go out and buy a picture?'

There it was again. His remarks were indifferent but each one seemed to spark endless possibilities.

Sally remembered the things she had done that day. 'No,' she said, 'I wasn't going to do that.'

She thought about the death at the Old Bailey and said again, 'No, I wasn't going to do that.'

'What were you going to?'

'I was going to do a day's work. But it was cut short. That's why I'm here.'

She knew he was about to ask another question and for a moment annoyance at being interrogated replaced her previous feelings. Astonishingly, he seemed to realise what she was feeling and instead said nothing.

He took a sip of wine.

'But here we are,' he said, 'surrounded by beautiful pictures and we're wasting our time talking.'

Wasting her time. She supposed Roger Nichols's wife was trying to deal with the death right now. What does one tell a child? Again sensing her preoccupation, he turned away slightly, not completely, but enough to give her space. She took the opportunity and stepped away from the table. Immediately she felt downright depressed. The feeling flooded over her as though the lights had been turned out. She could hear herself saying, 'Come, come, Mr Nichols. You don't mean that, do you?'

It hadn't been a question, it was a way of making someone look stupid. Scott was right. She remembered how Nichols had contradicted himself, eventually floundering, nearly breaking down. How guilty she had made him look. She stared at the picture in front of her without seeing it. She knew perfectly well that looking guilty had very little to do with whether someone was guilty. Nor did an inability to answer mean he wasn't telling the truth. She pretended that it did, pretended that cross-examination uncovered the truth. But it wasn't so. It wasn't so and it wasn't going to be possible to go on pretending that it was so, not any more.

She put her glass down and walked away from the table towards the door. As she did so the gallery owner entered.

'Are you off, Miss Donne? Your picture will be delivered tomorrow, to your chambers. Before midday.'

So he had checked up on her. No, of course he knew what an address in the Temple meant. She summoned up a smile and answered him. 'Thank you, Mr Brown.'

He shook her hand. Then she left.

She had spent the blood money she had earned that day.

It had grown completely dark outside. The road had become blocked with traffic coming up from Piccadilly, and what had earlier been a cheerful scene had now become angry and tense. A horn blew behind her where a car was being held up. She could see the drawn faces of the drivers. It isn't possible to drive home in a traffic jam relaxed. She walked down the street, slightly fusty from the wine. She glanced at her watch – it was well after seven. If she found a taxi she could be back in the Temple in twenty minutes. By now it was raining again and getting colder.

After a short while standing unsuccessfully looking for a taxi, she crossed the road to stand under the arches outside the Ritz, out of the rain. She was so distracted that for a while she did not notice that she was now looking for cabs going in the wrong direction. She would have to go back round the corner, so she ventured out into the rain again. A taxi swerved in towards her; she stepped forward but it stopped short at the steps of the hotel. A couple came down the steps and climbed into the cab.

Sally stood and waited; another cab came. She hailed it but then, annoyingly, the same thing happened. She found herself becoming angry. The cold was picking through her coat. She walked to the other side of the Ritz entrance and stood waiting. The porter had seen her. A cab appeared, seemed to respond to her wave and then, at the last moment, shot past her; again it picked up a hotel guest. At this she became really annoyed.

'What do I have to do to get a cab?' she said to the hotel porter, who was standing by her looking at the tip he had just been given. 'Do I have to become a guest?'

The porter wasn't in the least bit put out. 'It would certainly help, madam,' he said, holding the hotel door open.

Warm air and bright light washed down the steps towards where Sally was standing. Her head had started to ache. She should never have drunk anything on an empty stomach; she wouldn't be fit to drive for some time. On the spur of the moment she made a decision that changed her life.

'All right', she said, 'I will,' and she walked up the steps, a single woman, or at least a woman on her own, into the Ritz.

5

The air inside the hotel was soft after the sharp cold air outside. Warm colours and sounds began soothing her as soon as she heard the doors close behind her with a sigh. The hotel porter followed her in. He signalled towards the desk and a pageboy came to take her coat. Between them they almost smoothed and patted her down.

A manager, or at least a man in a tailcoat, walked before her, holding his arm out as if to clear the way. She walked after him down the main hall where it widened out with tables beneath the chandeliers. In the corner there was a pianist.

'I understand madam was unable to get a taxi? You must let us obtain one for you, but meanwhile may we offer you something?'

How the information had percolated through so quickly to this exquisite creature in the shining tailcoat she could not make out. She had not seen anyone talking about her. Perhaps this was always happening.

'A dry Martini,' he said, 'or perhaps something different?'

The idea of a dry Martini was extremely attractive; her headache was receding already.

'And may we offer madam something to go with it?' Already a waitress was approaching her carrying a small tray. Sally could see smoked salmon, olives, pieces of black on squares of toast – was that caviar?

'A dry Martini?' he repeated. Sally nodded and he immediately flicked his wrist above his head in a twisting motion. He said, 'I observed you from our window, madam. It is certainly no pleasant thing to stand outside in the rain, trying in vain to get a taxi.' He spoke in a strange, periodic English.

A table was placed next to her, a small tablecloth was flung out. There a plate, a small knife and fork. The man in the tailcoat moved the laid table slightly, just so, to his satisfaction, so that the heat from the fire was slightly diminished. Another porter appeared carrying an evening paper; it looked as though it had been ironed. He set it down before her with a flourish, snapping it straight, and seconds later a tray arrived with the dry martini, the glass frosted, with a twist of lemon.

The attendants surrounding her disappeared as quickly as they had gathered. She was left sitting in a comfortable chair, drifting in the light and luxury. She was tired. For a moment she felt she might even fall asleep. She took a sip from the glass: it tasted sharp and clear. She looked at the small pieces of toast covered in caviar. Could it be caviar or was it roe? She didn't know whether she could tell the difference. She took a piece. She could tell. The extra-ordinary taste cut through her palate, emphasising the cold intoxication of the gin. It was caviar, no doubt about it. She looked at the tray. Even the generosity of the Ritz hotel knew its bounds: there were only two more pieces covered with the small clusters of black.

She left them till later and tasted the smoked salmon, then a piece of Parma ham. She began to think she didn't want to move and found she was content merely to sit still. She looked at her watch. It was getting on. She had looked at the time moments ago outside, and had then been considering how long it would take to drive home, and how long she would have to wait till it was safe to drive. But now after drinking this cocktail it was going to be even longer. She'd be lucky to be home by eleven-thirty, and even then driving would be a risk.

Sally noticed she was allowing her thoughts to run, going nowhere in particular. She didn't feel anxious about being late, it was just something she was aware of. It had been years since she had been free to do this, be on her own, at her ease with nothing to do, no demands. She didn't even have to go to court tomorrow if she didn't want to. Someone else could do the case; all that was needed was a police officer to give evidence of having seen the body, so the whole thing could be finished properly. Even at this short notice someone else could cover for her.

She found herself slipping her shoes off, but stopped in time. It showed how relaxed she had become. Instead she picked up the paper, sat back and looked around. She was sitting in a high-backed chair, turned slightly away from the public area, a position from which there was a perfect view of the comings and goings of the hotel. Again she experienced that earlier childish feeling of looking out from a secure private place, watching the whole room, unobserved behind her newspaper.

*   *   *

Jeremy Scott said, 'I want to see the ditch.' The Kent police were finding the lawyer's intensity a strain, but since he was accompanied by a Metropolitan Police officer and a solicitor they didn't complain.

The big four-wheel-drive emergency car set off again from the morgue towards the M2. About five miles down the motorway, the driver switched on a blue light and pulled over on to the hard shoulder. He bumped the huge Land-Rover up, beyond the concrete on to the grass edge, leaving the headlights shining up into the black sky above the field. They looked down. Twenty feet below them there was a wide drainage ditch, half filled with water.

'Here it is,' the driver said. He shone a beam out of the window on to the ditch below. Scott could see marks where boots had muddied the edge.

'I want to go down and see,' he said.

Stephen said, 'Why?'

'I want to see. I want to see what happened.'

'But why?' Stephen repeated again. 'It's raining. It's wet out there. We can't do anything.'

Scott said, 'I want to see it through to the end. I'm tired of walking in and out of people's lives like a tourist.'

Scott climbed out of the car. The rain was coming down even harder now and without the light of the car they could not have seen how to get down into the ditch. Half-way down the light ran out and they had to pick their way in the darkness.

'Just there over to the right,' said the driver through his open window. He had no intention of stirring from the warm car. He called out, 'His head was half in the water, and his boots were sticking up in the air. They were yellow, otherwise we'd not have noticed him. He'd still be stuck there.' He flashed the beam to show them. 'And the rats would have come by now,' he muttered, pulling his head back into the car. There was no need to make people feel ill. He could hear them sliding down the slope cursing.

Terry Davies made a note of the time as they stood looking down at the edge of the drainage ditch. He'd have to give evidence of the body and where it was found to the judge. That would be a bit like reporting the weather to the speaking clock, for all the effect it would have on her. He walked along to the place which was lit up: there were dark marks on the grass which were clearly blood. He pointed them out to the barrister and the solicitor. Scott poked at the clump of grass with his foot. There were probably bits of bone in there.

Terry Davies watched them. God knows why they were here. All Scott kept saying was that he was fed up with not knowing about things. And twice he had heard him say it wasn't a game. They were both clearly upset about something. 'Something' – that was silly, obviously they were upset about the man's death, but more upset than you would have thought. After all it wasn't their fault.

'If only we had told him,' Scott said, 'and the reason he wasn't told was that everybody takes counsel's advice.'

He turned rather too suddenly and nearly lost his balance. Terry Davies held his arm and prevented him from falling. 'Steady,' he said. 'Don't want to go falling in, do you?'

'Not any further,' said Scott.

They started scrabbling up the bank, sliding backwards, becoming wetter and dirtier the more they fought to get to the top.

The police car smelt of wet clothes. There was a wet

scarf between the front seats, cluttered in with a torch and a map. Surreptitiously Scott wiped the mud from his hands on the back of the seat in front of him. The driver leaned forward and turned on a fan which began to hum in the background. 'Where now?' he said.

'We're going home,' said Terry Davies.

'Where's home?'

'The car's at the police station.'

'OK,' said the driver. 'Then it'll be easier to go back on the side roads.' He pulled off the motorway at the next exit. The rain poured down, the windscreen wipers slapped in time on the windows as the car swept down the small lanes. Scott sat in the back looking down at the spray the car threw up.

He felt the car slow down and looked past the driver's shoulder at a Mini which was driving in front of them. It fought its way through the wet, looking very tiny as though scuttling away in panic from the police car's headlights. The mere difference in size gave the feeling of a chase.

Scott spoke over the driver's shoulder. 'I suppose the moment they see you their driving improves.'

'If they see me,' the policeman said. 'Most people never look in their mirror. This one hasn't yet. And she's going too fast – at this rate she'll lose it at Topham Cross.'

They followed the little car zipping down the lanes.

'We'll pull her over just before she gets there, then she'll have to go into the corner slowly. Though I think she's seen us now, look.'

Scott leaned forward to see the back of the small car. From the tiny window he could see a child's face looking up at them.

'The kids are not strapped in anyway. We've got a reason for a pull.'

There was a short, straight stretch of road. The police car swung out and flashed at the Mini. Scott was relieved to see it pull over. The policemen climbed down and one went to each side of the small car. They towered above the young woman who got out. Looking back Scott could see small faces staring up through the windscreen. The conversation didn't last long, it seemed friendly enough. The second policeman leaned inside the car and Scott could see him chatting to the children. One of them threw herself back on the seat in a shout of laughter. Scott could see the other one slowly putting a seat belt on.

The two policemen came back and the Land-Rover pulled out ahead of the small car. Scott watched as the small faces stared up wonderingly at him.

They set off again in silence, then the driver said, 'First contact.' Nothing more, until Scott repeated, 'First contact?'

'First contact with a policeman. It sets the tone. If the first time you see a policeman he's kicking your mum's door in, then that sets the tone as well.'

Scott was surprised at the officer's remark, then immediately judged himself. That was arrogant. Why should he imagine that defence lawyers have a monopoly on understanding people? The driver spoke to his colleague. 'Her name was Anne Timms. That rings a bell.'

There was a moment's silence. Obviously both were searching their memory. Then the passenger said, 'Timms. It's that family from Topham. That was my patch once.'

'Those aren't her kids then.'

'No way, too old, she's not nineteen yet.'

'That wouldn't stop some of them in Topham.' They laughed. 'Isn't she the girlfriend of that Darren? The Topham toerag?' Then, 'Here's Topham Cross.' The road was suddenly brightly lit.

Topham Cross was a roundabout. Scott looked to the right and saw a large lorry coming down the ramp from the northbound motorway; it swept into their sight surrounded by a huge shower of spray. Almost before they were aware of it the whole thing crashed past the small roundabout at the bottom of the slope. The police car, which had hung back instead of insisting on its right of way, slowed up sharply. 'Bloody dangerous,' the driver said. Scott looked back to see the little Mini sweep over the roundabout after them. 'Think what it would have done to them.' Scott had no difficulty imagining the little car skidding into the path of the lorry, its tiny tyres unable to grip the slippery road.

They carried on in silence as the dark closed in on their car. Behind them Scott could occasionally see the following lights of the little car illuminating a hedge at a corner.

'Here's where one of yours lives,' the driver said over his shoulder.

'One of mine?'

'Big-time lawyer.'

The police car rushed past. Scott got an impression of a long white fence, a closely clipped beech hedge, a long sweeping gravel drive, lit at the top by arc lights showing off the whole clean façade of a large country house. He turned to look and as they turned the corner saw the lights of the little car making its way up the drive, delivering the children home no doubt.

91

'One of the successful ones,' Scott said to Stephen.

'Very successful,' said the policeman over his shoulder.

Two women picked their way down the central hall of the Ritz, preceded, as everyone seemed to be, by a man in a tailcoat. Sally watched them.

They were shown to a table just at the top of the steps, where they sat down, side by side, looking out, gazing at the hallway below them.

They did not speak to each other. One of the women reached down and lifted a small handbag on to her knees. She opened it and peered inside, apparently rearranging what was there, for she took nothing out, but shut it and, transferring her gaze to the hallway beneath her, put it down by her feet again. A waiter appeared with a tray. Two drinks, one of them a curious emerald green, arrived. The women nodded and the waiter glided away. Still they said nothing. After a long pause one of them took a drink.

Suddenly there was a momentary stiffening of their attention. Sally looked in the direction of the women's gaze. In the hallway an elegant, middle-aged, rather stout man was approaching. He was wearing a dark suit. His face and hair glistened. He held a cigarette slightly away from him between the thumb and forefinger of his upturned open hand: it was unmistakably a central European gesture. The position of his hand seemed to be one of deference. He stopped a little way before he reached the women and dropped the cigarette in an ashtray. Then he moved forward and stood with one foot advanced on to the steps the better to be able to speak to them. After a moment one of the two held her hand out. The man took it and kissed it. The other woman said nothing, hardly even acknowledging his presence. A few words passed, then the man ducked his head again receiving a slight nod in return. He turned round and walked away. As he did so he took his cigarette case from his pocket and tapped the end of a new cigarette on it, tamping down the tobacco. It was a gesture Sally had not seen for years.

The woman who had spoken said something to her companion, who acknowledged it by moving her lips for a moment. What had she said? What would fit? Maybe, 'The Baron, my dear.' Sally imagined that the woman would have placed the emphasis heavily on the second syllable. She repeated the words to herself, like the Eliot poem. Then she looked around to see if anyone had noticed her talking to herself. She was becoming slightly light-headed.

Again the women's attention was attracted by something in the hall. Sally watched. This time a procession approached. Four people, two couples, being led by the tailcoated attendant towards the central area, then past them towards the restaurant. Sally could just see the edge of the far room.

They walked in a stately fashion. As they began to pass the steps to the area where the women were sitting, Sally was astonished to see one of the two women half stand, move sideways from her chair and discreetly curtsey toward the group. The leading man, walking slightly in front, twisted his wrist in a half acknowledgement. The other three continued as though nothing had happened. Royalty had passed. Sally wondered which little country had spared its monarch for a life at the Ritz.

'May we find you a taxi now, madam?' The waiter

appeared at her side. Again on impulse – was it connected with the fascination of what she had witnessed? – she refused. 'No, I think I shall stay for a while.' And then she said – it seemed utterly natural – 'Is there a table I could have in the restaurant?'

The waiter didn't need to enquire. 'We shall prepare a table for you, madam. Will you be dining alone?'

'Yes.'

'It will be ready when you wish.'

'Could I . . .' Sally paused, she was committed now. 'Do you have a room?'

'Yes, madam.'

The waiter indicated the reception desk on the other side of the hall.

After a while Sally made her way towards it. Behind her the table at which she had been sitting was instantly cleared, the cloth removed. As she approached the desk she saw the face of the staff member who had first spoken to her.

'Have you a room?' Sally watched herself make the request. She had become detached, smoothed out by the calm. The pressure of the Old Bailey was being dredged out of her. Here there was nothing but compliance, there nothing but confrontation.

'Why, certainly.'

A register was turned towards her and a pen offered. As though in an effort to take part in her own adventure Sally opened her bag and searched for her pen, found it and signed the book.

'Room number . . .' The desk clerk turned away from her in a gesture she had seen in a thousand films, reaching towards where the keys hung. 'Here we are.' He handed

94

her the key while at the same time gesturing to a young porter who stood nearby, already holding her coat.

Sally remembered she had no suitcase with her. The hotel had realised this too, and a young woman from behind the reception desk was suddenly alone with her. 'Can I get you some night things, madam?'

I wonder what sort of person they think I am? Sally thought, then she said to the woman, 'That would be very kind.' She moved away from the counter. 'I must ring the children, they'll be worrying where I am,' she said out loud. Again she looked to see if anybody had heard her talking to herself, or had she said that because of what the staff at the hotel might be thinking? It was difficult to tell. She looked around but saw no trace of any disapproving judgement.

Sally stood at the window of her room. She looked out over Green Park and Piccadilly where the traffic was strung out below her in a ribbon of light. Over to her left Constitution Hill was lit by a gentler light, gas, occasionally flaring in the wind. Behind the lights, Buckingham Palace gardens were dark.

Her children were not at home. She had phoned. Anne Timms must have taken them out after collecting them from school, taken them maybe to Topham. She knew that sometimes she did that, but she was not normally this late home. Perhaps she had rung home, found that Sally hadn't got back and stayed out late.

Sally watched the traffic come to a stop on Piccadilly. A taxi suddenly decided to go back the way it had come. It was amazing how good-tempered the drivers were in London; at least they were if you played the game and waited your turn. Then someone would eventually let you in, but if you pushed, people got angry. The taxi made its tight turn and the ribbon of light started moving again.

The children did like Anne. They were always calm after being with her for a long time. Sally pictured it. It didn't seem the same when they spent time with her nowadays. Eventually there would be an argument, and sometimes she would end up shouting at them. She knew why, of course: they were angry she wasn't with them more. But what could she do? Her job was all or nothing.

She stared out of the window. The children liked Anne. No, that did not describe it. The children loved Anne. Sometimes she wondered if they loved Anne more than they loved her. Perhaps they were right to do so. After all it wasn't always clear that she was particularly good for them. Was that possible? Well, it wasn't long ago that it was perfectly normal for a mother's role to be taken by someone else, someone whose career it was. She laughed to herself at the hateful word. Someone whose career it was to be a mother.

There was a knock on the door.

She went over to answer it and two housemaids headed for the bed and started to turn the sheets down. One of them closed the curtains, as though telling her not to look out – what's out there is unfriendly. A waiter followed them in and set up a silver ice bucket; in it was a half-bottle of champagne. Behind them was the woman in the dark suit to whom Sally had spoken below, carrying a small packet. She stood and watched as the staff set everything right, then remained behind as they left.

'I have some things for you, madam, and for tomorrow morning. Something to wear in bed of course.' She smiled and put a tiny flask of Chanel on the bedside table. She didn't wait for a response, but picked up the small bottle of champagne and expertly flicked the cork out, dropping it into the wastebasket. Later Sally reflected that the waiter must have prepared the bottle, to enable his colleague to do it so easily. It was what she had seen below, the staff acting out a picture of perfect hotel employees.

The woman backed out of the room with a smile. 'With the compliments of the management, madam,' she said as she closed the door.

Sally turned away from the interruption. Of course it was possible. Generations of English children had been shuffled off by their parents, first to nannies and then to boarding schools. Boarding school – that was a problem she hadn't faced up to yet. She knew her husband assumed they would go. Should they go away to school? 'Sending them away to school.' You only had to repeat the phrase to yourself to understand exactly what it involved. People used the words without appreciating what they were saying. Sending them away. What was so odd about it was that most of the country would not even dream of doing such a thing, but to those who did, it seemed perfectly natural.

She took a glass of champagne and went to stand by the window, pulling the curtain back.

Of course it was possible for the children to love someone else more than her. That was the journey they were setting out on. All children left their parents; if they didn't there was something wrong. But not as early as this. Her husband had told her of the time he came home from a term away at school and called his mother 'matron'. Was that going to happen to her? She went to the phone and pressed the redial number. There was still no answer at home. She took another sip from her glass and looked at the bottle. Krug. They had given her the best.

The thought reminded her of the parcel. She opened it. There was a white cotton nightgown, very demure. Underclothes and a selection of shirts. Each of them carefully priced. She looked at the shirts, a couple each of two sizes. The woman at reception had sized her up, but hadn't made the decision. She smiled – well, that was the proper use of the expression, sized her up. And some tights, a complete change. Enough – after all they could hardly supply a suit.

She ran a bath, and took the champagne into the bathroom. The light reflecting from the mirrors on to the tiles was dazzling. There were beautiful towels, the floor was thickly carpeted, something that had always seemed to her the height of decadence. It was wonderfully warm and clean. Sally was beginning to enjoy herself. She lay in the bath. She didn't often have a bath, normally she only had time for a shower. When was the last time she had done this? Taken time off for herself. She thought back. She couldn't remember.

All that work had paid off: she could afford what she was doing now without even stopping to think how much it would cost. And she had bought the picture. In four hours she had spent what some people earn in six months.

But then, today was a funny day. Suddenly her mind was back on the man she had cross-examined. Blown the top of his head off. She shook the image from her mind and took a drink.

The phone rang.

Sally was out of the bath, dripping wet, before she

realised there was an extension within reach. She un-
hooked the phone. The hotel receptionist spoke to her,
'You asked us to reach this number, madam.' So she had.
Sally remembered.

It was Anne. 'Hallo, Miss Donne.'

'Anne, I shan't be able to get home tonight. Will you be
able to manage?' As she spoke Sally lost control of her
voice very slightly. The slip was like a momentary im-
balance on a polished floor, her voice skidded up the scale.

'Of course, Miss Donne,' Anne said.

Frisch gebohnert, a freshly polished floor. Sally noticed
that her thoughts were slightly disordered as well. The
heat of the bathroom was affecting her.

'Anne? I'm sorry, can I ring you back in another
moment?'

'Of course, Miss Donne.'

She got out of the bath, angry with herself. She dried
and put the Ritz bathrobe on. She sat on the bed and ate
some nuts, controlled herself and then picked up the
phone.

'Anne?' she said as the phone in Kent was answered.
'Anne, can you manage?'

'Yes, Miss Donne. Mrs Hicks will be in the cottage.'
Mrs Hicks was the housekeeper, living in the old cottage
behind the house.

'I can't get back,' Sally said. She was about to make
excuses, but thought better of it and stopped. It was all
right not to explain. Anne clearly thought that what was
happening was the most ordinary thing in the world.

'Will Mr Murray be back?' Anne said.

'I don't think so. Doesn't he have an appointment in
his constituency?' Sally didn't want to talk about her

husband, she wanted to ask, 'Where were you? Why weren't you at home?' But now wasn't the time.

'Are the children there?' she said. She could hear them in the background. Harriet came to the phone, slow and careful, feeling the pressure of being the older. 'Where are you, Mummy?'

'I'm in London.'

The child was trying to keep the disappointment from her voice. At least she was still disappointed. 'When are you coming back?'

'Tomorrow.'

'Oh, Mummy. We won't see you.'

'But often you don't see me.'

'But we know you're coming back.'

There was no answer to that. Sally wondered whether she could change her mind and get home. But a glance at the clock made her realise it would be pointless. 'You'll be all right with Anne,' she tried to reassure her daughter.

'Yes, Mummy,' then the child's momentary distress lifted as quickly as it settled upon her. 'Mummy, we went to Anne's. We made a cake.'

Sally pictured it. She knew that they had more fun in Anne's mother's tiny kitchen than in the whole expensive playroom upstairs at home. On that kitchen table they cut out paper, made cup cakes, painted wild pictures, while Anne's mother sat in the corner occasionally switching the channel on the TV. It wasn't the old-fashioned image of a cheery farmhouse but a small, rather nasty bungalow; nevertheless, on the occasions when Sally collected the children, it still had the atmosphere of the friendly kitchen of children's stories. 'Jenny made a paper bag go pop, Mummy.'

Sally could hear a voice in the background, 'Me, me, me.' There was a scuffling noise. Harriet said, 'Bye, Mum,' and her voice was replaced by the younger's. Jenny had not yet learned to adjust her voice properly for the phone and Sally had to hold it away from her ear to separate the meaning of the words. 'Slow down,' she said. It made no difference at all. 'I made a cake with Anne's mummy and Harriet upset the bowl and got – got – got –' She became stuck on a word, and had to take a deep breath: 'got flour on her face and she looked like a snowman, her face was white, and then she fell and she cried and Mummy' – she had to repeat the word Mummy, as though to keep contact with Sally's silence at the end of the phone – 'when are you coming back?'

Sally heard Harriet say, 'Tomorrow' in the background and then heard Jenny turn away from the phone and speak to her sister behind her. Sally pictured it, the tenuous telephone link between her and her child being over-shadowed by the actual presence of her big sister.

'Yes? Go on,' Sally said. Her daughter immediately changed the subject in the same sudden way that a baby opens its hand and drops something as its attention wanders elsewhere.

'Harriet hit me in the car on the way home. We spoke to a policeman.'

'What?' Sally said.

'Yes, he was nice and he told me he would show me his dog.'

That sounded a little like the kind of invitation the police themselves are always warning children against.

'Was Anne with you?' Sally said evenly, controlling her voice.

101

'Yes, she was driving the car.'

What was all this about? 'That's nice. Was he nice to you?'

'He had a big radio, like your phone, and he talked to his friends on it. He showed me. He kept ringing his friends. As he drove around looking for people to stop. He told me.'

'What did he want?'

'I don't know, he never said. Mummy, when are you coming back?'

Sally heard Harriet repeat 'Tomorrow' in the background, and heard Jenny move away from the phone to argue, 'Not tomorrow. When's tomorrow?'

Sally could see her standing in the large kitchen, trying to hold her own.

'Mummy, when's tomorrow?' She had come back.

'I'll come and collect you from school tomorrow.' Sally made a rash promise. How could she be sure of that? But it was the one thing that always set her children squealing with delight. The next day would now be a rising crescendo as going-home time approached and they rocketed into the playground towards where she stood by the big tree.

'Mummy'll come and get us from school tomorrow,' the child repeated. There was silence where Sally expected to hear a shout. Then Harriet came to the telephone again. 'Mummy, we can't come tomorrow. Anne's taking us to tea with her sister. It's Maisy's birthday. We're going to tea with Maisy.'

For a moment Sally nearly said, 'Well, I'm sorry but you can't go.' But that would make things worse. 'Oh, lucky you,' she said. 'That'll be fun.'

Her daughter was not to be deceived and said simply, 'I'm sorry, Mummy,' and put the phone down.

For a few moments Sally stood on her own in her white terry towel bathrobe, the emblem of the Ritz hotel on it, holding an empty glass in her hand, waiting for someone to speak to her. Then Anne came on the line and said, 'I'm sorry, Miss Donne, I promised to take them to Maisy's birthday tea tomorrow. Will that be all right?'

Again Sally thought how she could easily have said that they couldn't go, after all they were her children. She was in charge. But of course she couldn't.

'Of course, Anne,' she said. 'Anne, we're very lucky to have someone who loves the children so much.'

'Oh, it's only natural, miss,' Anne said, twisting the knife.

Sally put the phone down and immediately realised she had forgotten to ask about the policeman.

She dressed slowly, since she had no very clear idea of what she would do when she was finished; there was no one waiting for her downstairs. The fresh linen felt good against her skin, her head was clearing from the alcohol and the heat of the bathroom, and she realised that she was beginning to feel hungry. She had eaten nothing save the apple at lunch and the canapés.

Had she gone home her appetite would have been suppressed, if she got there in time, by feeding the children, reading them books and putting them to bed. More often than not after that she felt like eating very little, perhaps some fruit. But now she felt her senses sharpened by real hunger. She pulled on her stockings, cool against her skin. The new shirt crackled slightly as she unwrapped it. The gloss on the material shone in the soft

103

lights of the room. She felt like she was dressing for a party. Even her shoes caressed her feet as though massaging them.

She stood before the mirror looking at herself, remembering what she had been told. Never look in a mirror. Only a man – it was her father – could have said that. Her eye fell on the small bottle of scent. She always hesitated before wearing any other than her normal light scent, ever since one day she had bumped into Jane sweeping out of court, complaining about her opponent. 'My dear, it was like being in a Turkish bath,' she had said, holding Sally's wrist tightly. 'She was covered. I couldn't bear it any longer.' Then she had laughed her curious, coughing laugh. Sally loved that laugh and felt she would have liked to hear it now.

Sally touched the tip of the bottle on to her wrist, and rubbed her wrists together. 'The heat of your blood evaporates the volatile liquid, then it mixes with your animal smell, which entices stray men. Pure barbarism,' her pupil master, who thought he was entitled to tell her these things as well as teach her law, had warned her. 'We should seek to be above such artifice, Sally. We seek to avoid the heat of the blood,' he had said, and she had laughed at him. He was pleased to be laughed at. She could see him now sitting in a corner of El Vino. He was proud to have trained her. He had said so. 'I know how the job should be done, but somehow can't seem to do it properly myself. You do it for me, like I showed you.' Once she had seen him at the back of a court listening to her, but when he realised that he had been seen, he slipped out. 'On the other hand,' he said, 'I'm not sorry I was never good at it, because if I had been, then something inside me might have died. It usually does if you are good at this job.'

She used to think that what he said was just words, just excuses for his not achieving as much as others, but look at her now, what was she doing here, what was it that had made her end up in this hotel? It wasn't just that she was tired and didn't want to drive. It was more than that. For a moment she was stopped in her tracks. Had something inside her died, the thing her pupil master had feared would happen to him, and which never did?

She felt like smoking a cigarette. At least then there would be something for her hands to do. She sat down on the bed. She could smell the perfume rising from her wrists, mixing, no doubt, with her animal smell.

She said to herself, 'I think I may be in trouble.'

6

The dining room was busy, though as far as she could see, it wasn't full. A tail-coated attendant hung over a tall mahogany desk like a bird, checking and rechecking a thick leather book. He appeared so busy that Sally immediately expected difficulty: no doubt there wasn't a free table – especially for one. But then he looked up. He had been told she was coming, he had her room number immediately, her previous request had been acted on.

'Of course, madam. This way, madam.' He snatched up a menu and a wine list, and holding them before him like a warning, swept across the room towards the window. Long before she reached the table a waiter had begun to prepare it: the second setting of silver knives and forks were removed leaving only one place, and a huge linen napkin was shaken out with a snapping sound. A small vase with flowers arrived.

She found herself seated in a corner on one side of the huge room, looking out through the vast window over Green Park, with, on her other side, a full view of the dining room. She herself was not exposed, and she found that if she leaned back slightly she became almost hidden by the shadows of the twenty-foot curtain above her. She tried to remember when last she had been in a restaurant on her own but wasn't sure that she could. When occasionally she went out of London to provincial courts there was always another member of the bar at the hotel. On the train? Yes, she had eaten alone on the train while going to Exeter. But that wasn't the same.

She sat, preoccupied with her thoughts, and then suddenly looked up. A man at a nearby table was watching her. He was eating with two other men. Sally avoided his eye, though at the same time she found herself smoothing her clothes and touching her face. She became angry, with herself. Why was there always this double response? She knew she had no wish whatever to make eye contact, nor any contact, with this man, yet all the same there came, unbidden, this ridiculous need to preen. No, it wasn't preening, she was being too hard on herself. It was more a case of keeping one's equipment in order. She smiled and hid the smile behind the menu – don't let him see that; the smallest movement and he would use it as an excuse to come over. She looked again out of the corner of her eye: now the man was talking about her to his friends – that was obvious by the way they reacted, immediately looking over at her. She could almost write the script, so she had better avoid it.

The waiter appeared, blocking their view, and she took the opportunity to move her chair slightly backwards under the shelter of the curtain, out of their sight. The waiter didn't stay, he was concerned only to make sure she had iced water and some bread, but his arrival had been enough to give her the opportunity to avoid being so easily seen.

107

She picked up the bread. It smelt of olives. She sat still, there was no hurry. Clearly she could sit here as long as she wished. 'An aperitif?' Another waiter appeared. Sally refused. Just wine. She'd had enough to drink already; a half-bottle of wine would be all right.

She looked out through the window over the park. In the distance she could see the traffic at Hyde Park Corner, where cars swung around in a huge arc under Apsley House. A mist hung over the park itself. Here and there the soft whiteness was lit from within by yellow lights, where swan-necked wrought-iron lamps dotted the paths. Each created a little pool of light which people occasionally entered, holding the stage for a moment, then leaving again into the dark.

The whole park was criss-crossed with paths. Lines of desire. The tracks would originally have been created by people cutting across the grass by the shortest route, and continual repetition had created paths, 'lines of desire', architects called them, patterns of movement unassisted by planners. It seemed a shame to have wasted so poignant a phrase on such a mundane event.

A bundled figure, wrapped up against the cold, appeared, approaching the hotel and then turning away, disappearing into the gloom. She remembered Conrad's shadowy figures stealing through Greenwich Park between pools of light like these, carrying their packets of explosive. The very light felt cold and she shivered, until the warmth and colour of the dining room wrapped itself around her again.

A waiter was approaching carrying her wine. She settled back and watched what was happening inside the room. Behind the waiter someone else was walking towards her. It was the tall man from the art dealers.

Her first reaction was annoyance that she had been followed, but then it was clear that he wasn't approaching her. He wasn't even aware of her presence. He walked straight past, accompanied, as she had been, by the *maître d'hotel* extravagantly showing him his table. It had been obvious this was someone's regular table, she had already noticed it, set only for one, and on it something one often saw in France, a napkin, not folded, but rolled in a silver ring. Next to the table setting was a book, dark red, soft Moroccan leather, with a silk marker spilling from between the pages.

He sat down with his back to her, though when he turned in order to signal to the waiter she could see his profile plainly. He was certainly an extremely handsome man, with a strong, ridged face, dark hair, slightly unkempt. His suit was dark with a thin red stripe, hardly noticeable, and – Sally had spotted them immediately – he had beautifully made shoes. She watched him from her hidden place. He didn't seem to be aware of himself in the way that handsome men often are. She caught herself being pleased at that, but then thought, why be concerned either way?

Another waiter appeared carrying a small contraption. At first Sally, who by now was watching unashamedly, could not see what it was. The waiter stooped over and manipulated the pieces, unfolding it. It was a reading stand, carved from dark wood. He thanked the waiter, placed the book on it and held the open pages back with clips that folded out from the base. What ought to have been a rather precious action, arranging a book so that it could be read while he was eating, was relieved by his obvious and complete indifference to how he looked.

Under the table Sally saw him half kick off one of his shoes. A drink appeared at his elbow. He accepted it with a nod. No menu was brought, food just arrived.

He started to read and became engrossed. In what? Sally could not see. Other than that the book was bound in Moroccan leather and the pages were of the thinness of rice paper, she could not see anything of it. Whatever it was, though, it was clearly not Jeffrey Archer.

Sally ordered her meal. Fish. Dover sole with white wine, nothing too heavy. She was beginning to feel only tired now, less beset by what she had drunk before. Her mind wandered away.

By now the children would be in bed. She knew that sometimes when she didn't get back in time, the girls would sleep in the same bed, bundled up together under the Homer Simpson duvet. She could picture it with absolute clarity. The picture made her heart shift. It was bitter-sweet: she wasn't there, one more night gone, and after all, it only lasted so long. They grow and then what? For a moment she contemplated being without them, but shook the idea off. That was years away. On the other hand it was inevitable, so it was difficult not to be aware of it. Wasn't there a woman who jumped off the bridge in Bristol because her children had left home?

Sally allowed herself to taste that woman's despair. And that other woman. Sally touched another memory gently with her mind, as though insistently feeling an ulcer in her mouth with her tongue, that other woman, whose child fell into the river, and whose other two children, while she was trying to rescue the first, also fell in. All three drowned. Drowned. Later she also took her own life. Her death was reported with a complete lack of comment, because there was only one thing to be said: 'Of course she did, who wouldn't?' She would have done so herself.

Sally shut the memory down, as effectively as if she had slammed a door; after all, it was possible to become morbid, to allow one's feelings to swell and grow until a sense of proportion was lost. On the other hand it was events like those that set matters in proportion, or the other way around.

She was drawn back to them. We all carry a place in our minds where it is possible to stand looking over the brink. There was that mother in South Wales who gave her daughter a drink at a party. The daughter died from it, a single glass of wine. And then the mother was prosecuted, for heaven's sake. Sally could only too well imagine the atmosphere in that court, strained, righteous condemnation of a bad mother. At least that woman would have been protected by her grief. She probably didn't notice the arrogance of the system lecturing her, it would have been as irrelevant as a slap to a dying man. That woman had killed herself too. What did the judge feel then?

Courts.

Courts were her daily life. And they were snagging at her natural responses all the time, unpicking her, turning her away from being a woman into being a lawyer. Maybe she didn't want it any more, maybe that was why she was here.

In Lewes Crown Court she had cross-examined a man. No, he wasn't a man, he was a boy, only nineteen. He had killed a friend on the back of his motorcycle, crashing it into a road sign. Sally had read the prosecution papers and pictured the arrogance of him, driving too fast, too much to drink, overtaking a line of traffic and wham! his friend was dead. Now there he was in the witness box denying he

111

was at fault. She had cross-examined him, but the man she thought she was cross-examining, the arrogant young yob, wasn't there. Instead there was a young man breaking down, sobbing out how he couldn't sleep for dreaming of his dead friend. As the boy had lifted his bowed head from his chest to take a gasping breath she had seen his face and the pain, like a classic representation of grief. In the silence the dead boy's mother had run across the court and cradled him in her arms, looking at Sally, saying nothing.

What was she meant to do? Shrug that kind of thing off as just another day's business, or let herself feel the pain? If she didn't allow herself to feel, then she would be killing something which was still alive within her, like the man had said. But if she did allow the pain continually to enter her, what was it doing to her? How long can you stand it?

With an effort she recalled herself to her surroundings. The plate of Dover sole, half finished, a flowery wine, and suddenly, she realised, standing by her, holding his book, the gallery man. She saw the title of the book, *The Secret Agent*. Another spy.

'Can I sit down?' he said.

A chair appeared and after a pause, certainly long enough for her to refuse had she wished, he sat down. Sally was interested to notice that she had not been about to say no.

'I am sorry, you haven't finished your meal,' he said.

'I hadn't really thought about it,' she replied. 'I wasn't really eating from hunger. Just the taste.'

'Then if it's taste you're looking for, have a milena. Here it is only served for two people, and as you can see I'm on my own.' He gestured at his table. The room around her buzzed with conversation. The waiters contributed a quiet hum, with the occasional clash of silver on a serving dish.

'Do you eat here every day?' she asked.

'Most days. What made you think . . . ?' He turned round and looked at the table. 'Oh, the napkin ring,' he said, solving the problem.

'And you look at home,' she said. A waiter brought his half-finished bottle of wine from his old table. 'Somehow I hadn't imagined the Ritz using those.' She pointed to the rubber stopper that must have kept the wine sealed overnight.

He laughed. 'No, they weren't pleased, you could tell when I asked for it, but it really does keep the wine perfectly, and who wants to drink a whole bottle every night? So they do it for me. And do you know? They only charge me when I have finished the bottle. I don't understand that. You'd have thought I was liable for the whole price the moment it was opened, but no. Now you're a lawyer. Explain that.'

Sally nearly asked how he knew she was a lawyer, but didn't. He answered her nevertheless.

'Because you look like a lawyer.'

She decided he must have spoken to the owner of the gallery.

'Tough,' he said.

'What?'

'You look tough. On the inside, not on the outside. You look as though you can stand up for yourself. So I thought lawyer. You speak like a lawyer.'

'What's milena?' she said.

'It's their special pudding. Milena and wine, please,' he said to a waiter who appeared behind him. Sally watched.

113

He seemed miraculously able to attract waiters, so that he only need look up to speak to one.

'But first you must finish what you have,' he said, hoisting her half-bottle of wine from its ice bucket and pouring more into her glass. 'Don't mind me. Dover sole. Wherever he was, Alfred Brendel used only ever to eat Dover sole. All the time.'

'The musician?'

'Yes.'

'For breakfast too?' said Sally.

'Now there you have me. I don't know if he ate it for breakfast. My father liked Dover sole, but for breakfast he ate kippers. If he could rescue them from my mother. She hated kippers.' Sally started to eat again. She clearly wasn't expected to join in this reminiscence. 'My mother was aware of it the moment a kipper came into the house and she would go down to the kitchen to search when Cook wasn't there, or even when she was, and root it out. In the end the only way my father could get kippers was by having them brought over from the small house immediately before breakfast, because my mother wouldn't actually take them off his plate. Though once she tried when he was deep in *The Times*. Of course those were the days when you could read *The Times*.'

He watched Sally eating, though he did so with such indifference that she found that she was not at all put out.

He said, 'My father ate Dover sole a lot, but I suppose if a man only *ever* eats Dover sole, all it tells you about is his digestion. Perhaps Brendel had bad digestion. People with bad digestion wouldn't eat kippers.'

Sally saw the label on the wine he was drinking. It must have cost a fortune. She was watching him perform.

114

'You eat sole beautifully,' he said.

'That's the first time I've been complimented on the way I eat,' she said, now feeling self-conscious. 'Anyway, they boned it for me.'

'I don't ever remember their boning it for me.'

'That's probably because you didn't ask them.'

'At the table?'

'Yes.'

'How did you know they would?'

'How could they refuse?' Sally said.

'Why not? I asked for a tomato salad at the Criterion last week, and they refused. They said the computer couldn't handle it.'

'What?' She laughed.

'A tomato salad. And they said no. What they meant was that the computer wasn't programmed to charge for it. So they might have refused to bone your Dover sole.'

'They wouldn't say that. The impression I get here is that they'd do anything you asked them to.' She paused. He was laughing at her. 'Wouldn't they?' she added.

'Well, they always have for me.'

'Look at the way you have them keep your book for you overnight, like your wine.' He opened it and looked at the pages, listening to her. She said, 'Do you think they read it?'

The waiter cleared her plate away, took her napkin, and flicked out another one as though he were cracking a whip.

'Milena, madam?' he said, laying the cloth across her lap.

'No, they don't read it, I don't think so. It doesn't feel read. The wine too, please,' he said to the waiter.

She wondered whether to ask his name, but decided not to.

'They just look after it. I've never asked what happens to it overnight. There's probably a bookshelf.'

'You really eat here every night? Where do you live?'

'There are some flats in the block, that way.' He gestured backwards. 'They're always spoken of as the Ritz flats. I live there during the week and, given that that's where I live, where else would I eat?'

'Well, you have the view,' she said, and they looked out over the park.

'Are you a lawyer?' he said.

'Yes.'

'What kind?'

'Guess.'

'Intellectual property?'

'No such luck. Miles away. Crime.'

'Crime?' He seemed genuinely surprised. 'Are you a barrister?'

'Yes.'

'Prosecuting or defending?'

'Mostly prosecution.'

'Where?'

'At the Old Bailey.'

'Well, I was right about tough then, wasn't I?'

'Yes, I suppose you have to be tough.' She admitted it. For a moment she remembered Roger Nichols. 'I don't suppose there's any alternative.'

The waiter arrived, placing two plates in front of them. Sally looked at the extraordinary colours. The blackberries shone with a glaze, and what was the green leaf – mint? It had an odd shape, not like the mint she knew.

116

'The thing is to crush the mint,' he said, crumpling the leaf in his fingers, 'and then while the taste is in the air, drink the wine.' A waiter was settling a bottle of dessert wine into an ice bucket. He pulled it out. 'We don't want it too cold, do we?' It was a bottle of Château d'Yquem. He smiled at the waiter, who left the bottle to him, and he poured it into her glass. He held the bottle by the neck, gestured with it and said, 'Hold a bottle by the neck and a woman by the waist. But I've never seen a waiter hold a bottle by the neck.'

The golden wine ran into her glass. It seemed to flow slowly as though it were denser than an ordinary liquid, curling around the inside of the glass like a Japanese wave. The scent of the wine and the herb on her plate mingled for a moment, then separated. The soft colours and sounds seemed to hold them both poised, sitting at the table, in a detached moment.

'Jasmine,' she said, tasting the milena.

'Mint from Vojvodina. A special mint. See how well it goes with the jasmine. It's almost not a mint at all, it's so sweet.'

'And the wine,' she said. As she tasted it, the flavour rippled into her mouth. It was indulgent to allow herself to become so entranced by taste, scents and colours.

'Your father sounds an important man,' she said.

'He was.'

'Famous?'

'Very.'

'Did you admire him?'

'Not much.'

They looked out of the window. The mist had grown thicker and the globes of light within it more mysterious.

117

'It looks like a set for a film.'

A couple stopped under one of the lights, turned and talked to each other. It was not possible to tell what they were saying, though by her expansive gestures it looked as though the woman were arguing.

'There you are,' he said. 'This is the scene where the intense and happy life they have been leading in a garret together is destroyed by the death of their young son. The relationship can't withstand such a blow. They separate.'

'Does he hear from her again?'

'It depends. If it's a Somerset Maugham story then he might come across her in a tenth-floor flat in Atlantic City, married to a timber importer, wearing too much make-up. If it's real life, then no. He just has a long ache in his heart for her.' As he spoke the couple separated, the man walking back towards them, while the woman's figure disappeared into the mist.

'This is the best time of year,' he said. 'In the summer you can see people so clearly that they lose all individuality and become merely boring. A paradox, that.'

There was an interruption. 'I have a message for you, sir.' Sally looked up. It was the magnificent hall porter with whom she had spoken earlier. 'I haven't written it down, since I had thought you would be on your own.'

'That's all right. What is it?'

'It's very short, sir. I'm to tell you that the submission will be made to the Cabinet tomorrow. That's all.'

He nodded and the porter walked away.

'How intriguing,' she said. 'I feel like a woman in an upper-class Edwardian play hearing the distant sound of male government. The Cabinet? Are you a politician?'

'No,' he said. 'Nothing like that. Sometimes what I do

is affected by government department decisions. Government is a very distant sound for me too. Did you decide where to hang the picture?'

Sally paused with the spoon half-way to her mouth. 'The picture,' she said as though dealing with a hazy memory. Roger Nichols, the man with the trestle table, the woman on the iron bedstead and her companion at the Ritz all mixed together for a moment in a strange pageant. 'No,' she said. 'I've been thinking it's the kind of thing that one would like to carry around and put up wherever one happened to be.' She reflected on what she had said. 'That's an odd remark. It makes me sound like a wanderer and I'm certainly not that. I can't remember the last time I slept away from home. But if I were a traveller I think I would like to carry it with me.'

'Why is that?'

'You know what you said about the difference? That I bought it because of the difference. What did you mean?'

'Because this woman in the picture, she, she . . . I don't know if I ought to say this.'

'Go on. I remembered it, so I think it matters. Tell me.'

'Because she has got something that you neglected.'

'Freedom? Is it freedom?'

'Nearly, but not quite. What I meant was that she has no role. She isn't anything else but herself.'

'That's remarkable,' Sally said. She remembered how she had decided that one of the aspects of the woman was that she didn't need to be somebody – she just was. 'And you think that I am different because I go around being someone.' The phrase sounded odd when she spoke it aloud.

'I think,' he said, 'that's probably what you think about

yourself. Because you're fed up with it. Is that right?'

This was going too far. 'No,' she said, 'I'm not fed up. I don't know why you think so, and,' she continued before he could reply, 'I'm not going to ask you why you think so. Today I find myself taking a rest, and this seemed a good place to come.'

'What's it like to be a barrister?'

Sally immediately dreaded the next question – the one everyone asks a barrister. 'How can you defend people you know are guilty?' But he didn't ask it. He said, 'It can't be very good for your personality.'

Was that what Scott had been trying to say to her? Again this stranger had asked a question that impinged on everything that had happened to her that day. She looked back at him, not saying anything for a moment. The fact that he was asking questions that seemed particularly accurate probably only meant she was feeling vulnerable, not that he had any special insight.

'Well, I suppose I can't really judge that,' she said. She didn't want to go on with this.

Again he seemed to respond to her unspoken feeling and he changed the subject. 'Do you play?' he said.

For a moment she did not know what he meant.

'Roulette,' he said. 'There's a club downstairs. Why don't we have a try?'

7

'The main aim when you play is to make sure that if you win, you win big.'

'I imagine it would be,' Sally said. She might as well have sniffed at him, acting the disapproving piano teacher who knows that success comes only from knuckling down to practice.

'Yes, well,' he said, looking at her from under the lids of his eyes for a moment, 'we all have to try to let go sometimes, but there are ways and ways of doing it. Your way is to spend the occasional night in a luxury hotel.' It was the only time in the evening when she saw anything but perfect unaffected manners from him. Until later.

Sally wondered whether to try to correct him and point out that her being in the hotel was pure chance, accident in fact. But even as she began to formulate a reply she realised that her stay at the hotel was more complicated than mere accident and not easily explicable – even to this man who seemed to understand what she was saying before she said it. Anyway it wasn't any of his business.

Immediately he went further. He stopped her at the

entrance to the casino, putting his hand on her arm. His hand was warm and it was a gentle touch even though intent on conveying a kind of urgency. She hardly caught what he said in the moment of contact. It was clear he was physically a strong man. 'It's not unlike fishing,' he said. 'All you can do is be properly prepared for when something big comes along.' Sally did not respond. After a moment, slightly tightening the pressure of his hand on her forearm, he asked, 'Do you fish?'

'No,' she said, 'I've never done that.'

She wondered whether to shake his hand free – wasn't it intolerable that he should hold her so openly? – but she did not. After all, what did openly mean? Was what he was doing so odd, was she like the Queen, someone who could not be touched?

'What about your husband?'

'No, no, I don't think so. How do you know about my husband?'

'The man who likes pictures of stags at bay.'

She remembered what she had said and felt her disloyalty again at having let slip such a phrase. After all he was more than that. He was – well, he was her husband.

'You implied that he is someone who would probably not approve of elegant watercolour pictures of women who are no better than they ought to be, sitting naked on iron beds in the south of France. Well, here we are.'

They stepped through the entrance door of the casino. Sally looked around, but her mind stayed with the idea he had conjured up. It had never occurred to her that the girl in the picture might be a – what was the French for it? She searched but couldn't find the word. A soubrette was it? She wasn't sure. For a moment she reflected upon

122

whether this changed the picture for her, then decided it did not.

'Royalty here tonight,' he said. He seemed to sniff the air in explanation, like a countryman justifying his declaration that it would shortly rain. She looked around. At one of the tables she recognised the small group that had earlier made the procession down the main hall of the hotel. 'And money,' he added, 'a good mixture.' He indicated the stout man sitting near the group, the man Sally had earlier decided was the baron. 'The Crown Prince and the Banker. It sounds like a novel by Bulgakov.'

The man he had identified as the Crown Prince, the man who had been at the front of the procession upstairs, leaned forward and spread some chips around the table. Sally thought she saw him glance, as though for reassurance, at the stout man to his left. Perhaps he got what he was looking for, since the stout man leaned forward and covered the chips with larger ones.

'A thousand a go,' he whispered to her. 'He's only got to hit one number and the Prince's expenses are met for a week.'

The wheel was spun and Sally felt the tension in the room increase. She had always wondered what caused the applause at the end of a big auction. After all, what was being applauded? Someone spending a large sum of money. But it was the same here: even those who had not bet anything shared in the tension.

The ball bounced around the circle. It was an immediately recognisable noise, provoking the same shock of familiarity that one experiences when seeing a famous face. She looked at the table. If those chips were a thousand,

123

then the annual pay of, say, a nurse was riding on the fall of the ball.

There was a soft sigh as the winning number was called. She couldn't tell whether the sigh came from the winner or from a general release of tension. The woman next to the Prince put her hand on his, as the croupier pushed a pile of chips towards him. The Prince took no notice of the gesture, nor of the money, and got up, leaving his winnings in place. He nodded to the other people at the table, as though they were merely acquaintances and, with no further acknowledgement to the man whose money he had just won, he left. It was a suitably princely, disdainful gesture. No doubt he thought that was the proper way to behave; perhaps if you were a prince it was.

'The banker's name is Zaric. He secured the Macedonian crossing points. Luckily for him there were Nigerians posted there from the start,' Sally's companion said.

He was watching the small events at the roulette table intently. 'It's as good as a show. Most weeks the Prince comes here, either with Zaric or one of the other brothers, and he gets paid. It should be posted for tourists, like the Changing of the Guard.'

'What's he paying him for?'

'Insurance money.'

'Insurance?'

'Yes. It all started at Claridges. The Crown Prince announced that now there had been changes in the new order, he might like to go home. He said, "If it be the wish of the people then I shall return." They really do think like that, these people. When Zaric heard it he said, "To do what? Drive a taxi?" Of course over there taxi driving is the occupation of the dispossessed. There are

124

more taxi drivers with Ph.D.s in Vlastanjagrad, than there are Ph.D.s in Cambridge. Naturally the Prince got to hear of the remark and Zaric suddenly found it more difficult to buy the things and the people that he was used to. He had especial trouble with the London community.'

He and Sally were standing by the table now. 'Let's sit here,' he said. They sat down.

'So one day Zaric found himself sitting near the Prince at this table. He covered the prince's bets, and when the bets won he got up and walked away leaving the money for the Prince. Now Zaric wins both ways, by plundering what's left of the state and by buying the monarchy. Since then his problems have gone away.'

He spoke to the croupier. 'Three thousand, please.'

The other players had risen one by one after the departure of the Prince, and Sally and the tall man found themselves almost alone save for a player opposite, who was slowly reducing an untidy pile of red chips.

'We'll play like this. First work towards a stake, but don't do that for more than an hour or so. That's the first stage: if you get it, bet it all and walk away. If you don't get to a stake you also walk away. It's all in the waiting, like fishing.'

She watched him. He divided his chips. The light glittered on his hands, and on his nails which she noticed were polished. Were they lacquered? It was a tiny shock. She looked again at his clothes: gold cuff links and immaculate cuffs, a white shirt and the dark, almost black suit, made of a rough material. He managed a perfect mixture of formal and informal.

He became conscious of her gaze and turned and smiled. Charm, she thought, the gift of the psychopath. This man uses people.

125

As though he was aware he was being judged, he spoke to her. 'Now, work with the four number sets. If one of the four comes up, then it pays nine to one. Obviously you don't aim to beat the odds, since in the long run they even out and are slightly weighted against you, but by definition they don't even out over a short run. So what you're looking for is a win before either the zero or the long run destroys the odds for you.'

While he was saying this he was placing chips on the board, one hundred pounds. 'Subdivide your stake, but always think of it as one bet. That's where the hour comes in. If you haven't got past the first phase by then, go home. Don't stay, staying is the way to become a gambler. You don't need that.'

The ball began its noisy, ricocheting journey round the wheel.

'We've only got so many bets, but with the occasional win, that'll keep you going for a bit.' Number six came up, one of his set of four. He received a thousand from the croupier.

'That win goes into the second phase. Don't touch it. With any luck . . .' He waited as the wheel spun and the ball fell into the fourteen. 'There we are, that goes aside too. And we start again. Now we've got two thousand for our stake. I'm sorry,' he said, interrupting himself, 'I'm talking too much.'

Sally was becoming involved: the compelling quality was the precision of his actions. Everything else in the room conspired towards headiness: the colours, the carefully controlled lighting, the lowered voices, the jewels, the clothes, the thrumming noise of the wheel punctuated by the click of the ball. But he was showing her how to cut

126

through it. She was the plain girl at the party, secretary to the rich lady, sitting watching Mr de Winter, cool, controlled, measuring his fate.

'Of course you're not,' she said.

There was silence as the ball clattered from ridge to ridge. 'Of course not, it's very interesting,' she heard herself saying again, and saw him lose, and then on the next play of the wheel, gather in another thousand.

He separated it, took another chip from his original pile and placed it on the table. The croupier glanced at him and was about to call no further bets, when he gestured, gathered his bet from the numbers and allowed the wheel to continue without a stake on the table. He turned to her. 'You disapprove?'

'No, no,' she said. To her surprise she found herself gushing. 'You're wrong there. I was just beginning to approve. Though why, I don't know.'

'It's important you maintain your distance,' he said. She realised she did not know what he meant. Distance from the gambling, or distance from him, or he from her? There was no doubt that he was an extremely attractive man, and dangerously she was beginning to like the oddities about him, his vanity for instance. She had thought him free of it when she had watched him in the restaurant, but now she could see she was mistaken; he was driven by vanity.

He leaned towards her and whispered, 'Look at them opposite. What do you think? He owns a curtain shop in Marylebone, making up material from Selfridges, and she paints her nails for a living.' It was a florid piece of prejudice, chiefly memorable for Sally because of the lingering touch of his cheek brushing her hair as he whispered.

Opposite them the red chip man had been joined by a young woman, who sat down fluttering, putting her chin on her hand, saying something with a broad smile.

Sally watched as the man responded automatically to her presence. Here was a couple who did not think very often about themselves, or if they did, did so only with surprise when things went wrong.

After a few murmured words, the man gestured towards his chips and pushed a pile of them over to her. She took her elbow off the table and started to place them at random around the table, although beneath the apparent frivolity Sally thought she could see a tense determination.

Sally reflected. All bets were random and any attempt at logic at the roulette table which didn't take into account the nature of the enterprise was absurd. On the other hand it was this background of chaos that enabled one to see behaviour so clearly.

'The test is to remain untouched. Here, you try. Take some.' He took the chips from his winnings pile. 'Use the method. If you start winning hang on, it will feel like the Big Dipper, but don't stay on too long, or hang on too hard.'

Sally hesitated. Was this money being given to her? It seemed churlish to refuse to play on the basis that she couldn't accept a gift. But to say out loud, 'Whose money am I losing?' would seem as out of place as any other piece of bad manners.

'Don't worry,' he said. Again he knew what she was thinking. 'I'll get it back.' She placed a hundred on a set of four as he had done. One of her numbers came up. She had got back a thousand pounds.

'Beginner's luck,' she said.

'You haven't reached the difficult bit yet,' he said. 'Now work the system, and remember it's a method of controlling yourself, not the wheel. Put the money in the working pile, then bet it.' She did as she was told. This time she lost it, and the next.

He said, 'If you're working a system, a losing bet is as important as a winner.' Then she won again, and again, twice in a row. Out of five bets she had won three times. She transferred money as he directed her.

The money reserved for the stake rose. Now she had well over two thousand in front of her. She tried again and lost, then twice more, but on the next won another thousand.

'You've got a stake now,' he said. 'Remember this is not your money yet, it's an abstraction. It only stops being an abstraction if, when you stop, you've still got it.

'Wait a minute.' He put his hand on her hand as she was about to play. For a moment his hand lingered there, but when she looked he was intent only on the other couple, the touch was nothing else. 'Let's let the slow players move over first.' Again he brushed her hair with his lips. For a moment Sally's whole experience was the pressure on her hands and the sensation in her hair. She seemed to swell with feeling.

'Now,' he said. 'Go for it.' He gestured with his chin, and she felt a surge of excitement. 'We're coming,' he said to the table, 'we're coming.'

'Half the money on thirteen to sixteen.'

She pushed half the pile forward. The roulette wheel spun and the ball skipped then started to slow. The slow fall of the ball into number sixteen was as relentless as the back beat of any rock band. She felt the blood threshing in her neck and cheeks.

'Keep that. Now the rest, all of it. Twenty-one to twenty-four.' The ball began its roll again. She wanted it to hurry, to come quickly. 'Wait,' he said. 'Wait. It'll come. Gently now, take your time.'

'Twenty-three,' said the croupier.

Sally's throat caught.

'Put twenty thousand on one side.'

His voice came from a distance amidst the singing noises in her head. Twenty thousand? She put her hand on his arm as if to prevent herself from falling. 'And double the rest. Scarlet or black? Black, I think, for my lady of the law. Last bet of the three, double what's left.' He put the chips by her hand. 'Good luck.'

She put the money on red. This is me.

The ball jumped and fell. Red.

'That's it. Sit still,' he said as she began to rise convulsively. She felt unsteady.

'Sit still for a moment. The first time is always a little distressing.'

He touched the back of her neck. She was aware that a thin film of perspiration had broken out on her, and aware that the touch of his hand was warm and dry. It was his most intimate touch yet, but seemed merely restrained after the place they had visited together. Opposite them the woman who painted her fingernails for a living was staring at them open-mouthed.

'Shall we do it again?' Sally heard herself saying. She felt drained, but wanted the relentless beat to start again.

'No. Now you stop,' he said, 'and there is a way of guaranteeing that. Waiter,' he signalled, 'a bottle of wine, thirty-eight on the list, the Avrache champagne please, to room number . . .' Her key was on the table beside her

130

bag; he read the number. He said to her, 'Now get up immediately. Don't think about what you are doing. Just leave. Those are the rules.'

In a daze she did as she was told, and they left the table. The man with red chips looked after them, then he turned and said something to the croupier, who shrugged and didn't reply.

'Get the money in cash, with a receipt. You'll need the receipt for the revenue.'

She collected the money, and as she tried to fit it and the room key into her bag she stumbled and fell against the banister rail. He put out his hand too late to stop her falling, but she fell no further when he caught her just before she hit the floor. His sudden grip almost lifted her off her feet.

'You're still throbbing with it,' he said. 'You can see why they say never drive a car or work dangerous machinery after winning a lot of money.'

She rubbed her arm and shoulder. The fall combined with his grip had hurt.

'I haven't woken up yet,' he said.

They reached the main hall and passed the now empty area where the two women had sat. There was no one about. She said, 'I have to look at it.' She pulled a bundle of fifty-pound notes from her bag. As she did so her key fell to the ground. He picked it up. The money was in a thick packet, five slabs, each slightly thicker than a pack of playing cards. They stood in the lift. 'Astonishing,' she said. 'Does the hotel mind?' Was this guilt at getting something for nothing? Perhaps it was the piano teacher speaking.

'No,' he said, 'the money was won from other people

who lost it, not from the hotel. The couple opposite for instance.' He laughed. 'Did you see them? She was angry with him that you had won, almost as if it were his fault.'

There was a waiter already at the door of her room, holding a silver tray above his shoulder. On it stood a bottle of champagne and some sandwiches. The waiter stood back as the door was opened. 'I don't think I can eat anything. After that I just want to go to bed,' Sally said.

He gave the waiter five pounds.

They went into the room, and he sat in a chair near the dressing table. 'It's funny, one of the reactions to winning big is always tiredness. It's the release. Have some wine, just a little, but you must eat as well.'

'I will, yes. My God, how much did I win?'

'About thirty-three thousand pounds.'

'What does that look like again? Put it on the table. I'm going to change,' she said.

She felt as though they had been involved in a conspiracy together, something secret. What was she going to tell her husband?

She went to the bathroom and looked at her face. She was slightly flushed. She loosened the collar of her shirt, took her jacket off and splashed water on her face. She rubbed a towel on the back of her neck. A thrill ran down her back as the warmth of the towelling cleared away the tension. He had touched her there, but it wasn't an intimate touch, she told herself. What was it like? More like a driving instructor touching her hand on a gear stick. After all, he had guided her through it; she could not have done what she did on her own.

Her shoes seemed tight: she kicked them off and slipped off her tights. She began to calm down. Thirty-three thousand pounds. How was she going to explain that? But why explain? Just put it in the bank. But her tax returns. It would have to show up. Her mind skittered to and fro. She hesitated at the door – for a moment she had forgotten he was out there – then she put the bathrobe on over her shirt and skirt.

In the room he had spilt the packets of money out on to the bed, on the pillow and on to the turned-down sheet. By the side on the table were two glasses of wine. She sat looking at the money. He handed her one of the glasses and lifted it in a toast. 'Here's to a holiday!'

'Holidays?' she said. 'My husband doesn't believe in holidays.' The moment she said it, she felt the same disloyalty. But it was true, a country cottage in Norfolk where she worked on legal papers in the garden was as far as they went.

He disregarded her remark and carried on. She noticed that her attention remained for a few moments on what had just been said, following his words with a slight time delay. She had to make an effort to switch her thoughts from one idea to the next.

'Well, the Ritz won't forget that in a hurry. The ice-cold prosecutor is in their casino for just over an hour and walks away with the pot.'

'Was it an hour? It seemed so quick.' She put the wine down and leant forward to pick up some of the banknotes and he took hold of her and kissed her. Again there was a momentary delay before she reacted. The bundle of money she was holding fell and spilt on her legs as she was pulled across the bed. He was incredibly strong, stronger than she had experienced in any man. The thought lingered in her mind, long enough for her protest to be delayed. By then he had his hand behind her back and he lifted her up towards him like a toy. 'No,' she said. Money fell all over the bed in a cascade.

Once or twice she had experienced helplessness before power. She remembered being caught by a big wave once, on a surfing beach; it had tossed her in the air then pounded her down on the sand for what could only have been seconds, but felt like minutes. It was the same here: everything was in slow motion – she had time to reflect and even compare experiences. Another time she had been in a crowd which had broken a barrier at a concert and raced across a field. She had to run with the crowd, desperately trying to keep her footing. This was the same, though this was not just brute force, it was also skilfully applied. She thought, no. Then she thought, He is doing the same as he did downstairs, just taking over, leaving me no choice. Or is it only that?

She didn't feel frightened, but found only that she was intensely annoyed that decisions were being taken away from her. After all, had she been left to decide she might have decided yes. Maybe not now, but perhaps some other time. She was aware now that she had even thought of this during the evening. But she had wanted to draw it out, come back to the hotel, meet him again, and then slowly, perhaps after a long time, one day go upstairs with him. He would help her with her skirt, and look away as she slid her tights off. But she wasn't prepared to have the decision taken from her. 'No,' she said out loud. He held her down. Should she scream? 'I'll scream,' she said.

'Go ahead,' he said. 'It's all right to make a noise. Lots of women do.'

Did he think she was warning him that she was noisy during sex, that she was being polite and warning him? Then she realised that this wasn't just a heavy session, where she might be able to slap his face and have him stop at any time. She was about to be raped.

Or at least he was about to make love to her without asking first. He was about to take her clothes off and fuck her. Give her a good seeing to. Different ways of describing it went through her head as she tried to stop his hand by holding his wrist. Even now she had not broken loose from the ordinary way of reacting, still constrained by manners. She had heard of this. The reason it is difficult to fight back immediately is not always fear, but an inability to break out of the normal. He was lifting her skirt up. Her hand moved with his, unable even to slow him down.

In that play on television the frustrated housewife had shouted out, 'I need a man who will give me a good seeing to.' And her husband, sitting with his knees together, had laughed. This man was acting out a male fantasy, and hadn't asked her permission at all. He thought she needed a good seeing to, and he was wrong. He turned her over; she kicked at him and he laughed. Her suit was being creased. There, he had torn the skirt where the button had come off earlier that morning. 'No, don't,' she said. If they were going to make love they wouldn't do it like this. Not that she was going to do it at all. This was rape.

'Just be still.'

He pushed her head into a pillow and putting his hands on her waist he lifted her bottom up towards him, sliding her knickers down. She was totally exposed. She flailed with her arms behind her, then she felt his weight on her, the rough suit on her skin. He pressed his hand on to the

135

back of her neck and she was pinned down; he could do what he wanted with her. The cloth was a kind of tweed material, wasn't it? No, bird's-eye, that was it, bird's-eye. She would need it for the identification. It wasn't too rough, it had a warm feeling.

Was this the detachment that she had been told about in lectures on rape? The reason, apparently, why some witnesses remember incidental or irrelevant things very clearly. That woman who had spoken about her experience of being raped for hours by three men – she described how she had become completely detached, and speculated that the detachment was a kind of protection. And then she had gone on to admit, which was quite courageous, that detachment like this occurs during normal sex as well.

'No, no –' Sally was shouting now. Not that. His penis was right up against her, it felt warm, hot. She shook herself, all the time her face grinding into the pillow. What was that in her face? It was money. She opened her eyes and twisted her head round. It was money piled up against her face. 'No, not that.'

'You don't like that?' he said. He was surprisingly courteous. 'Your husband doesn't do that? Then we'll do it properly then. Here we are.' He lifted her and entered her. She felt herself subside on to his penis, slowly and then completely impaled; any movement she made stirred her up. She was astonished to feel the ease with which she became filled with him. She was moist. Her body had betrayed her. She shook and struggled. 'Oh, you bastard. Oh.' She was making noises like a heroine in a bodice-ripper. He moved smoothly. She could feel metal against her skin, what was that? His zip? He hadn't even taken his trousers off. For a moment she wondered

136

whether he wore underpants. Perhaps he did not, he had been sitting next to her with only that rough material separating her from his genitals. It was an odd thought. The more she struggled, the more his movement dominated her; her struggling became weaker and eventually she gave in. After a while she screamed out. Then he was gone.

She was lying on her face. A fifty-pound note had twisted itself up against her cheek and mascara had blotted the picture on the paper. She struggled to remember what had happened. All she could really remember was the money in her face, and it was still there. It was proof of everything that had happened. She had won all that money. The exact figure jumped into her mind: thirty-two thousand, nine hundred pounds.

She allowed other events slowly to drip back in. The lady who painted her nails for a living. His hand on her neck, as though he was calming a horse; the memory of it was disgusting. Then upstairs. She remembered wondering how she was going to explain the money to her husband. But then she had been attacked. The attack – she had been pushing it to the back of her mind. She sat on the bed. She felt sore. She looked at herself in the mirror, and saw the woman in the watercolour looking back at her, but now wearing a crumpled skirt, under a Ritz bathrobe.

Court. She reached over to her watch which was lying on the bedside table by the wine. It was half past eight; she had been totally asleep. By God. She had been asleep, was that possible? She thought back and remembered a time after the attack when she had tried to get up, but she had just lain there. How could she have fallen asleep, after that? She was due in court. She had little more than an hour to get there. She was never going to make it.

8

Sally only just got to court in time. She clung to the strap of the taxi, leaning forward anxiously as it dashed down Fleet Street. It got caught up in traffic just past Ludgate Circus where the road narrows at the police barrier to the City.

'Don't worry, you're all right, miss,' the driver said. 'These jams seem to last for a long time but when you look at your watch it's only moments. The more anxious you are the longer it seems.' As he spoke the traffic cleared and they swung round into Old Bailey.

There was another queue at the main gate of the court: defendants and jurors waited to be sniffed at for any explosives they might be carrying. She looked for Ted, caught his eye and he opened the side door. 'There you are, Miss Donne,' he said as she went through. He added, 'You know, you left your car here last night. You should have told us you know.'

'Sorry, Ted.'

She had no time for more. She ran up the main stairs to the ground floor and took the lift, but it stopped at every

139

floor, reminding the occupants in a bored voice which floor they had reached. While the doors were open at the third floor she heard a call for all parties in the case of Nichols. She was going to be late. She had never in all her time at the bar been late for court.

She ran to collect her wig and gown from the women's robing room. Jane was there smoking. She always seemed to be there. 'Late today?' she said.

Sally didn't stop to talk. When she arrived at court number eleven, the judge was being slowly escorted towards the bench by a man carrying a sword. He in turn was accompanied by another attendant. Sally blessed the ceremonial which had given her a few extra seconds to get to her place. Everybody bowed to each other. Sally adjusted the bands at her neck and the case was called on.

An usher stepped to the door of the court and called the dead man's name. Immediately the Clerk of the Court stood up, turned his back and started to speak to the judge. The stenographer stared vacantly into space and Sally was able to beckon to Terry Davies.

'Is it OK?'

'Yes. I went down last night. Mr Scott came too.'

'Did he? Why?'

'Dunno.'

'Did you see him?'

'Yes.'

'The body I mean. It, not him.'

'Yes.'

The court clerk sat down and the usher returned. 'No reply, milady.'

The judge spoke. 'Miss Donne, is there anything to be said?'

'Yes, milady. I will call Mr Davies.'

The detective gave evidence. 'Last night I confirmed,' he said, 'the dead body was that of the defendant Roger Nichols.' He looked around for anybody who might contradict him. No one did.

After a pause the judge said, 'I see that Chapman J. laid down the procedure to be followed when evidence is given that a defendant who is the subject of an indictment is prevented by death from answering the indictment.'

Scott, sitting at the other end of the bench from Sally, considered the image that the judge had conjured up: 'prevented by death'. But there was better to come.

The judge said, 'Now what should be done when, instead of preventing the defendant from attending his trial in the first place, death intervenes to halt a trial before it has run its full course? Chapman J. gives no assistance on this point. Is there not a problem here? I have discharged the jury. I hope I have not done so too quickly. Miss Donne, have I acted prematurely?'

Scott watched the judge wrestling with the problem. It was of course not of the slightest importance. He remembered a similar look of intense concentration on his tutor's face at Cambridge, as they had analysed the problem of whether one was able to steal the air from someone else's bicycle tyres. One could steal the bicycle right enough, but the air in its tyres? Surely not. Dead bodies, arguments about rape, dirt and disgust, all the stuff in the cases they studied, they were all clever word games back then. It was the outside world that was exotic, and now he had travelled a long way to find the same absurdity at the centre of the real world.

'I think we can disregard that difficulty,' the judge said.

'I am satisfied by Detective Constable Davies' evidence. I shall follow Chapman J.'s precedent and 'order that the indictment be endorsed as aforesaid, declared now to be of no legal effect, and that the file should be closed unless and until this court, on cause being shown, otherwise orders.' I hardly think there is any need for any reference to the Court of Appeal?'

It wasn't clear to Scott whether the judge was being serious or whether she was making some sort of arcane joke. He assumed she wasn't, since it didn't seem the kind of thing she would do. He felt her eyes upon him; she wanted an answer.

Sally was on her feet. 'No, milady, there is no need for such an order.' Scott noticed she didn't give any reason.

The judge seemed satisfied and for a moment Scott thought her face was going to crack into a smile. 'It's odd, isn't it, Miss Donne, that this procedure should have been formalised so recently? I see Chapman J.'s ruling was made not very long ago, in 1978 in St Albans.'

Scott was beginning to get angry with this crablike behaviour. He got up. Sally had not been there before for him to say this so he might as well say it in open court.

He said, 'Well, milady, one method might have been for Miss Donne to offer no further evidence in the case.'

The judge looked at him in total astonishment. 'But why should she do that, Mr Scott?'

'Because the Crown now has a statement which conclusively demonstrates the dead man's innocence.'

For other people this might have been the occasion of some surprise or interest but for the judge it wasn't. She was interested only in procedure. 'But if the defendant is deceased, how could such a procedure make sense, Mr Scott?'

142

'It would make sense to his wife and children,' Scott replied. He knew his remarks for what they were, merely venting his anger. There was silence. Scott started again. 'The defence served a statement on the Crown which demonstrated without the shadow of a doubt that the allegations made in this court yesterday against Mr Nichols were invented. I understand the Crown confirmed the truth of the statement yesterday afternoon.'

'Invented?' the judge replied. 'How can they have been invented? The defendant admitted he was there, did he not?' The judge was clearly trying to recall the facts of the case, having already dismissed them from her memory.

'No, the statements demonstrate that the allegations of what happened at the hotel were wrong.'

For the first time since her dash in the taxi Sally thought of her night in the hotel. In the mad race to pay her bill, money spilling from her bag, in trying to make herself presentable and get across town, she had shut it from her mind. Her handbag lay beside her on the floor of the court; in it was over thirty thousand pounds. She was startled to think that the first thing she remembered was the money, rather than what the man had done to her. Was that because it was less important or more so?

The judge took a grip. 'A man may not be acquitted in his absence.'

'I have seen the senior judge do it here myself,' said Scott.

The judge watched Scott. This confirmed everything she had thought: he wasn't reliable and lacked judgement. What else could one say?

Scott went on. 'In that case the court had the choice of arresting the defendant to bring him to court to acquit

143

him, or of just acquitting him. They acquitted him.' More silence.

He went on, 'So Miss Donne can perfectly well offer no evidence.'

The judge ended the argument by the simple expedient of disregarding him. 'This indictment is closed,' she said. Scott sat down.

As is always the case with unreasonable behaviour, it didn't make you feel any better. On the other hand, was what he had said so unreasonable? Just because the rules are clear that doesn't mean one can't suggest they are wrong. He felt Sally's eyes on him. It was difficult to imagine her upset, or losing control.

They left the court and went upstairs together.

'Coffee?' Sally offered.

'No thanks. I've got to get going.'

Scott saw himself being abrupt. Who are these paragons who can say what they think and yet not annoy everyone? After all it wasn't Sally's fault this had happened; she'd only been doing what she was paid to do. 'Are you sure?' she said. Although of course it *was* her fault, it was her cross-examination that had done for Nichols, and that cross-examination was – he searched for the word – factitious. Like the air in the bicycle argument, artificial. It didn't reflect truth, it reflected only what one was able to do with words, the weapons that lay to hand in a court. He should know, he'd done it himself enough.

Sally wanted someone to talk to. As a lawyer Scott could be a complete disaster – he'd just demonstrated that in court – but maybe she could talk to him. Maybe she could even talk to him about what had happened to her. But he didn't want her company.

144

'Thanks for the offer,' he said, for a moment almost grasping that this woman, normally a bit distant, a bit too successful, was in fact asking for his company, 'but no thanks, I think I had better go. See you soon, Sally.'

Had he accepted the offer of a cup of coffee things might have been different.

He left Sally standing by the staircase.

'Paul, I'm going home. I'm not feeling well.'

Sally had collected her car, packed her things in it and driven down Ludgate Hill towards Blackfriars Bridge. She had parked where the road widens opposite Queen Victoria's statue, a place to stop without blocking the traffic, so that she could phone her clerk.

Paul was surprised, but there we are, in the end the women always behave oddly. She rang off and he realised he had forgotten to tell her that a package had arrived.

Sally rang her husband's clerk. He was on constituency business. 'I had to stay away last night unexpectedly.' Sally was surprised to see herself lie without a thought. 'I wasn't able to get in touch with him.'

She rang his constituency secretary at the House of Commons, and was put through instantly. The new switchboard hardly gave her time to gather her wits for the story. But there was a message for her. 'Your husband asked me to say he would be away again tonight.'

That made things easier.

She started the car and eased it out over the bridge. The Thames was at high tide, with the water being blown into little white caps by the wind. As she came off the bridge, she glanced to her left and pulled over to the filter lane.

The editor's car park at the Express building was fuller

than normal with Jaguars. Her mind ran on over things that didn't matter. Perhaps one could forecast the profitability of the Express group by watching the car park? Would that amount to insider trading? Although of course the more Jaguars there were, the more likely it would be that the company was losing money.

She glanced at her bag in the footwell beside her. She could buy one of those cars for cash. 'I seem to have this new car,' she would have to tell her husband. What would he say to that?

While her thoughts skittered on there was a background of worry. What was she going to do? She began to come to herself as she relaxed. She noticed that her arm and side were throbbing. Her head ached. How much had she drunk last night? She remembered waking and smelling the wine on her bedside table. It had been revolting.

The scene at the hotel that morning came back to her: frantically gathering things together, phoning the desk to have a bill prepared and a taxi called, and each time when she turned to pick something up, finding another fifty-pound note. There were notes under the pillow, and – thank God she had looked – down the back of the bed head. What on earth would the maid have thought to find a wad of fifty-pound notes under the pillow? Of course there would be only one thing to think. Even in the Ritz these things must happen.

Then the question she had been avoiding appeared, fully formed – she could keep it at bay no longer: Am I going to report this to the police?

A van blew its horn as she sat at the pedestrian crossing just outside the newsagents. For a long moment she didn't move. When was she going to report it to the police? She was going to, wasn't she? She pulled the car over to the right and cut down through the back streets. Under the railway bridge there was a cabbies' garage; she needed some petrol. She eased in under the offices built overhead and had to wait. There were four cabs filling up.

The longer she waited before going to the police, the more the delay would be used against her. In rape cases . . . Rape – she had been raped. I'm sure of that. As the words formulated in her mind she knew it meant she wasn't sure. A pump came free. Of course she was sure of it, don't be so damn silly. After all she hadn't gone to the Ritz in the hope of a bit of sex, had she?

She got out and stood filling the tank. She stared vacantly at the man filling his cab on the other side.

She had not invited it, she had not agreed to it, she had protested at it. He had used force. She was raped.

'Not today, love,' said the cabbie, putting his petrol cap on. She coloured. She had been staring at him hardly seeing him. She walked over to the office to pay. The man who had spoken to her was buying a large roll and joined the queue to pay behind her. She was uncomfortably aware of him and could feel him watching her back.

'You don't remember, do you?' a voice said quite equably. 'You were my fare last night, from the Old Bailey. You said you worked there, but you're not working today?'

'Oh, I'm sorry.' Sally had busily to readjust. 'Of course I took a cab.' Last night. Was this only last night? 'No, I've finished today.'

'Working a night shift then?' he laughed.

'No, no night shifts at the courts,' she said.

The cashier pointed to the amount she owed and she

opened her bag. How she hated it when women only started to look for their money when they were asked for it, while men always had it ready. She fumbled in her bag. Oh God, she had taken the hotel key with her. A wad of fifty-pound notes surfaced while she looked for her credit card. It was odd, somehow she hadn't thought of the stuff as money that could actually be used for day-to-day things. Give him a fifty-pound note. She tried to slip one of the notes from under the rubber band and of course couldn't manage it. The whole thick slab of money shot from her hand and landed at the feet of the cabbie waiting patiently behind her.

'Good Lord, miss, you don't want to be doing that all the time,' he said. He was already picking up the money. 'Not for everybody to see. On the other hand I can see why you packed it in for the day.'

She laughed, took the money from him, gave a fifty-pound note to the man behind the counter and turned away. 'I didn't earn it, you know,' she said, forcing wads of money back into an already stuffed handbag. It must have been clear to him that it was full of money.

'Oh,' said the cab driver. 'I suppose it depends on what you call work. But you be careful.'

She left the shop. As she walked to her car, she looked behind her, ostensibly to see if it was clear to cross over to her car, and she could see him leaning on the counter looking at her. He was saying something. The cashier replied, put the cabbie's change on the counter and looked over towards her as well. He said something and laughed.

She got in her car and cringed. 'I didn't earn it, you know.' What sort of remark was that? What did it actually mean? She looked up. They were still watching her. She started the car and pulled out of the petrol station, replaying the conversation in her head. 'Working a night shift then?' He must have thought she was a prostitute. If he thought that then 'I didn't earn it you know' would have confirmed it for him. 'She gets her money on her back, she doesn't earn it,' a policeman had said to her about a witness.

'Men think of nothing else.' She could hear a shrill voice inside her. Then she thought, Women think men think of nothing else. After all, she thought the cabbie was saying 'Not today, love,' as though she was propositioning him, and all he was saying was he had seen her before. People's capacity for misunderstanding each other is infinite.

She pulled the car to the left past Borough Crown Court. In the distance she could see a familiar short-haired figure cross the road towards the door. It was Sasha – she could speak to her. Tell her the problem. Sally waved as she approached, but just at that moment Sasha turned her head and spoke to someone coming out of the door. She didn't see her, although to Sally it felt as though she had been ignored. A ridiculous feeling of rejection flooded over her. She wondered whether to stop and run back, but by then it was too late.

She turned to the right past the old fire station then across the road, and there on the right was the Chilean Coffee House that people from the court used. It was a warm day, despite the cold snap in the air, and some chairs had been put outside on the pavement in the sun. Sally became aware of her surroundings. Why not have a coffee and sit for a moment? She pulled over to the right and parked outside the shop. She'd be able to watch for traffic wardens as she drank it.

The owner was standing outside. He was a bulky man though only five foot six tall, completely encased, save for his trunk-like legs, in a long white apron. As Sally sorted herself to get out of the car he reached over and opened the door. He smiled broadly, his whole face lighting up. He had a thick black moustache. 'Just a coffee, please.' She said it as she crossed the pavement, and the owner called to the counter inside, 'A coffee for madam, please.' The girl behind the counter – was she Chilean? Beautiful, with a slash of lipstick and shining eyes – said, 'Espresso?'

'With hot milk,' Sally said.

She felt drab. Drab. Drab was an Elizabethan word for a prostitute. Yes, she felt dirty. That was one of the things she had heard said. After rape you feel soiled. But she had felt soiled after some ordinary sex.

She remembered the occasion with Tozer; she'd felt pretty soiled after that. Tozer, who used to ask every woman he met to sleep with him, on the basis that if he got his face slapped twice for every ten he asked, nevertheless he got lucky with three of them.

She'd felt soiled then, but not like now, even though the man clearly was a good lover. He could obviously be good if he wanted to be, couldn't he? What was this? He'd bloody raped her, hadn't he? She snorted and slapped her coffee cup down in the saucer. She looked around. No one seemed to have noticed.

Sally turned her car into her house at about lunch time. The place looked empty but she knew that the house-keeper and Anne would be there. As she came through the

150

gates and pressed the remote for the garage door to lift, she beeped her horn to warn them. It was unfair just to walk in the door.

They were sitting at the kitchen table, a small lunch spread out before them. Mrs Hicks greeted her for them both. 'Welcome back, Miss Donne.' It was a way of saying everything was all right, so Sally didn't need to ask. If Mrs Hicks was content then so should she be.

'Will you have something with us?' Mrs Hicks asked, indicating the food that she had laid out on the table. Sally slowly sat down at the table, so that her refusal would not be seen as unfriendliness. 'Do you know, I won't, Mrs Hicks,' she said, using a roundabout and rather formal way of speaking, 'I'm very tired and above all I need to get out of these things.' She indicated her suit. Mrs Hicks's eyes took her in.

Sally wondered if Mrs Hicks had ever really approved of her. She had been with her husband's family for more years than they could remember, had lived in one of the family's cottages. From there she had looked after the family, and then, after Sally's marriage, helped her and the children.

'I'm very tired.' Sally repeated herself, noticing that it was true.

'And you've torn a button from your skirt.' Mrs Hicks's eagle eye noticed it. 'You put that out for me, Miss Donne.'

They both of them called her Miss Donne, the name by which she had been introduced to the house. It had stuck even after her marriage, maybe because they still had to answer the phone for her in that name. To Sally it seemed slightly odd, as if she had never really attained the position of wife, if such a thing was an attainment.

'I'm going upstairs to change, and I may lie down for a while. What time are you going for the children, Anne?'

'Half past four. They've got country dancing with Miss Gallagher today.'

'I'll go and get them. If that's all right with you, Anne.' She always felt the need to apologise for this interference with routine.

Sally noticed a fugitive glance between Anne and Mrs Hicks and, as Anne made to reply, she understood, remembering what had been said the night before while she sat in the Ritz. It was embarrassing for them all, for here was the nanny apparently putting her relationship with the children before that of their mother. For fear of letting it get worse Sally spoke quickly: 'But of course, Anne, I forgot, you're taking them to Maisy's party.'

'Yes, Miss Donne.' Anne was so pleased that the moment of difficulty was past that she unwittingly aggravated it. 'They were so looking forward to it, Miss Donne.'

'Well, perhaps it's just as well, since I will probably fall asleep.'

But Anne kept her for a moment. 'I shall have to come into your room, Miss Donne, to get the things from the basket.'

'Things' meant the washing, so Sally was able to nod, say, 'Of course, Anne,' and leave on an easier note.

She sat in her bedroom and looked out over the ploughed hill at the front of the house.

It was a large room, with a window stretching the whole length of one wall. To one side there was a bathroom, well lit and welcoming, making the room, which was anyway large and airy, even more spacious. When she sat there she

152

felt in her own world, protected. The delay seemed to have settled the question: it looked as though she wasn't going to say anything about what had happened. She slipped off her jacket and skirt, and put her tights and underwear into the basket, just before having a shower, aware of course that to do so would be to take another step away from a complaint – since she would be destroying evidence that might be found by forensic examination of her body.

Often she had read of, and in fact had read out to juries, details of intimate examinations, with their high vaginal and low vaginal swabs, the draining of semen and sometimes the tearing of the entrance to the vagina. It was strange to imagine this describing her now.

She was sitting in the Ritz cotton slip on the edge of her bed. She had laid across her knees the skirt which Mrs Hicks had noticed, and was examining the damage where the button had been torn. It wasn't quite clear what had happened to it. She thought there was a tear, but could not find it.

She was feeling sore and noticed an occasional twist of pain. She was wondering, had she been injured? Her mind dwelt for a moment on illness and infection. But no, he had not been the type – but of course, who knew? All rape victims are advised by the police to go to hospital for a check.

Perhaps she had better – what was the phrase that the doctors used? – 'refrain from anything' with Brian for some time. Then she smiled. That was a joke: when was the last time they had made love? Come to that, when had they ever made love – certainly it had never been like the whirlwind which took possession of her in the Ritz.

For a moment the image of her body bent like a bow,

lifted towards this man's, flashed in her mind. That didn't happen in this room, even with consent. She pushed the thought away.

There was a knock on the door. It was Anne. The girl entered apologetically. 'Thank you,' Sally said, as she crossed the room.

'I'm sorry about today,' Anne said, insistently opening the subject of the children again. The distress which this caused Sally was quite beyond Anne's understanding. Sally nearly let her control slip since a sharp reply came to her lips, but she managed to stop it.

'Really, that's quite all right, Anne. If I choose to lead an unpredictable life, then I can't really expect everything to fit in for me, can I?' She looked up smiling, the more to emphasise that the subject was finished with, but she was astonished to see that the young girl had stopped half-way across the room and was staring open-mouthed at her.

'What is the matter, Anne?'

'Miss Donne . . .' The girl could say nothing.

'Anne, what is the matter?'

'Your shoulder, Miss Donne.'

Sally stood up, laid the skirt aside, went to the mirror, and in the light of the window examined her shoulder. There was a livid bruise stretching right down her arm. It stood out against her white skin like a stain. She lifted her arm, looking over the uplifted point of the elbow, and was shocked to see outlined, like a child's hand painting, the marks of four fingers, dark and clear. In the mirror she could also see Anne standing with her hand to her mouth. Then a curious transformation took place: the girl stepped forward and took over. She led Sally back to the bed, she said, 'Why, that's terrible, Miss Donne,' and then stepped

154

into the bathroom. Sally heard the sound of water running. She returned with a soft flannel, warm and comforting on her arm, which Sally now realised was aching and tender to the touch. Why had she not noticed it before?

'That's awful, Miss Donne. Your beautiful skin, what have they done to you?'

Later, when she thought about it, it was not clear to Sally what it was – perhaps the girl's unaffected tenderness, perhaps her uncomplicated ability to touch her, the feeling of being gently touched maybe, or Anne's simple assumption that Sally was also a victim of 'them', people who push young women around with impunity, any of these things – she did not know what caused it, but she found herself in tears.

Softly she started weeping. It was a quiet business. Had she begun sobbing then she might have been able to control it, but this weeping happened to her: as the bruising had come out, her body was speaking. The same body that had betrayed her in the money-strewn bed the night before. Clearly it had rhythms beyond the reach of Sally's discipline.

She found Anne's arm on her shoulder. Her hair was being smoothed back. The flannel wiped her cheeks and face. She put her hands over her eyes and wept. She wept for herself, but she also wept for her children, and her marriage.

'I wanted to collect the children,' she said, trying to stand up.

Anne said nothing. This was something to which she was used, the silent despair of women who do not have the outlets that their men have, the drink, the noise, the violence. She was only surprised that the same applied to

Miss Donne, who she had thought was free of such things. In the end she was not surprised though, because this state was so common amongst her friends and her elder sisters' friends that she could not really believe that there were women who were free of it. And this proved she was right. All that nonsense you see, advertisements for Tampax and stuff, full of girls in white trousers stretching to show they are unaffected. The public pictures never show the real thing, the pain, the depression, the whole burden.

Anne sat Sally on the bed and said, 'Of course you can collect the children, Miss Donne.'

'I rang you last night from the hotel.'

'I know, I know.'

'I wanted to be with them, but they didn't want me.'

'That's not right, Miss Donne. They love you.'

'They didn't.' She didn't know what she wanted to say, she closed her eyes. She didn't need this to happen. Then she heard Anne's voice change the subject back to the thing that was going to destroy it all.

'What happened, Miss Donne? What happened to you?'

Anne clearly suspected what had happened. They had not known where Miss Donne was last night, only knowing she wasn't with her husband.

Sally said nothing. She sat looking at the ceiling. Occasionally her hand crept across to feel her arm, which, now that she had seen the bruise, throbbed insistently. 'I was stuck in London late. I couldn't drive. So I phoned you.'

'Yes, I remember. But what happened to you?' Anne's eyes flickered across the slim body on the bed. There were no other marks, but then she saw the skirt, where Sally had put it down, the button missing from the waistband. She picked it up. 'What did he do to you, Miss Donne?'

Again it was Anne's natural assumption that this was the work of some man – 'he', after all, is only a smaller part of 'they'.

'I took a room in a hotel. And a man somehow got in and he raped me. He had sex with me. I didn't want to.'

It was nothing more nor less than Anne expected.

'Did he hit you?'

'No. No, he didn't. But he must have held me hard.' Sally touched her arm.

'Did you know this man?'

'No. No, I didn't.'

'How did he get in?'

'I don't know. I let him. No, I don't know.' Sally tried to picture the moment when he entered her room. She remembered he had her key, but she couldn't remember how. 'I don't know, he got in somehow. He had the key.' She didn't want to tell Anne about this.

But of one thing Anne was sure. 'Have you told the police, miss?'

'No.'

'You have to.'

'No, Anne.'

'But, Miss Donne, if you don't tell the police when this sort of thing happens to you – if you don't, what hope is there for anyone?'

Anne knew this. If you let it go on, then the end is certain. It happens again, and if it happens again it will go on happening, until it is just normal.

'You must, Miss Donne. If you can't stand up for yourself then who can?'

157

Sally heard what Anne said and knew it was true.

She waited a moment before she spoke, but she knew that there was now no way out. 'All right, Anne. I'll do it. I'll do it now.' She got up. Now she had made the decision, it was easy to regain control of herself. She went to fetch the clothes she had discarded from the laundry basket, because she knew what happened next.

'I need to speak to someone. I want to make an allegation of rape.' Sally had telephoned, not the small local police unit, but the larger district police station.

'Just one moment.'

There was a pause. The policemen played music to her while she waited. She waited. The same voice came back. Sally paused for a second, then she gave her married name. 'Sarah, Sarah Murray.'

Her married name seemed the proper thing to do, as though it emphasised she was someone else's. Of course it was towards her husband that she had been disloyal with all that stuff about the picture. Was she going to have to tell the police all about that? For a moment she reflected that she had not thought about what she was going to say and what not to say – the money, what was she going to say about the money?

'Miss Murray?' a voice said, and when it didn't get an immediate reply, it repeated, 'Are you there, Miss Murray?' Of course Sally realised the voice didn't know to whom it was speaking: there might be an hysterical person at the other end.

'No, I'm here,' she said. 'It's Mrs Murray.'

'Are you all right, Mrs Murray? It's Angela here. I

158

understand you have a problem.' Sally was already being touched by the new rape-friendly police procedures.

'No, I'm all right, but I need to tell you about something that happened last night.' Again she was amazed that this was all so recent; it already seemed like at least a week ago. 'Something that happened to me.'

'And what was that Mrs Murray?'

Sally didn't want to have to use the word again, but she did. 'I was raped,' she said. 'I thought you had been told.'

'Yes, we were, Mrs Murray, but I have to have it said before we can set the motions in . . .' The voice paused confused by her use of the expression. '. . . in motion.'

There was silence as they both got over the difficulty. 'It's Angela here, Mrs Murray. Are you in a position to come to see us?'

'Yes,' said Sally, then, 'Where are you?' Angela named a town nearer London. 'All right. When shall I come?'

'Whenever you want. There are no times.' Sally picked up a faint tone of surprise, it was as though she had enquired whether there were set times for reporting rape. 'And, Mrs Murray . . .'

'Yes?' said Sally.

'Have you had a bath since – since the event?'

'No.'

'Then please don't, and have you changed your clothes?'

'I can bring what I was wearing.'

'Good.'

'And one final thing, Mrs Murray?' Slowly the Angela voice began turning every sentence she spoke into a question. Sally was beginning to hope that she was not going to spend much time with that voice. 'We may not

159

be able to get a woman doctor. Do you mind being examined by a male doctor?'

'No,' said Sally. 'It was only one man who raped me, not men in general.'

'Yes, Mrs Murray, but we have to check in case.'

Angela was not amused.

Long ago Sally had had a burglary at her flat in London. The burglar had come into the flat in the night while she slept. She had called the police in the morning and, standing in her dressing gown in the kitchen, she had told the officer what had happened, how the burglar must have got in, what he had taken. She had not been upset, not even frightened by it; it was too much like her day-to-day life, then a diet of burglary prosecutions. The thing seemed too much like a caricature of itself. But the officer at the time had noticed this lack of distress. No doubt he was always on the alert for the unusual. 'If you don't mind me saying so, miss,' he said, 'you don't seem very upset.' Perhaps he thought she was setting up an insurance fraud. Sally reassured him. But she had learned. Don't tell policemen who were doing their job that you know how it's meant to be done. They will not be pleased. Don't be too coherent, they need you to ask their help, otherwise they don't feel in control.

Sally drove north, looking for the exit that would drop her down to the police station. She would stick to her married name. She needn't tell them who her husband was, nor what job she did. She would deal with that if the problem arose.

The whole thing would take some hours. She would have to make a statement. What else would happen? She'd

160

have to give details of the man. She thought about it. She would certainly have enough information to find him, in fact he would probably be eating at the same place tonight, watching out for someone else maybe.

Now she had made the decision to report the attack, her feelings were changing about what had happened, and about the man. She was becoming more sure about what he had done. He was obviously on the lookout for women on their own. A thought struck her. Was it all true about his being at that table so regularly? Perhaps he had followed her and made the whole thing up.

For the first time she felt frightened. She had accepted his story so completely that maybe she had overlooked what he really was. Maybe he was on the prowl. Of course she had been tricked. He was a rapist. Only now was she beginning to feel properly about this, only now appreciating what had happened to her. Perhaps it was the shock wearing off, and the fact that having to manage that morning had kept her from thinking about it. After all, she couldn't just skip going to court, so she had pushed it to the back of her mind. But once you start to drop your guard then the pain sets in. She had heard of that before, but not experienced it.

No, she wasn't going to have to pretend in the police station that she was upset, she was never going to have to pretend. She was angry now. How could she let this happen to her? After being in control of her life all this time, how could she let it happen to her?

9

Scott was on the phone listening to Archie protesting about the unfairness of it all. 'I didn't know it could happen. I got him bail, but then the prosecution lawyer popped up and said they were going to appeal. Apparently they can if they organise it within two hours, and just before time was up' – Archie spread the word 'just' over several syllables – 'they came up with the paperwork. So now he's remanded in custody.'

Archie swallowed. He was having difficulty overcoming his anger. 'That means over the weekend, and even then they tell me that the appeal needn't come on until after forty-eight hours, so it doesn't have to happen till Tuesday.'

Scott listened. He was used to this response to the workings of the criminal law from solicitors who only ever do polite crime, solicitors who don't get much involved in the nasty bits.

'Just like that,' Archie protested again, 'he gets locked up for four days.'

Scott reflected. He was always being told, mainly by

judges, that the criminal law was fair, but when people came to it new they didn't think so.

'And I wasn't able to see him after the hearing – they took him away before I got down to the cells. He's in Pentonville prison, and as far as I can make out the people who run Pentonville don't even answer the phone. And when they do, they put you on hold. And then the line goes dead. I haven't even been able to arrange a time to see him.'

Scott knew that phoning Pentonville prison had become a joke in the profession. On occasions it took a whole day to get through and arrange an appointment.

'I'll just have to speak to him at court when the case comes up again on the appeal.'

Scott rather enjoyed this in a flat sort of way. He said, 'I should write to him, Archie, because they won't even bring him to court.'

There was silence at the end of the phone. Eventually Archie said, 'What?'

'Yes,' said Scott.

'Not to court?'

'No.'

'They won't bring him to court to hear his own bail application?'

It was good to hear the reaction, since it confirmed Scott's own feelings. After all, it's possible to get so used to something that your responses become atrophied.

'No.'

'But it's a bail application. Aren't people entitled to be present at their own bail application?'

'No, apparently not. The public aren't allowed in either, and that includes the man's wife for instance.'

'Why not?'

'I have no idea, Archie. None. My guess is it's done that way because it's more convenient.' Scott attempted no sort of defence, nor any complaint. It wasn't possible to express indignation all the time. The way it worked was the way it worked. He felt older.

Archie said, 'Convenience? Whose convenience? What's convenience got to do with it? What are you talking about?'

'Nothing. I was listening to you tell me about this case.'

Archie gathered himself together and said, 'Well, he's charged with rape. He's a perfectly decent person, we've known his family a long time, and here he is charged with raping some bloody woman he met. The police arrested him at his flat. He was packing his bag to go abroad, so they objected to bail, even though I could show he goes abroad every year at this time for a party. The police refused to believe one can go abroad for a party.'

'And?' Scott was curious about whether this conversation was going to result in a brief.

'He's coming up at the Old Bailey, or at least his bail application is going to be heard next Tuesday. Can you do it? It's cash on the nail.'

At last. Good old Archie. He didn't come through with very many cases, but when he did they were generally quite good ones. The last one was a footballer who had driven his Ferrari too fast.

'You'll have to speak to the clerk's room, but I think I can manage it. I'm at that court then anyway.'

'I'm told that the case is going to come up very quickly, fast track, or some such phrase?'

'That's what they say,' said Scott.

*   *   *

164

James Reid of counsel was not someone Scott trusted. He was overexcitable and today Scott could see it in his eyes.

'Are you in this case?' he asked Scott.

Scott said, 'Yes.'

Scott wanted to say, 'Let's get it over with quick,' since in about half an hour he had to address a jury in court ten on the floor above and he needed to be on time, but he decided not to say anything. He remained detached. 'What are your objections to bail?' he said.

'Same as in the court below,' Reid said.

Scott watched him. 'And what were they then?' he said.

'Are there no notes?'

Scott shrugged. He didn't have to tell Reid what he knew; he was entitled to be told the objections out loud.

Reid didn't reply immediately, and again Scott nearly said something, but he restrained himself. It was clear Reid was not going to volunteer anything. Scott repeated the question: 'What are your objections to bail?'

'The likelihood of his absconding.'

'Based on what?'

'On the seriousness of the offence – the rape of a woman completely unknown to the defendant. If convicted likely to result in a long sentence.'

'And?' It was like drawing teeth. Reid didn't want to tell him, but he had to. Courts were still run by lawyers who had to talk to each other, though no doubt even that would disappear soon and Scott would be told by a bureaucrat to look at the papers and guess.

'And he was leaving the country. I have a copy of his ticket. He was running.'

Scott said nothing.

165

'And he said to the arresting officer, "Another half-hour and I would have made it."'

Scott thought it would happen. This scrap of conversation was new; nothing like this had been said in the proceedings before. Obviously the prosecution appeal had needed a little help, and any court hearing that remark would take a very dim view of bail. But if the defendant had really said that to the police at the time of arrest, why had the first court not been told of it? It wouldn't be something that you would forget.

'And who gives that evidence?'

Reid made a pretence of looking at his papers. He knew all right.

'Angela Deakin, she's the arresting officer.'

'Why wasn't it given at the court below?'

'Don't ask me, I wasn't there.'

'And who can I take instructions from on whether it's true, or whether only something like it was said? My client isn't here. What do you want me to do, ring the prison up and ask him to come to the phone?'

'Jeremy, I'm not responsible.'

'I know you're not, James. But you're in charge now.'

'Not nowadays, Jeremy, you know what it's like now. I do as I am told.'

'Have you got a statement from the officer?'

'No.'

'A copy of any note she made?'

'Nothing. I believe he said it in the car on the way to the police station.'

'So it was information that was available at the lower court, but not mentioned?'

166

'I suppose so,' said Reid, who knew he was talking too much.

'Is the officer going to be at court today?'

'I don't know. She may be.'

'So we may not even have an explanation for the sudden appearance of this damning remark.'

'No.'

Scott was turning away when Reid said, 'There's something more.'

Scott whirled round.

The prosecution were going to fight tooth and nail to keep this man inside till his trial, and they were going to use all the advantages the pre-trial position gave them to do it. These were in effect secret hearings: the public had no access, and with no record kept, no evidence given on oath, the prosecution could pretty nearly say whatever they liked. The defence at this stage were not even entitled to see the witness statements. The situation was exactly what Scott had described earlier to his solicitor – a complete disgrace.

'It's not entirely clear, but your client seems to have equipped himself to commit this offence in advance. The key to the hotel bedroom was not accounted for the next day, and if you look at what the victim said when she made her first complaint, the defendant seems to have got hold of the key to her hotel room somehow.'

'Are you saying he broke in?'

'No.'

'Tricked his way in?'

'No. It seems they had a drink there. So we can't go that far.'

'You can't go anywhere.'

'Well, we feel we properly ought to raise the question of the hotel key. If he can get hold of one key, then he can get hold of others. We may be completely wrong but it is worrying, and we think there is substantial ground for the belief that he may commit similar offences.'

'What does the – the . . .' Scott did not want to use the word victim; who the hell knew if she was a victim? 'What's the woman's name?'

They both looked in their papers. Reid came up with it first. 'Sarah Murray.'

'What does Sarah Murray say?'

'I haven't got her full statement, only a summary. She says she does not remember how they got into the room, but she said to the woman she first told about the incident, Anne Timms, the next day that he seemed to have a key.'

'You can't say that.'

'Why not?'

'It's not nearly certain enough. The only result will be to scare the judge into thinking that this guy is prowling hotel corridors with a bunch of keys.'

'Perhaps he is.'

'Well, what does the statement say? Did she wake up and suddenly find him at the end of the bed about to jump on her?'

'I don't know. As I said, we only have a summary, but, no, it's not like that. All we say is that she is alleging rape and told her friend the next day that she thinks he had a key.'

'Well, either she is saying he tricked her or broke in, or she isn't. That's different from letting him in and having a drink before hopping into bed together.'

'Scott,' Reid began to demonstrate that he was a serious

168

man with responsibilities to society, 'these are my instructions. It may be it was explicable—'

'What's explicable? You haven't produced anything that
needs explaining yet.'

'The victim's confusion about the key.'

'Maybe she's just confused.'

'Well, maybe she is, but we'll let the judge decide that.'

'How can he?'

'How can he what?'

'Decide that.'

'That's his job.'

'But you're not giving him anything to decide it with,
just someone's summary of what someone else thinks
might have happened at some time. What's the use of that
to anyone? All you'll do is frighten him into not giving
bail.'

Reid said nothing.

'Which I assume is not your intention.' Scott began to
realise he was on a loser. 'Who's the judge, anyway?'

'Teflin.'

'Oh Lord,' Scott said. 'He lives his life plagued by the
belief that there are substantial grounds for believing that
everybody is likely to commit further offences. I don't
know how he sleeps at night.'

His Honour Judge Teflin blinked at Scott through his
rimless spectacles. 'But Mr Scott,' he said in a flat and
rather plaintive northern voice, as though speaking to
someone behaving in a foolish and illogical manner, 'Mr
Reid is quite right to draw this to my attention. I really
can't see why you are complaining. I have the statement of
Miss Anne Timms and she says that Mrs Sarah Murrray

169

said to her in answer to her direct question –' he interrupted himself and smiled pityingly in Scott's direction, 'it was a direct question, Mr Scott, so we may suppose that Mrs Murray's mind was on the subject – she says, Mrs Murray says, that she did not know how your client got into her room. And we know that the next day she found the room key in her own bag at home, so he is hardly likely to have used that one is he?'

These propositions seemed such blatant nonsense to Scott that he hardly knew where to start. Anyway, why did the judge have the witness statement when he didn't?

'But we have had no evidence of any sort that would enable us to make a proper decision, and certainly not one against the defendant.'

'Nor shall we have evidence, Mr Scott. Please remember. I think I have it correctly, "in bail applications strict rules of evidence are inherently inappropriate in a court concerned to decide whether there are substantial grounds for believing something."' Teflin quoted the passage from the law reports word for word. The passage had always been completely incomprehensible to Scott, and he had never found anyone who understood it.

'No, Mr Scott, I will hear no more. Bail is refused. There are substantial grounds for believing that the defendant equipped himself with a hotel key, and if that is so, then one must wonder why. I conclude that there are substantial grounds for believing that your client would commit further offences. He shall be remanded in custody.'

That afternoon, after he got back to chambers, Scott reached Archie on the phone. He stood looking out of the window and told him what had happened.

'No good, Archie. They came up with some information that implied our chap had got hold of a hotel key
from somewhere. It wasn't a direct allegation, in fact they
accepted that she had a drink with him in the room, but
the implication was that the whole thing came about
because of his access to a key.'

'But he told us he was invited upstairs.'

'The trouble is he wasn't there to give me direct
instructions on where the key came from. Not that it
would have done any good, I don't think. Nowadays
judges are terrified of making mistakes in rape cases,
because they know the police have an open telephone
line to the *Daily Mail*.'

The rain hissed against the window, and dripped on to
Middle Temple Lane immediately below where Scott
stood. He could see umbrellas moving like little black
scarabs up towards the archway. It had been dark for a
good hour now and the contrast between the warm yellow
of the lights from the buildings lining the lane and the
glistening wet of the cobbles increased as the darkness
deepened. A bicycle tottered up the lane.

'When can you see him, Jeremy?'

'Whenever you like.'

'I've got an appointment arranged tomorrow.'

'I'll see him by all means, but the evidence won't have
been completely served yet, will it?'

'No, but at least you can establish contact.'

'All right then.'

'Pentonville at six?'

Tomorrow was going to be another late evening and if
the weather was anything like this, then even getting to the
prison was going to be awful. 'All right,' Scott said.

The rain poured down.

Scott put the phone down and turned away from the wet outside. He watched a game of solitaire being played on a computer screen. In the background of the same screen he could see an indictment laid out: 'Count 38. False accounting.' Thirty-eight counts of false accounting – it would have to be a benefit fraud. No doubt there was another crackdown. Well, at least crackdowns are of benefit to some. Chambers was just beginning to empty, and indictments were being replaced by computer games. More fun than the law.

Scott said goodbye to no one in particular and made his way down the staircase into the street below.

He stood in the shelter of the arch of the Middle Temple gateway and watched the rain. A small group of people straggled up the hill towards him, all criminal lawyers. One of them turned and said, 'Are you coming, Jeremy?' as they bunched up to go through the narrow wicket gate out into Fleet Street. The speaker didn't wait for a reply.

Then Scott saw Bob on his disreputable bicycle. He was wearing a crash helmet apparently made of sausages, and his trousers were clipped, revealing his socks. He pulled up out of the rain under the arch, tipped the bicycle slightly over on one side and leaned on it to talk to Scott.

'Too wet for that,' said Scott. Then he added, 'Bicycling.'

Bob was non-committal. Then he said, 'Do you like the tie?' He turned it over to show Scott the label. 'Tootal, 100% Polyester.' It was made of a stiff, red plasticky material. 'It's the kind of tie one might have worn to greet

172

Harold Wilson's first election.' Bob was pleased with his eccentric purchase. 'And the socks.' He looked down and leaned his bicycle away from him, showing his feet more clearly. Scott looked: the socks were a savage mixture of jagged colours.

'Just awful, Bob,' he said. For Bob that was praise indeed.

'Where are you going?' Scott said.

'The chief's giving a lecture.'

'Where?'

'Old Bailey bar mess, starts at six thirty.'

'So that's where everyone's off to.'

'Are you coming?'

Scott had known there was a lecture, but had forgotten it was tonight.

'What's it on again?'

'The right of silence. Should be interesting.'

'Yeah, I think I'll go.'

'See you there then.' Bob wheeled his bike away, scootering it with one leg through the gate into Fleet Street. A girl taking a short cut down Middle Temple Lane to the tube was prevented from coming in. She stood aside as Bob wheeled himself out into the street. Scott remembered a time when, had a woman been obstructed in such a way, she would have assumed an air of outrage. Was he wrong about that? Had things changed? It seemed to him they had; people were easier in their manner. Nowadays taking offence wasn't the full-time occupation it had once been for the English.

He had to get rid of his papers and move the car, which was on a parking meter. The rain fell steadily. He set off down the lane and cut across Pump Court, working out where he could find another parking place. In front of him was another group of people he knew, sheltering under umbrellas, clearly heading for the same place. He got to the car. He was lucky, the penalty warning was flashing, but there was no ticket. He drove it straight down the road and left into Blackfriars, over Ludgate Circus, then he had to do a U-turn right across the busy road, otherwise he would have had to drive all the way up to Smithfield. Traffic stopped for him. It really was true that driving in London was easier than in the rest of the country: people realised that you had to give way. It was something that had always struck him – how amazingly good-tempered drivers were, not the opposite.

He reached Old Bailey. There was a meter free and he dived for it. The rain swept up the road as Scott struggled with his change, trying to manage an umbrella at the same time. A figure was approaching, hunched against the rain, and as Scott straightened he saw it was Sally Donne. He offered her the umbrella and she sheltered under it with him. They set off towards the court.

Scott looked at Sally's clothes: not a court suit. 'Not been in court today?'

'I've been at home. I've been away from work for a few days.'

'Time off?' Scott said vacuously.

'No,' Sally said, 'I've not been feeling too good.'

'Oh, I'm sorry.' He glanced down at her. He wasn't tall and she wasn't very short, but she seemed to have diminished slightly. She was looking down at the pavement as she walked. Then she looked up at him. An unexpected wave of protectiveness swept over Scott. For him it was an unusual emotion – nowadays he had no one to look out for – but there was little he could say. The time when he and Sally had been friends was long gone.

'What has happened about Nichols?' she said.

Scott replied, 'I only know one side of it. Though I have been told I may have to give evidence at the inquest.'

'Why?'

'I was the last person he spoke to, apparently. Or at least the last they can find.'

'And what can you say?'

'How depressed he was.' They were veering near something Scott did not much want to talk about.

'He told you that?'

'Yes.'

'When?'

'When we last spoke.'

'He hadn't said it during the trial?'

'No.'

'It was my cross-examination?'

Scott had to admit it.

'And that's what you were telling me about, that evening – no that day, during the break. You were complaining. You were saying I was being unfair.'

'Sally, it wasn't you being unfair, it was what you had to do.'

'You mean cross-examine a man into looking guilty, even though he was not?'

She had said it pretty damn accurately. So accurately that Scott found himself pleased that by now they had reached the top floor and had to go into the lecture. They couldn't carry on the conversation.

The room was packed. For a few moments they looked around, trying to find seats from which to see the speaker, but there was standing room only. At the front of the room Scott could see that most of the permanent Old Bailey judges were there and, sitting in the same row, the senior prosecuting barristers attached to the court, Treasury counsel.

'Everybody's here,' he said.

But Sally wasn't to be put off. 'You were complaining that anybody can be made to look ridiculous. Anybody can be made to look guilty.'

'It's true,' said Scott, 'you know it. I've done it. Everybody here has either done it or is going to.'

'No one has ever complained to me, or said it out loud during a trial.'

'That's because we don't examine what we do very much. For example, is anybody going to spend a moment enquiring into how Nichols was nearly convicted of something he didn't do? The really big cases get looked at sometimes, but there's a different agenda by then. Any sensible modern system would be examining a random selection of court cases to see . . . Well, that's the problem. To see what? We have to keep it a mystery whether the verdict was right or wrong.'

Then Sally said unexpectedly, 'You're not saying it's my fault then?' Scott remembered the self-confident opponent who had dismissed him, saying 'Jeremy, it's not a game.'

'Of course it's not your fault, Sally.' Again he was struck by her appearance, how diminished she was. He risked the question: 'Don't feel bad about it. Is that what's worrying you? You don't look well, you know.'

Barristers don't ask questions of each other like that.

'No,' she said. She risked talking to him. She realised

176

how much she liked him. Perhaps it was because he was a weak person, so he didn't condemn weakness in others. 'That's not what's bothering me, but I did worry about it a bit. I've had other problems as well. I want—'

For the second time she was about to tell Scott something but wasn't able to continue; she was interrupted. 'Come on, Sally, you should be at the front with me.' Jane's instantly recognisable voice cut between them. She took Sally's arm. Immediately she also spoke to a young man with fair wavy hair who was standing by them. 'And you, Piers, what are you doing skulking at the back?' For a moment Jane's attention was elsewhere.

'It's only a game,' Scott said to Sally, 'and we're hired to play it. You shouldn't be worried about playing according to grown-up rules.'

'Game? What game?' Jane said to Scott. He noticed she wasn't inviting him to the front.

'The rape game, Jane. Sally and I have been playing the rape game.'

'What on earth could you mean? That's no game,' Jane said as she shepherded Sally away.

The schoolboy atmosphere began to swell.

A well-known voice said, 'Can we smoke?' and a chorus shouted back, 'No, put your cigarettes away.' 'Vile habit,' someone shouted. Great laughter greeted this refusal. The atmosphere was like those few moments before the arrival of the headmaster to address the upper school. Someone else shouted, 'Of course you can,' then 'Give us one!' and there was a cheer as a cigarette flew with notably bad aim towards the judge who had asked whether he could smoke. 'We always smoked in my day!' he snorted, throwing up a cloud of blue tobacco smoke.

177

Attention turned to the arrival of another latecomer. 'Slow bus back, John?' someone cried as a tall, elegantly dressed man threaded his way to a seat being kept for him, and there was another cheer. John Starling had been to the Falklands and the acquittal he had obtained had made national headlines. The latecomer gave a bow and settled down with his friends.

'Easy acquittal?' someone shouted.

'It was on the cusp,' he said, which resulted in a roar of laughter. The phrase 'on the cusp' had echoed around the Bailey since a sensational acquittal some years before.

John Starling was a notably careful dresser and someone called out, 'John, did you take your tailor with you?' He got up and resettled his jacket on his shoulders. 'I can manage on my own, thank you,' he replied. 'I only took my solicitor.'

'And did she help you with your clothes?' Another cheer.

One of the permanent judges walked over to Jane, who was sitting on Sally's right, and crouched down in front of her. There was a little whispered conversation. No one could hear what was being said, but everyone could see it. The little display ended and he got up, then the judge saw Sally, stopped and spoke to her. That too ended with a shared joke.

Someone next to Scott said, 'See that? The laying on of hands.'

Scott said, 'What do you mean?'

'A new Treasury counsel list is out in a month or so.'

Before Scott could reply, there was a stir in the crowd. The Lord Chief Justice had arrived. There was a change of tone, the headmaster silencing the sixth form. Here was the man who presided over a court where the slightest expression in a judgement, misplaced or unintended even, could change the balance of a hundred verdicts in the lower courts.

He had not been long in office, but already a small change in direction could be felt, as though slowly the impulses of many years were changing. Was this a real change or something only imagined? This had added to the nervous excitement, as though the oracle had agreed to mingle for a few moments with the crowd.

He was introduced.

Scott listened to the introduction, staggered. Behind him there was even some suppressed laughter. 'Wherever one goes, one meets him, he is at all the parties.' The rather stern, even ascetic features of the man being introduced did not sit well with the notion of a round of constant party-going. There was a growl behind Scott: 'He's not been at any of the parties I've been to recently.' Scott turned and saw Barney. Barney's parties, despite their widespread fame, were certainly unlikely to be graced by the Lord Chief Justice.

The introduction over, the Lord Chief started his talk. As he continued, the audience's disappointment became palpable. Where Scott stood people became restless and started to whisper. They had hoped that this would be a convincing intellectual display, dealing with the fears over the change in the law. 'Is this what senior judges say to each other over tea?' someone said out loud. One or two people turned round, as though acknowledging the speaker's courage in bearding the headmaster. But Scott looked towards the front. He was sorry he had come: what he was hearing confirmed what he feared was always the case. It would have been better not to have had it confirmed. This was the face of power. There was no room here for personal experience. Here was the law at its most unforgiving and rigid.

Scott left, having to pick his way through the crowd. What did he expect, some sort of subtlety? These people were lawyers. He stood at the door for a few moments, unwilling to take the final step outside. In the front row, just opposite the speaker, he could see Sally. In a short moment she looked up, directly at him, and their eyes met.

She had started to say something to him and had been interrupted. What was it she had been trying to tell him?

The next day Scott went to Pentonville. 'I tried,' he said, 'but the judge wasn't buying it.'

'That's ridiculous.' It was the only occasion before the trial when Scott saw his client express any emotion.

'They produced a statement which could imply you had obtained a key to her room from somewhere.'

'Balls.'

'And you understand what that means?'

'Of course. They're trying to say I'm stalking the corridors of the Ritz looking for spare women to rape.'

'How did you get into the room?'

'I opened the door with her key.' He paused as though picturing the event. 'She dropped it while fiddling with her bag and her money. I picked it up for her. Obviously she didn't notice. Anyway, I opened the door in her presence.'

'Can you remember it clearly?'

'I can remember the whole thing clearly. Word for word.' Scott was used to having clients who were so befuddled by life that they couldn't have told him on Monday where they were on Sunday. This was a pleasant change.

'What happened as you went into the bedroom, for instance?'

'We arrived at the door. She was carrying her bag, I was holding her arm. She had nearly fallen over. I think it was the excitement of winning the money. She was trembling all over. I had the key. Martin was waiting with champagne.'

'Who's Martin?'

'The floor waiter that night.'

'You know him?'

'Of course.'

'Would he remember you?'

'Yes. I ordered a bottle of Avrache. He brought two glasses. No ice. It must be drunk at room temperature – surprising for a champagne, but I didn't have to tell him that, I've ordered it before.'

Scott wanted to say, 'When you give evidence, you can leave that bit out.' Juries are very unimpressed by the niceties of serving champagne. But this was a first meeting, so he just listened.

'The waiter had some sandwiches. Smoked salmon, I think. You'd have to check.'

'Where would we check?'

'My bill of course.'

'Of course.'

'It'll be on my desk. My secretary will give it to you. The bill arrives on the third Tuesday of every month. It will have got there by now.'

'What happened then?'

181

'She said, "I don't think I can eat anything. After that I want to go to bed." Or something like that.'

'Something like that?'

The man looked at Scott with a lazy smile. 'Exactly that.' Scott began to measure him. He was going to have to deal with this client entirely differently from those he normally worked with.

'Did the waiter hear her say that?'

'He must have done so.'

'Do most of the staff at the hotel know you?'

'Yes.'

'Would we be able to track your movements that night through the staff?'

'You should be able to do that.'

'Would you object if we tried?'

'No. Why should I?'

Scott wondered whether he should say what he often thought. He decided he would. 'One of the difficulties of this job is that most of the people we defend are guilty, guilty of at least something. It would be surprising if they weren't. And sometimes investigating too hard doesn't help them.'

'Well, that doesn't apply to me.'

'All right then. We shall need to know exactly what happened, from the start of your meeting this woman, everything that was said, everything. Everything anyone else said. Who made this suggestion, who made that suggestion. The whole lot.'

Scott turned to Archie. 'You don't mind me saying this, Archie?' Archie was only too pleased. He was much more at home with wills and the domestic arrangements of his rich family clients than with taking instructions in rape cases.

182

'Your case will depend upon two things: your own evidence, of course, but more than that, the cross-examination of the woman.'

Scott made a mark in the notebook in front of him. He had done dozens of cases like this one and he could remember the feeling as he rose to his feet to cross-examine the woman. 'Her evidence may only last half an hour. Most of what happened will be left out of it, not intentionally, but because giving evidence is in chief an attempt to establish the complaint in all its nastiness. And one thing to remember, complexity is the death of a rape allegation. Complexity is our friend. Life is complex, not likely to be simple, and the more we show that, the better.'

Scott's client was listening to him. It was clear he could understand exactly what Scott was saying. What a difference.

'I need to bring out her motives. I don't mean her motives for crying rape, but what motivates her, what are the circumstances surrounding the whole business? Is she married? What was she doing in the West End on her own? It's important we don't attack her on that, there is absolutely no reason why women should not stay in expensive hotels on their own in the West End, but why was she there? You spent an evening with her. Somewhere in what she said we shall find the answers.'

Scott's client paused. 'Well, for a start I know she was worried about not seeing her children enough.'

Immediately Scott started working on it.

Sally had told her clerk that she was not available for court, although she agreed she would go to Holloway to see the extradition client. Paul did not object; the overrunning of the rape case had put a hole in Miss Donne's diary, so she

183

had time to spare, otherwise he might not have been so understanding. But since she wasn't in court he sent some work down to her home in Kent. They were papers he had been expecting for a while, and he told her what they might mean. 'Miss Donne, you should bear in mind that you might have to do this case on your own.'

'This is Treasury work, Paul,' she said when she saw the papers, work which could only be done by lawyers nominated as Treasury counsel by the government.

'That's just what I meant, Miss Donne,' Paul said.

Sally thought about it. Was Treasury counsel something she wanted any more? Of course it was. She had been working towards this for years. She wondered whether to talk about it with her husband. But there were more important things to talk to him about, and she had not found the right moment for that yet. She wondered whether she wanted to tell him at all. He had not noticed that she was feeling off-colour, only that she was not leaving for work. 'A big set of papers,' she said.

'You know you're ready for it, Miss Donne,' her clerk said.

'Thank you, Paul. But it's a shock when it comes.' She was quiet. There was something irreversible about an appointment like that, a final agreement that they owned you.

'We should know soon', Paul said. 'Meanwhile I've arranged another conference for you in your extradition case.'

In Holloway prison Monty Bach was all ebullience. He seemed to swell with pleasure when he saw Sally, his huge coat straining to cover it, his words making no effort to do so at all. 'My dear, a joy to see you.' He bowed over Sally's hand.

I'm in the real world now, she thought. She remembered what Scott had said. Being a defence barrister means getting on with your instructing solicitors. She and Monty sat in the small room waiting for Gaynor. 'We haven't that much to talk about, since not all the formal papers have arrived yet, but my dear, our client does so enjoy a visit. She asked about you,' said Monty.

Sally said, 'But Monty, what's her defence?'

'Defence? Well now, in extradition matters we don't concern ourselves with defences. All we need do is demonstrate that the other side's papers are not in order, and hope for a friendly magistrate.'

This was a new idea to Sally. Magistrates were normally on her side, the prosecution side. 'Are there such things for the defence?' she said.

'Oh yes.' Monty grinned conspiratorially. 'Especially where the Americans are concerned. But what I do say is this. I will be very curious to see how they prove identity. I think they may have trouble with that.' He whispered it, looking around, as though to make sure the warders could not hear what he said. Sally looked up. No one was paying the slightest attention to Monty's secret pieces of information.

'How do you know these things, Mr Bach?' said Sally.

He sat back in mock alarm. 'Why? Don't call me Mr Bach. Call me Monty,' he said. And then he put his finger beside his nose and grinned at her, like Disraeli holding the key to the canal. 'We shall see if I'm right.'

Gaynor arrived. She had exchanged her T-shirt for a full

185

roller-blader's outfit. 'Why hi, Sally', she said, 'how have you been keeping?'

The question immediately took Sally back. It would have been good to be able to answer properly, even to have asked Gaynor about what had happened to her. It was absurd of course, but people outside her usual round seemed likely to be of more use to her in this. She had a feeling that Gaynor would have known exactly what to do with thirty thousand pounds and a man on a hotel bed for company. The way she put it to herself momentarily shocked her, but then she realised what she was doing and doing all the time: distancing herself from it.

Monty surprised them. 'Ladies, ladies, I must be going now. I have an appointment with young Janey Welch, just down the corridor.' 'Janey Welch', it sounded like arcane nineteenth-century slang for something disreputable.

'Well,' said Gaynor after he had gone, 'that's just like Monty, he's always seeing someone else.'

'How often does he come?'

'Most days.'

'What do you talk about?'

'Anything. But most often about change.'

'What change?'

'I underwent a change.'

'You what?'

'I underwent change. I tell him about it.'

'Tell me too,' Sally said simply.

'It's easy to say. It's all about not wanting anything, about how you haven't got to want anything, and if you hanker after what you were, then you are not ready for change. The man says, "it's the questions you ask that

186

define you, not because of the answer you get, but because of the answers you hope you're going to get." '

'Who's the man?'

'John Lorne. I have his book.' Gaynor fished in her bag for a scarred paperback book, which from reading and rereading had taken on the suppleness of cloth. 'It says here, "Some questions that show you are not ready."'

'Give me an example.'

The girl put her finger on the book. '"*Can I contact some of my friends, to let them know how I am doing?*"'

'And that's not allowed?'

'No, Lorne says it the same as in the Bible. "*I come not as a friend, but with a sword.*" He divides families, you see.' Sally could see that the Bible reference had been written in next to the text.

'What were you doing, Gaynor? I don't understand.'

'Changing, Miss Donne. I didn't like who I was and I needed to change.'

'What were you?'

'I try not to talk about it too much. John Lorne says, "*Once the change is made, then don't talk about it, because talking is being.*" He also says, "*A description of a thing is, however minutely, actually that thing itself.*" That's Duns Scotus. John Lorne is hot on Scotus. "*What you say, for that moment you are.*" '

The sudden spurt of philosophical enquiry took Sally aback. She listened and realised that she was hearing the repetitions of a true believer, a true believer in this Lorne man: '"What you were remains what you are if you relive it." "To describe is to inscribe." '

'What kind of thing were you, Gaynor?'

'There was a woman once, living in a house with two

children. She was unhappy.' Gaynor's voice took on a sing-song quality.

'Is this the way you talk about it, then?'

'In order to avoid being drawn back, you must see your previous life as someone else's, then it has no power to touch you. Do the same for the present, and you'll be completely free.'

'The same for the present?'

'Well, the present is a state of mind. The first change you make is to try to escape the whole weight of a lifetime which bears down on your present. That's called karma in the Eastern religions.'

Sally couldn't catch the tone, it seemed to vary between eminently down-to-earth and plain nutty.

'Dealing with the present is a practical activity, but like all practical activity it contains another truth.'

'Which is?'

'That you are responsible. Any baggage you carry around with you is of your own making.'

'This man John Lorne, who is he?'

'He's an attorney in the States. You can contact him on the Net.'

'So you changed?'

'Yeah, I did that.'

'And if you can change once, you can change again?'

'Yeah.'

'Does it matter what you change into?'

'That's your choice. All we say is that you are not bound to remain the way you are. You can get off the train, or the bus, as you say here, any time.'

'And once you get off the bus?'

'Your choice.'

They looked at each other.

'Look, John Lorne says, the whole nature of society is the restriction of one person to one role if possible, then they become reliable tools, they become owned.'

'What if your choice is to be a reliable tool?'

'Great. The whole thing wouldn't work without those people. But if you choose not to, then you should be able to do so.'

'What if you end up here? In prison. How does one deal with that?'

'There are different ways of being free. One way is to have nothing left to lose.'

'But –' Sally felt the question was insulting but she asked it anyway – 'you would prefer not to be here?'

'Of course. There was a Buddhist lama who taught non-attachment, and one day his student found him weeping. The student asked, "What are you crying for?" and the lama replied, "My child has died." "But Lama, you teach us not be attached, to be untouched." "Yes," he said, "but this is my child. If your child dies you weep for it." '

Sally said, 'I don't understand that.'

'You got it,' said Gaynor.

On the way out of the prison Sally met Monty. She said, 'I understand why you said it might turn on identity, Monty. That's almost all she talks about once you get her going.'

'Well, who we are is always the most difficult thing, isn't it, Miss Donne? And the most interesting,' Monty said.

'Have you got access to the Net, Monty?'

'Certainly not,' he said.

Part Two: Trial

10

'This court sits from ten-thirty to four-fifteen. I ought to say, I am told it sits between those hours, since I am not regularly here, and I don't know anybody here, neither counsel nor court staff.' The judge smiled at the jury who, relieved at finding a human being in the robes, smiled back at him.

Why did he say that? Scott thought to himself. He knows me perfectly well. Scott had often been to the judge's court on the south coast.

'And of course you know nobody either. One of the advantages of the system is that on the whole we gather here together to make one decision and then disperse, never to meet as the same group again.'

What's all this about knowing people? There's something up, thought Scott, but he had no time to follow the idea through. The judge nodded to prosecuting counsel and Reid rose to his feet to open the case against Scott's client.

'The Crown says that this defendant raped Mrs Sarah Murray in the hotel bedroom where she was staying in the

West End of London,' he started simply. 'I am now going to set out a few of the facts that the Crown says demonstrate beyond doubt that this offence occurred, and that the defendant committed it.'

Scott contemplated Reid. It was clear by now what his attitude to the case was – people even accused of rape are too dangerous to be allowed out, a notion exactly in accordance with prevailing public opinion, or at least pubic opinion expressed in the newspapers. The saving grace was that the only group who did not seem to share in this particular piece of hysteria was juries.

It was also clear that James Reid was anxious to continue receiving work from the prosecution authorities, and was naturally determined to convict Scott's client by whatever means available to him.

Scott surveyed the case ahead.

Reid was going to be able to cause Scott trouble over various things, for instance the injuries the woman had received. He had already begun playing fast and loose with the medical evidence outside court before the trial had even begun, changing his position on the doctor. 'I know we agreed the doctor need not come,' he had said, 'but I am thinking of getting her here nevertheless. I do a lot of these cases and in my experience an injury to the posterior fourchette such as the one in this case is indicative of violent penetration.'

Scott blinked at him. 'The doctor doesn't say that.'

'No, she has left that bit out. So I want her to come to court to say it.'

'Are you going to tell her she left that bit out?' Scott asked innocently. Of course for Reid to do anything like that would have been completely wrong.

194

'Of course not,' he said. 'I shall just ask her whether it is the case.'

'You mean remind her that she's got it wrong?'

'Nothing of the sort.'

It was obvious that Reid didn't like being questioned like this – he regarded it as impertinent.

Scott said, 'But previously you agreed that it was neutral evidence and you were going to read it.'

'Yes. Well, on looking at it carefully I have changed my mind. I am entitled to do that, am I not?'

People who say 'am I not?' in an offended tone are a pain in the arse. Scott said, 'Of course you are, James. Of course. But don't do it too often or we won't know where we are, will we?' He started to laugh but stifled it. He didn't want to antagonise his opponent completely. After all, there were advantages in having a prosecutor with no imagination, and he didn't want anger to focus what limited powers Reid had.

'The victim in the case,' Reid continued his opening to the jury, 'a Mrs Sarah Murray, decided to spend a night at the Ritz hotel in London. She registered there on the evening of . . .' Scott didn't bother to listen.

Reid was a plodder. He had written his opening out, paragraph by numbered paragraph. It was the way people were taught to do it now. If Scott had bothered, he could have followed it on the original with a pencil. There was nothing in the man's voice which acknowledged that the jury was being told a story, a story in its way as surprising as any fiction, nor did there seem to be any recognition that the jury was sitting waiting to be captured by the first person who seized their imagination.

Well, if Reid didn't want to do it then Scott would.

'She met the defendant at supper. They sat for a while at the same table.' Scott relaxed slightly, this wasn't a picture of a man stalking his prey. That had been something he feared, the image of his client on the lookout for inexperienced suburban housewives, unused to the glitter of the naughty world. He was nervous of it because he was concerned there might well be a little truth in it, his client was so damn sophisticated. At last it did come, but when it did it was so weak it was only just noticeable. 'He took advantage of her being alone in London.' Hardly worth worrying about.

Scott stared up at the public gallery and drifted away. It was extraordinary, this ability to turn off. He'd noticed it before and had been a bit frightened of it, until he worked out it must be a protective mechanism. Only fight when you have to. But on the other hand – his mind slipped sideways to something else – he had been putting on weight recently and that was the tension of the job. He'd been drinking a bit more, so he wasn't relaxing properly. It couldn't be good for you, this continual tension – that kind of thing induced heart attacks. He could turn off in court but not outside it. Odd.

Reid droned on, and Scott lived inside the private time. It was a feeling similar to that which a child experiences while sitting silent, unnoticed and able to observe what is going on around him.

Scott looked at Reid: he was a bit overweight too, but younger than Scott. He had a kind of stoop; was that something he affected or was he unaware of it? What kind of guy was he? It was difficult to judge. Scott had been prosecuted the other day by someone who had seemed utterly normal, but then Bob had told him that in another incarnation he had been one of the stars of Frank Zappa's *Hundred Motels* – and that had certainly been an odd movie.

Scott's attention returned. Reid was saying something about the defendant ordering wine. He listened for a moment to reassure himself that the man was sticking to his script and then he drifted away again. Wasn't there another case where the question turned on who ordered the wine? He couldn't quite remember. That was the trouble with using short-term memory so much: once the memory wasn't needed, it went, it was wiped. Actually that was wrong, it was archived and only needed a hook of some sort to bring it all back in a flood. Wasn't it a bottle of champagne? In old computers some of the memory used to disappear when the computer was shut down. He couldn't get a hook on it.

'Used a key,' Reid said, and Scott's attention came back quickly, 'maybe her key, but how had he got it?' Here Reid attempted a bit of oratory. 'Members of the jury, one of the matters we shall be asking you to consider is this: would Mrs Murray allow a man to come to her room, or did the defendant by sleight of hand inveigle his way in?'

Good Lord, that was weak. Why did Reid think wine had been ordered? But then the prosecution didn't know about the evidence which the defence had confirmed with the floor waiter: how the waiter was standing at the bedroom door with wine and glasses. 'I don't think I can eat anything. After that I just want to go to bed': the waiter had remembered her words clearly.

Scott reflected that one of the dangers of this case was the possibility that he would win all the arguments so completely that it would leave the jury free to come to whatever conclusion they wished. That was always a problem. It was something he would have to guard against: he was going to have to leave something for the jury to discover for themselves.

'Violence. Injuries to her arm. Clear signs of finger-marks. Photographs.'

Reid produced a set of photographs, six for the jury and one for the judge. Scott had his already; he fished for them amongst his papers. They were photocopies and looked pretty innocuous, but he saw that the copies being handed to the jury were original glossy photographs.

He stood up. 'May I also have a copy of the originals? Mine are photocopies, milord.'

It was the first time the jury heard his voice, maybe the first time they properly appreciated that there was another lawyer in the case – Reid's introduction of him had been very perfunctory.

Reid was about to take this as another opportunity to complain, when the judge intervened. 'Of course you must see the original, Mr Scott.' And then, turning to the jury, 'Mr Scott will have originally been supplied with copies, but at the trial he is entitled to the same documents as yourselves.'

It was only a piece of ordinary good manners, but it was cheering.

Scott knew the judge to be a decent man and he was reassured by it: he was not going to have to fight this case on two fronts. But he was not reassured by the photos: the glossiness made them particularly vivid, showing finger-marks on the woman's arm much more clearly than his photocopies had. Here was another complication, especially if the prosecution were actually going to bring their doctor to court.

Reid dealt with the fingermarks: 'No doubt these were caused in the act of the defendant holding down the victim' – there was the word victim again.

Scott watched to see what Reid would say about the mark to the fourchette. Was he going to say it was the result of violence even though there was no expert evidence to say it was? Scott had seen such marks before and doctors didn't always say they were the result of violence, so Reid could hardly open an explanation to the jury which was his own rather than his witness's. Reid went on, 'I must also deal with an internal injury suffered by the victim. She received a tear to the posterior fourchette, an internal tear, ladies and gentlemen, no doubt also as a consequence of the attack that evening, since the victim had had no sexual relations for a little time.'

He had implied that the mark to the fourchette was a result of violence without actually saying so. What he had not been able to say out loud he had still said in a way that the jury would assume meant violence.

Reid moved on to the evidence of the woman's complaint. 'When Mrs Murray returned home that day, she was seen to be distressed. She spoke to her nanny, who saw the marks on her arm.' Nanny? Scott repeated the word to himself. The court papers had not referred to her as a nanny, and the statement of Anne Timms only said, 'I was present when Mrs Murray said to me that she had been raped.' Scott glanced at the jury. There was no reaction he could see.

'The defendant was traced by his booking at the restaurant and arrested. He was in the process of leaving the country.' Scott looked up sharply at the judge; their eyes met.

In its present form this was obviously inadmissible and Scott had not thought it necessary to tell Reid that he objected to it. Perhaps Reid thought that sort of behaviour was proper. If he thought it was, then Scott was going to have a few things to say about it during the trial.

'The defendant was interviewed. He steadfastly refused to give an explanation for what had happened, only telling the police that he had indeed, as he put it, "made love to" the complainant that night in the hotel. He said, "I assure you, officer, that she was as willing as I was."

'He refused to go into details. At one time he accused the detective charged with investigating the offence of being impertinent. It is difficult to see how an enquiry into rape can be impertinent.' Reid tried a leaden piece of humour. The jury looked at him stolidly.

'He refused to account for the marks on her body, and did not explain how he got into her room.'

Well, there it is, thought Scott. He's going to make a meal of the police interview and of course nowadays he's entitled to try.

Scott smiled to himself at what his client had done in the interviews with the police investigators. The biggest offence you could commit in a police officer's eyes was not to show proper respect, and his client had certainly done that.

Reid started winding up his address and Scott began marking up his notebook. It was something he always did at this stage. A line down the side of the right-hand page, each page numbered on the bottom right, and on the front an index. At the top 'Opening, 10.55 to 11.20'.

It was a steadying thing to do, since this case was almost certainly going to turn on what happened next. He would only have one chance to cross-examine, and his client's life for the next few years would depend on it.

Scott didn't know whether his client was guilty, or whether there was something else in the complainant's life which had caused her to make this allegation; certainly she had not made it till she got home many hours later. But he was only going to have an hour at the most in which to find out. Perhaps she was frightened of her husband, and unable to tell him where she had been that night. Or maybe she hated herself for sleeping with a stranger and now wanted to deny it even to herself, and once an allegation like that is made, it has to be pursued to the bitter end.

He had discovered that the reasons for false allegations, or at least exaggerated allegations, are endless. But of course it could also be true. He kept his eyes down, carefully preparing his notebook, giving himself an area of calm within which to work. Now he had to concentrate. He couldn't let his mind wander any more.

Sally had come to London by train. For her it marked that this was a different day.

She had hoped that the case might be transferred to another court in London, but had done nothing to ask for it. Asking wouldn't have helped anyway – where could the case go? She went to all the London courts all the time. At first she had said nothing about what her job was, and had decided she would not, but then the officer had found out.

Sally didn't like Angela Deakin. She didn't like the way she spoke of her evidence as though it were something that

201

was independent of her, rather than her own experience. She wondered whether she herself did that in court, and decided she probably did. So she was being unfair.

But that didn't dispose of her feelings. The police-woman also spoke of the event as though the man involved were some sort of automaton, a thing. Sally felt she wanted to say to her, 'But I liked him. He was witty and charming. He was original.' But of course she could not, because to Angela he was the enemy. To Angela everything he did and said had to be a lie, as though there were no such thing in life as mixed motives, or contradictory personalities. Again she thought to herself, Maybe I think like that when I am prosecuting, but this time she decided she did not.

But she was being unfair nevertheless – after all, Angela had to get involved, arrest people, and you don't have space to allow for the complexities of life when arresting someone, you just watch out for a knife. Not everyone is detained at the door of an expensive flat next to the Ritz.

But most of all Sally thought about the trial.

She knew her evidence was going to be a gift to defence counsel. Staying on her own in the Ritz. Not reporting the attack until well into the next afternoon. All that money. She was going to have to admit to that. She wished she could discuss it with someone, but there was nobody.

She had at last managed to tell her husband.

He had not understood at first what she was saying and then had refused to take in how serious it was. That of course was Sally's intention, since she didn't tell him everything, and when he didn't grasp it she didn't help. She let him get the impression, which he was anxious to do anyway, that this was a minor assault and that, if anything, Sally was only one among other witnesses.

'I had to stay up in London, it was difficult, I had agreed to go to this private view, and once there it was impossible not to take a drink. And you were at the constituency meeting, remember? So there was no point in going home.'

It was surprisingly easy to lie. They were talking in his chambers; she had figured it would be easier to speak about the whole thing on territory where there was a professional tinge. 'Get me a drink,' she said.

Her husband had few ways of expressing sensitivity towards others and fixing a drink for someone was the nearest thing to it. 'Look, you don't want to hear the details, it's the kind of stuff I deal in,' she said, 'criminal hack work.'

She took the gin from his hand. 'Ooh, that's good. Why do your drinks always taste better than anyone else's?'

He seemed less baffled, not threatened by the news; she could feel his balance coming back. Now was the time to make it seem unimportant. 'Look, with this new women-friendly approach, everything has to be dealt with as though it were as serious as it can be. Even something as absurd as this. It's the only way.'

The whole event was diminishing in his mind, and more so when it was associated with political correctness. By this time his responses were so muddled that he quickly backed off the whole subject, and Sally could see the relief in his eyes, relief now that he realised she wasn't asking anything of him. 'Are you all right?' he said. She said she was. They were sitting by now. Then she found herself saying, 'I am sorry.' Why was she saying she was sorry? There was nothing to be sorry for. He didn't regard her as damaged goods, but perhaps that's what she felt about herself?

He had clearly not seen the other changes she was going through. She had been losing more weight. As she caught sight of herself in her looking glass she could see she was beginning to resemble a model, something a lot of women would die for, but not if they were sensible.

'There's nothing for you to be sorry about,' he said.

It was the moment when he might have been expected to get up and come over to her. But he did not. 'You'll have to give evidence?' he said instead. She managed to make a joke of that. 'Well, it'll make a change. But it's all under control now. You needn't do anything.' She got up and went over to him. 'Thank you for being so supportive.' She offered him release. What he really wanted to talk about was how it would affect his career, so she answered the questions he dared not ask. 'Very few people will know. The press won't be allowed to report it. And you know the Old Bailey, what a tiny closed world it is. Nothing will get out. Just another assault.'

But then the effort of putting it right for him became too much because what she really wanted to talk about was the hurt. She realised that she had not been able to talk about what was hurting for as long as she could remember.

The children had sensed her distress. She noticed how they stayed close to her, handing her things and holding her skirt when previously they would have been running and playing. But when Anne was there they ran off, whooping and shouting as they had done before.

Eventually, as Sally realised might happen, the police-woman asked, 'Why didn't you tell me who you were, and what you did?'

'I didn't want to make it seem that I was asking for any special treatment.'

It was a good answer. She had calculated it and she could see that Angela accepted it, but she could also see the policewoman reviewing the contact she had with her, trying to work out whether she had done anything that Sally would have thought wrong.

Sally decided to help her. 'Of course I didn't need to ask for it. It's clear to me that all the women you help get special treatment.' She saw the worry wash away from Angela's face. Her ability to handle those around her, instead of being pleasing, now only reminded Sally of the shallowness of relationships.

Angela said, 'Now I realise where it was I saw you before. I heard you lecture the Police Federation on sexual offences.'

Sally thought back to that sea of serious, committed faces and wondered at how far she had travelled since then. 'Well, the next lecture I give will be a bit more interesting, won't it?' she said.

Now Sally was free to ask the question that she had been wondering about for some time. 'Who is prosecuting the case?'

'Reid. I don't know him, you probably do.'

Sally did. There was no relief there either.

'And who is defending?'

'A barrister called Jeremy Scott.'

That hit her.

'Do you know him?' Angela said.

'A little. I meet him now and again, but I used to know him.'

She thought about the occasion when she had been at a Temple party with him. That was the evening he had picked her up and carried her on to the dance floor.

205

Afterwards everybody had gone on to a nightclub, but he had gone off with another woman. She had not thought about that incident for a long time. Even longer ago they had been in the same chambers together. Scott had moved on, they had each moved on.

She had seen him a while ago at that lecture meeting, but she didn't speak much to him, only to ask about the man who had shot himself. Of course he had done that case against her, the one the very day of her assault, the one that caused the trouble. And the next morning she had wanted to speak to him about what had happened to her. She remembered it clearly now; she had pushed it from her mind at the time. Why had she wanted to speak to him? He had refused and that had upset her.

They brought Sally down to a seat outside the courtroom just after the case began. She knew that Reid was making an opening speech. That would take about thirty minutes. Even Reid – God, how he loved the sound of his own voice – couldn't take much longer than that, could he? And of course there was the jury to swear in, so – she looked at her watch – it would be another twenty-five minutes or so. She would obviously be the first witness.

Tony Powell walked by. 'Hi, Sally.' She nodded. Did he notice she wasn't wearing her court suit? Men didn't really notice these things.

Scott had. That time outside the Old Bailey when it was raining. And he had immediately realised there was something wrong. There was no doubt he was different. He had left the lecture early and as he did so he looked around at her. She remembered the look; at the time it felt good. Perhaps she did feel something for this man.

'Is Jeremy Scott still defending?' she said. Angela got up to go to the court door to find out. It isn't the questions you ask, it's the answers you hope to get. Who said that? She hoped – what? She hoped he was defending, and she hoped he wasn't. She really didn't know. If he wasn't, maybe he had decided he could not cross-examine her. If he was, it would at least be someone she liked doing it. But it would also mean that he didn't care. Didn't care? What on earth did that mean? Why should he care?

She put her hands together and dropped her head. Then she hugged herself and sat back against the right angles of the uncomfortable marble bench. God, what a damn silly design they were.

'Hallo, Sally.'

She looked up. Philip King was walking past.

'Hallo, Harry,' she said. Why was he called Harry, when his name was Philip? She didn't know.

Angela came back from the main hall. 'Yes, he's defending. I recognise him from the bail application.'

'Bail application?' said Sally. 'Why should Scott have been at a bail application?' Then she understood. 'Surely the man got bail?'

'No. He was remanded in custody. Locked up.'

Sally was staggered. Now this was real.

'Best place for him, I say,' said Angela.

An usher came to the door of the court and called her name. Sally's stomach turned over.

11

Court four at the Old Bailey is a wooden well into which the participants descend. Only the defendant, sitting in his cage, and the judge up on the bench are above everybody else – until a witness climbs up into the witness box at their level. Then everybody looks up, and watches from below.

Scott looked up and saw Sally Donne.

Sally saw Scott look at her. He stared at her. It was immediately clear to her that he had not known it was she who would be stepping up here. He started to get up and then stopped and sat still as she took the oath.

She saw everything with complete clarity and understood everything. You may not move in a court while the oath is being taken, so he did not move. You may not speak and he said nothing. She read the oath out and listened to her own voice, and heard something different. What was different about it? It was purposeless. In the silence of the room it sounded completely without purpose. Her mind raced on. Why purposeless? Because normally when she spoke in this room it was to persuade.

There was one thing she had not done, what was it? She looked at the defendant as the words came out of her mouth, 'nothing but the truth'. He looked at her. She hardly recognised him. He looked gaunt and grey, nothing like the calm assured man she had met in the hotel.

She stood there waiting for the first question. But now Scott was up talking to Reid. Then he said, 'There is a matter I must raise with the court. I apologise for doing it so early in the trial, but it would be better if this were done in the absence of the jury.'

Sally snapped back into the present, and the event stopped being a kind of dream. She had heard variations of this phrase dozens of times before. Scott was being careful not to let the jury know what it was about. She watched from her vantage point.

'But of course, Mr Scott.' The judge turned to the jury. 'These things happen, ladies and gentlemen. Matters of law are for me to decide alone, and Mr Scott wants to raise such a matter. May I therefore invite you to leave us for a moment? The jury usher will tell you where to go.'

The jury, looking suitably bewildered at the interruption, left the court, some gathering their coats, others merely following. There was a long silence as they left. No one said anything. The door closed behind them and the court attendant waved an arm to confirm they had all gone.

The judge turned to face Scott. 'You did not know the identity of this witness, Mr Scott?'

That was a relief: the judge was already a step ahead of him. 'No,' said Scott.

'You want to speak to your client about it?'

'Yes.'

209

'I observe that the witness's occupation is not given in her statement, and the usual procedure has been followed, so there is no address in the witness statement. I also understand that Mrs Murray is not using her professional name.' The judge was not asking questions, he was asserting facts. 'There was no information in the written opening note from the Crown, and the matter was not, Mr Reid, raised in any pre-trial hearing, was it?'

'I thought my learned friend knew . . .' Reid was not convincing.

'Of course. Mr Scott, I understand why you did not know who the witness was. Ten minutes, Mr Scott. We will then sit without the jury and you must tell us of your decision.'

Scott said, 'The prison authorities will not allow me to speak to my client in the dock. We shall have to go downstairs – that will take time. May I have five minutes more?'

'We shall sit in a quarter of an hour, then.'

'There are two questions: firstly, whether the rules of the bar allow me to continue given that I know Mrs Murray, but also, and this is not for me to decide, whether you are happy for me to continue to act for you.'

He went on, 'I know Miss Donne – that is the name she uses as a lawyer. I have worked with her. Once we were acquaintances, not close enough to be called friends, but we knew each other to speak to. What may concern you is whether in those circumstances you feel you can rely upon me to act without any reservation.'

Scott's client listened carefully to him.

'Clearly I have to attack Miss Donne, and of course I

210

have to suggest that the allegations she makes are not true. Do you feel happy for me to act for you in these circumstances?'

'Do you? Do you feel happy?' Scott's client asked back.

Scott paused before replying. 'Miss Donne means nothing to me. She is an acquaintance. As you have seen, I do not even know her married name. I think I once danced with her at a chambers party. We were in chambers together but only for a very short time. If we hadn't both been at the bar then I would not have known her, and I know nothing about her really. I do not think my knowledge of her will affect me.'

'If this trial were to stop now, when would it restart?'

'It would take at least a month to brief new counsel and find a gap in the court list. But that's only a guess.'

'Then let's go ahead. We've done too much work to waste it.'

Scott looked at his client. It wasn't correct to say he had grown to like him over the hours they had spent together, but he was certainly easy to work with. But he hadn't said anything about the identity of the woman. Why was that? Perhaps he didn't know.

'All right. That's the second question answered. I have to go and find the answer to the first.'

He went upstairs. As he left the cells Scott bumped into Rock. He said, 'I'm in a case where the main prosecution witness turns out to be a member of the bar whom I know. Do I have a problem?'

Rock stopped and thought. 'Do you have any personal knowledge that would make it unfair on your client?'

'No.'

'Or give you an unfair advantage over the witness?'

211

'No. I don't think so.'

'Then no problem.'

On reflection Scott thought it typical of Rock that he had the self-control not to ask, 'Who is the prosecution witness?'

'He didn't know it was me,' Sally told Angela. 'He obviously doesn't know my married name. He must have gone to tell his client, and to decide whether he can still stay in the case. I don't think if he had known it was me he would have accepted the brief.'

'He's a friend of yours?'

'No. Not really. But I can talk to him.' Angela knew what that meant.

They were standing in the lift area well away from court four. Of course it was the way Scott would come back from the cells, but they did not think of that till he emerged from the lift. As he stepped out Sally was directly in front of him. Neither showed any sign of recognition.

'My name is Sarah Murray. I am married. I have two children. I live near Topham in Kent.' Reid started taking her through her evidence. 'On that Tuesday I went to an art dealer's near Piccadilly. I had not arranged it. I happened to be free from work. I bought a watercolour.'

Scott watched Sally. Was he doing the right thing? He didn't know her, that was true. If he had not come across her for a year, say, then he would not have noticed, but he was aware of her. No. He was right, that wasn't enough to stop him from acting in the case, and the test that Rock had suggested was good too: he knew nothing about her that would make it difficult to represent his client properly. Or at least he knew nothing he could put to her as a question.

Sally said, 'I met the defendant in the art gallery. I did not ever hear his name. I did not ever ask him. I did not know him. I had never been to the gallery before.'

She spoke clearly. Of course she did. And she wasn't nervous at all.

Sally could see Scott waiting.

'On the spur of the moment I decided to remain in London. I was tired.' She didn't mention her fear of driving having drunk alcohol – why not? She should have done so. But it was too late.

'He sat down with me at my table.'

Reid was hurrying her on. 'I don't suppose you expected that?' he said.

'Well, no.' Sally was surprised Scott didn't object. That was a leading question.

'Yes,' said Reid. 'Unusual, perhaps.'

Scott even let the comment go.

Sally said, 'We ate part of our supper together. I had nearly finished when he sat down.'

Scott was curious to see if she was going to tell them what they talked about. She did not, she only said, 'We talked of this and that.'

'The casino?' Reid asked.

'It was in the building. He suggested I go and look at it. Rather, he suggested we go to look at it.'

'And of course that would mean remaining safely in the hotel?'

'Yes,' said Sally, who had never even thought of it.

Again Scott could have objected, but oddly enough the effect of the leading questions, putting words in her

213

mouth, was reducing the strength of her evidence. But there was something more important he was beginning to see. He had suspected it when reading the witness statements: Sally had been perfectly happy, she had even been impressed by being with this man, the man who was now his client.

Scott looked up at his client, who was leaning forward intently. He was reduced. Scott had seen him shrivel slightly while in custody from the time he first met him. He had been a handsome, attractive man; he still was, if diminished slightly.

He could see how Sally might have been attracted to him.

He looked at the jury. It was a well-mixed group of people. There were one or two for whom the Ritz and Piccadilly art dealers were a completely foreign country, but for others it might not be completely alien. There was a man at the back, easily, casually dressed, sitting sideways, looking at Reid and at the witness sideways, the classic body language of scepticism. Scott had seen the same posture many times before, even to the extent that he guessed that the man was carrying a rolled-up newspaper which he was tapping against his leg.

In the front row there were two women. Clearly they now knew each other – obviously they had struck up a relationship in the jury room. And they looked similar: well dressed, unaffected by the court atmosphere. What were they? Once he would have said personal assistants, top-level secretaries, but now those sorts of women had broken free. They could be anything. How about mathematicians? Well perhaps not. Any suggestion that Sally was taking liberties by prancing around the West End on her own without her husband to protect her wouldn't go down well with them. But on the other hand they would know all about how to handle themselves, and handling oneself meant not giving people too good an opportunity to take liberties.

The Mike Tyson defence. How Tyson was ever convicted of rape he couldn't understand. The sharp suits of the defence lawyers probably didn't help. What he had really needed was a cornpoke attorney. Cornpoke – was that the word? Scott thought he could fancy being a cornpoke attorney. Though once Tyson bit the guy in the ring everybody immediately understood the conviction – that's how near the edge this sort of case was.

'No, I had never been to a casino before,' Sally said. Scott was surprised Reid had asked her that; for a start, how did he know what the answer was going to be? Had some questions been asked privately beforehand? But maybe he was trying to present Sally as some kind of innocent abroad, which of course she was not. Scott guessed that she was a very tough person indeed, but nevertheless Reid was delivering her straight into his main line of attack.

'I won some money.'

Reid fluffed that one too. 'It was quite a lot, I think, Mrs Murray.' He had obviously thought about what to say.

'Yes.'

'We needn't go into that.'

Well, if that was the way he had decided to treat the matter then he had got it wrong. But did Reid know how much she'd won? Did he have any *idea* how much she had won?

Scott noticed that the man sitting sideways in the back

215

row was indeed holding a rolled newspaper. He had leaned to his side and whispered something behind it to his neighbour.

'When we left the casino we went to my room.'

Reid interrupted. 'I think you do not know how the door to your room was opened?'

Sally looked at him and said, 'That's right. I do not know how we got in there.'

That was enough. Scott got up. 'That is a leading question. Please could my friend exercise more care.'

'Yes, I think you're right, Mr Scott.' The judge was not going to get any more involved than that.

Scott hadn't objected because the question was leading, but to put down a marker. It was clear that the idea that Scott's client had got into Sally's room unexpectedly had become so embedded in the Crown case, probably because of the bail application, that it was being persisted with, in the face of common sense.

'I changed. I came out of the bathroom. He was sitting on the bed. He had some wine. I am unable to say precisely how what happened next began, but I found myself on the bed, underneath him.

'He tore my skirt . . .'

Reid interrupted the evidence to have the skirt found. Naturally it had disappeared. It was somewhere at the back of the court. The officer in the case was waiting outside so she couldn't help. When the exhibits were discovered they were all in big plastic bags. Which one contained the skirt? They were sorted through. The usher tore at the tough plastic ineffectively. What on earth was going on?

Scott had sat through this kind of farce dozens of times. The witness was hanging there, about to describe her own rape, and the usher was looking for a pair of scissors to open a package.

'There we are,' said Reid. He meant 'at last'.

The skirt was produced for everybody to see. If the jury were expecting to see a huge gash where the rapist had ripped this woman's clothes from her unprotected quivering body, then they were disappointed. There was a button missing. Archie had examined the skirt earlier and had reported the missing button in triumph. Obviously Reid had not bothered to look.

Scott allowed no flicker to cross his face; he couldn't have hoped for better. He looked at Sally. She looked back at him.

'He was very strong. I threatened to scream. He said, 'Go ahead.' I objected to his trying to come into me from behind. He was able to turn me over.'

'How did he get your underwear off?'

'I don't know. The whole thing was so surprising that I was confused for the first few seconds. He was very strong.' She added, almost under her breath, 'Very strong.' Scott doubted that the jury even heard it, but he realised that this was the point at which the case might start to run away from them.

He looked at Reid, who did not seem to have heard what his witness had said. Scott looked up: the judge had.

A trial is not likely to be decided by one moment, though Scott had occasionally seen that happen. But a decision can grow slowly out of one moment, particularly if that moment is repeated again in different ways.

'He was very strong.' Reid was not going to build on it, and Scott was certainly not going to repeat it, because if it were repeated often enough it would make everything else, the money, the room, the late night drink, seem irrelevant.

Scott waited. He tried to look unconcerned.

'How long did this take?' Reid carried on with another asinine question. Who cared? How could it be measured? Did it matter? Sally responded as Scott feared she might. She started taking over.

'I've no idea. I've nothing to compare it with. All I know is I was not able to do anything to stop it. I tried hitting him, but without any weapon it is not really possible. I think he got pleasure from my struggling.'

The jury's heads swivelled almost as one towards the defendant. Scott underlined his note. He would have to deal with this. This was the rough sex bit.

'Rough sex, do you like rough sex?' It was always coming up in rape trials, and the point was never really challenged, as though it was a truth universally acknowledged that all sensible people like rough sex. Was it? He looked at the lady third from the right in the front. He doubted whether she had ever been the prisoner of uncontrollable desires for rough sex. But who knew? The juror looked at Scott, directly, in the eyes. He dropped his head.

Sally said, 'I am not a young, inexperienced woman. I know about these things. I was aware of what he was doing, and I was aware he was not interested in my co-operation. And, after all, co-operation is what sexual intercourse is about. Mostly.'

There, she had said it. It is extraordinary how difficult it is to present things in black and white. 'Mostly.' Perhaps that was the word which would get him off the hook. Sally would not be able to justify that word.

218

Sally looked at Scott. He was a different prospect. She was beginning to get annoyed with Reid, but she had to face Scott yet.

'How was he dressed?'

'He still had his clothes on. I could feel the zip of his trousers against my skin. I remember being surprised. I also remember thinking at the time that he was not wearing any underwear.'

Sally had told the police this and when Scott's client was arrested and his clothes were taken for examination it was correct, he had no underwear. But what did it mean? It was information she would have come by however she slept with him, rape or not. Although it was the curiosity of it that made it dangerous.

'I don't know why, but I remember nothing after that. I remember waking up in the morning. I do not remember his leaving, though of course he must have done so. I myself woke on the bed still half dressed. I remember panicking, and then panicking some more when I picked my watch up, because I had an important appointment, and somehow rushing to make it, and trying to act normally.

'I didn't think. I didn't want to think. I put off thinking about it. I am very good at dealing with things in order.' She stopped. Had she left it like that she might have seemed rather cold and calculating, but she rescued it, not intentionally Scott thought, but just because she was like that. 'Though not necessarily in the right order.'

Scott thought of the times he had come across her, how attractive she was. He turned his mind away from that.

'I went to work. I left early. I drove home, and sat on the bed in our bedroom.'

219

'Did someone come into the room?'

'Yes. Anne, Anne Timms. She looks after our children. The children love her. We were talking and then I saw her looking at my arm. I got up to look at it and I saw the marks he had left on me. I told Anne what had happened. It was then I decided to go to the police station.'

There, she had said it. She knew that she would be asked, 'Why not go straight away?'

Reid took her through the remaining exhibits. Her examination by the doctor. 'The doctor will tell us that you had an injury on the posterior fourchette. For the moment I needn't deal exactly with that.'

'I know where the posterior fourchette is, Mr Reid,' Sally said. She suddenly seemed intensely grown-up. What a ridiculous idea. We are all grown-up. But Scott knew he had seen something that he would have to deal with – it wasn't just the momentary correction of Reid, but more. Here was a woman who if she wished could exert power; she had energy. Where was it all going? Into her work of course. Scott's thoughts were immediately confirmed.

'Could that injury have been caused by any other recent . . .' Reid stumbled over the next word, 'by anything?'

Scott looked at Sally. He was directly opposite her; the jury were to one side. He could see directly into her eyes; he saw her hand at her throat. 'No,' she said, 'nothing. No. Not for a long time.'

'Lunch break,' said the judge.

This last bit mattered, Scott knew. This mattered to women. For men sex was often just a relief. Not for women. Where did she find her justification? In her work?

No. In her children. That was it. But whom did the children loved? They love Anne.

There it was again. The children. She had said it. 'They love her.'

12

'At what time did you enter the Ritz hotel?'

'Between six-thirty and seven.'

'At what time do you normally set off home?'

'Sometimes then, mostly later, about seven-thirty.'

'So it wasn't the time that prevented you from going home?'

Sally said nothing. Then, 'No.'

'Had you seen your children that morning?'

'No. Not awake.'

'Would you normally have seen them that evening?'

'Yes. Sometimes I do not get there in time.'

'And put them to bed?'

'Yes.'

'So something kept you away from your children?'

'Yes. I didn't want to drive home.'

'Before the hotel, you had been to an art dealer?'

'Yes.'

'And you were invited to stay on at the dealer?'

The jury watched curiously.

'Yes. There was wine.'

'Had you drunk any wine?'

'Yes.'

'Was it a wine tasting?'

'Yes.'

'But you drank the wine, and didn't just taste it?'

'Yes.'

'How were you feeling?'

'I was upset.'

'Was the cause of that something other than the events of this case?'

'Yes.'

'Might this be part of the reason you drank wine rather than tasting it?'

'Yes, it might.' Sally thought, and went on, 'But it was probably more that I cannot get used to the idea of spitting it out.' There was a ripple of amusement.

'At the art dealer's you bought a picture?'

'Yes.'

'Is that something you often do?'

'I have done it.'

'Mrs Murray, buying a picture by a French Impressionist at a Piccadilly art dealer – is that something you often do?'

'No.'

'Is it something you have ever done?'

'No.'

'And did you pay a lot of money for it?'

Sally started to say, 'It depends what . . .' and then just said 'Yes.'

'Five thousand pounds?'

'Yes.' The jury stirred slightly.

'My client helped you decide on the picture?'

It was a weak question and Scott immediately regretted it.

'I wouldn't say he helped me.'

'He discussed the picture with you?'

'Yes.'

'For some minutes?'

'Yes.'

'Then he left?'

Sally remembered how he had suddenly left the room. She said, 'Yes, he did.'

'He made no effort to continue the acquaintance that you and he had struck up while you looked at the picture?'

'No.'

'You didn't get his name?'

'No.'

'You dealt with the manager of the gallery about buying the picture and were then invited to the wine tasting?'

'Yes.'

'You might equally have refused? You might have said, "I have to get home to Kent to see my children"?'

'Yes.'

'But you did not.'

'No.'

'You went into the wine tasting which was in another room. There was no way anyone could have known you would choose to do that?'

'No.'

'And there you met my client again?'

'Yes.'

'While you were at the art gallery you confided in my client that you found your husband's taste in paintings stifling?'

224

'Did I use that word? I don't think so.'

'What you said, I suggest, to my client was, "My husband's taste runs to stags at bay and that sort of thing," and you laughed.'

Sally remembered. She had said exactly that. When she had said it, it was intended to be a joke. But here it was being strung out for everyone to see. 'I did say that.'

'Why?'

'Because it is true.'

'Was there no other reason?'

Sally thought. 'What other reason could there be? No.'

'Your taste however is softer. Pictures of young ladies on beds.' Scott held up a reproduction of the picture she had bought. 'Henri LeBasque, is it not?'

'Yes, that is the picture I bought. I didn't know there were reproductions.'

'It is from the catalogue. Later you discussed with my client why you had bought it?'

'I think so.'

'You said—'

'He discussed it,' she interrupted.

'It was he who discussed it, was it? Are you saying he did so without your consent?'

'No. It wasn't. It was just he that discussed it.'

'He remarked upon the dissimilarity between the girl on the bed and you?'

'Yes.'

'He said he thought you liked it "because of the difference"?'

'Yes.'

'What did that mean?'

'I don't know.'

225

'What could it mean?'

Sally thought about the conversation and said, 'We discussed how the woman in the picture seemed content in herself.' Then she thought this was getting a bit personal. 'It was nothing,' she said.

'It wasn't nothing, was it?' said Scott. 'In fact it was a very personal remark.'

'Yes,' said Sally.

'Did you protest?'

What? Sally couldn't remember. Anyway how would one protest, how would one say it? 'No. I don't think I did.'

'What, you didn't say, "I'm not talking about that to strangers"?'

How ridiculous. Could one say such a thing? But she realised that in the false atmosphere of the court it was just the kind of thing one could be criticised for. 'No, I just didn't.' Then she remembered that she had felt annoyed when he made the remark and that she had said so. 'Yes, I did.'

'You told him?'

'Yes, I did.'

Scott knew he was on dangerous ground here, but he pushed on. 'What did he do?'

Again Sally could not exactly remember. But he had not been aggressive to her. She had to be fair. Then she remembered how he had obviously been very aware of her feelings. 'He was very sensitive. He wasn't being aggressive.'

Sensitive. One of the women on the jury nodded slightly. Sensitive was a code word for women. Scott knew he could use that.

'He was sensitive, was he?'

226

'Yes.'

Now was the time to change the tone again.

'Let me ask you again. Why did you not drive home?'

'You did not ask me that.'

'Mrs Murray, you are probably right. But certainly you did not tell us, did you?

'No.'

'Why did you not drive home?'

'I had had too much to drink.'

'So you stopped off at the hotel?'

'Yes. I decided to stay in the hotel later.'

'Why did you stop off at the Ritz?'

'It sounds silly, but it was raining and cold, and I could not get a taxi. Two taxis stopped where I was standing but rather than me they took hotel guests. They jumped the queue and I protested to the hotel commissionaire. He invited me inside the hotel to stay warm. It does sound silly.'

'You had taken a little too much to drink.'

'To drive, yes. Not otherwise.'

'And you dropped off at the Ritz because the commissionaire asked you to?'

'Yes. I said it sounds silly.' Sally began to wonder what sort of person she was beginning to look like.

'So you might have gone home had it not been for that invitation?' Scott knew he had gone too far. Sally would merely say, 'No. It was because I was over the limit.' But she did not.

'Yes,' she said. Now Scott knew he was beginning to dominate her.

'So what prevented you from driving once you had gained the shelter of the hotel? They presumably could have got you a cab?'

'I had another drink in the hotel.'

'On top of the wine?'

'Yes.'

'Had you eaten that day?'

'An apple I think.'

'So what did you drink at the hotel?'

'Dry Martini.'

'And some caviar?'

'Yes.' How did he know?

'Did you order that?'

'No. They just brought it.'

'They just brought you some caviar,' Scott said.

He stood still for an extra beat.

'Mr Scott,' the judge said, 'no need to pause.'

Scott didn't stop to argue – it was enough. He could leave the drink now. Till later.

'You chose to eat in the dining room of the hotel?'

'Yes.'

'Could anybody an hour earlier have forecast that you would do this?'

'No. I was there by chance. The whole of this thing happened by chance.'

Silence. The slow build-up was affecting her. Scott could feel it.

'You were there by chance, but you became aware that my client was a regular guest at the hotel, didn't you?'

'He said so.'

Scott risked it. He paused, looked up and said, 'When you first saw him in the dining room you probably thought he had followed you, didn't you? – this man, who a little earlier had been a bit too forward.'

Sally thought, how did he know that? But then she immediately saw his reasoning. She must have thought something, and she was hardly likely to say she was pleased to see him. She could feel the trial lawyer's brain working beneath the questions. What could she say? She had to be honest. 'Yes, I did.'

'No doubt that can be a problem if you are an attractive woman?'

'Are you asking me to remark upon my own appearance, Mr Scott?'

'Mrs Murray, you must know.'

'Yes,' she said. 'Women can have that difficulty.'

'But not now?'

'I am married now.'

'And you don't often find yourself in good hotels, or any hotels, on your own?'

'No.'

'And therefore not the annoyed object of unwanted attention.'

'No.'

'But the point I wanted to raise is this. My client is a regular at the hotel, is he not?'

'So he said.'

'Mrs Murray, it seems that for the first time during these questions we may differ. It wasn't just that he said he was a regular, was it?'

No reply.

'You yourself commented on it, did you not, Mrs Murray? You said to him, "You look at home." '

Sally remembered now. She had forgotten about the table. Her whole memory had been altered by her subsequent anger at the man. 'Yes,' she said, 'you're right, I did. I commented upon the way his table had been prepared for him.'

'A napkin and a napkin ring?'

'Yes.'

'And a half-drunk bottle of wine was produced. It had a rubber stopper in it?'

'Yes.'

'All the signs of someone who regularly dines at the same table?'

'Yes.'

'And you remarked that you were surprised that the wine waiter would agree to the replaced cork?'

'Yes.'

'You probably said *"sommelier"*, didn't you, Mrs Murray?'

Mistake.

'You're attributing a degree of sophistication to me that I do not possess, Mr Scott.'

'Why did you say to me a moment ago that your knowledge of his being a regular depended only upon what he told you? When I asked you if he was a regular at the hotel dining room you said, "So he said."'

'I don't know.'

'Was it because you later convinced yourself he had been lying about himself all along?'

Scott was right. Even Sally was surprised by what Scott was demonstrating about her memory and what she had thought.

'I think you're right,' she said.

'Did you later change your mind and decide he must have followed you?'

'Yes, I did.'

'But you must be mistaken about that?'

'I don't know.'

'You still think that?'

'Perhaps.'

'But Mrs Murray, by pure chance you go to the dining room, and take a table near his regular spot. He comes, as we shall prove, as he does nearly every day for supper, where his things are laid out, and you still think he followed you?'

'No. I don't say he followed me. I just don't know that he didn't.'

Scott paused and then said, 'That's your evidence is it, Mrs Murray?'

Sally had used the phrase herself many times, but until now she did not realise just how devastating it felt – and unfair. She opened her mouth to reply, but stopped herself. To reply would make it worse.

'He sat with his back to you?'

'Not quite. He was sideways on.'

'You remember it well?'

'I remember it.'

'He saw you and walked over?'

'Yes.'

'You invited him to join you?'

'No, I think he said, "May I sit down?" '

'But did he not give you time to refuse, or to indicate your unwillingness?' Scott's client had said to him. 'Count five before you sit down at another person's table in a restaurant. That's what my father always told me.'

Sally remembered now that he had paused. But the man could still rape her, couldn't he? Just because he had good manners. 'Yes. He did. His manners were impeccable.'

Impeccable manners. Sensitive. Scott knew that the difference between a shit who took exactly what he wanted and a romantic hero was very small. He had to be very careful.

'So you were willing for him to sit down?'

'Yes.'

'You were happy to have company?'

'Not really, it wasn't like that.'

'I don't understand. Were you not happy to have company?'

'No, what I am saying is that I was not in need of company.'

'I hadn't suggested that. That's the next step of course, isn't it, needing company?'

'Yes.'

'And you hadn't reached that stage?'

'No. Nor was I going to.'

'And you drank more alcohol?'

God, that sounded brutal. Scott looked at Sally and, for the first time, his heart went out to her. She saw it happen. They each knew exactly what he was going to do to her, and that they were powerless to prevent it.

At lunch, before he began his questioning of Sally, Scott had been told to behave himself. He had seen Reid talking to John Marriott, and had noticed how Marriott had looked over at him. They were obviously discussing him. Marriott followed Scott into the small library.

'Sally Donne is well liked in this mess, you know,' Marriott said.

'I'm sure,' said Scott. *Well liked in this mess, you know* – it sounded like a line from a stiff John Mills movie. But he

232

knew he was not going to be able to produce the reply which would stop this.

'Don't try any tricks on her, Scott.'

At least Scott didn't try to affect an air of injured dignity; he just turned his eyes away. Is that what the cad in the movies always did before dishonouring the Colonel's lady?

'Yes, I did.'

'More alcohol? What exactly?'

'A half-bottle of white wine.'

'Added to the champagne that was in your room upstairs when you arrived?'

Sally realised that Scott knew everything that had happened. 'Yes.'

'Then some more wine, which my client ordered?'

'Yes.'

'A Château d'Yquem?'

'Yes.'

'What's Château d'Yquem?' That was cheap and Scott was immediately punished.

'You obviously know what it is, Mr Scott, you mentioned the name,' said the judge. The judge wasn't going to protect Sally, but he would if Scott didn't do it right.

'Then you took more to drink in the casino.'

'I don't remember.'

'And more in the bedroom later?'

'I don't think so.'

'I suggest you drank more wine in the bedroom.'

Sally thought: she had picked up the wine when she sat on the bed. 'Yes, I probably did.'

'In total a lot of wine?'

'Is that a lot?'

'Is it, Mrs Murray? You tell us.'

Sally could not say yes, as she didn't think it was. But nor could she say no without compromising herself. She said nothing.

'Mrs Murray, please don't think I shall pester you. But my question was "Is that a lot of wine?" '

'No,' she said.

Scott had not looked at the jury once. He had not raised his voice once. He had not emphasised a word once. She had never dealt with such an implacable series of questions. Is this what it is like? She adjusted her thoughts. Is this what I am like? Am I this kind of person?

'Do you often drink dry Martinis?'

'No.'

'Was the atmosphere in the dining room comforting?'

'Comforting? No. It was comfortable, yes.'

'Is that why you confided in this man your dislike of your husband's taste in pictures?'

'Don't be so ridiculous.'

'Then why did you do so? It would not be something you ordinarily tell a stranger?'

'I can't say. You make it sound as if I was saying I didn't love my husband.'

'I am not making it sound anything, Mrs Murray. I am merely asking you questions.'

That was so obviously right that it silenced her. He returned to her reply.

'But I will ask you this, since you invite the question. You were saying, weren't you, that you didn't love that part of him?'

'No. No.'

'Do you not remember the phrase that men are supposed to use? "My wife doesn't understand me?"' It was the first really aggressive question.

'Mr Scott, it was not like that.' Sally bridled.

'Might a disinterested observer have thought it was like that, Mrs Murray?'

'She can't answer that question, you know,' said the judge. This time the judge's intervention helped Scott. It left the question unanswered.

'You were invited to the casino?'

'Yes.'

'Counsel for the Crown remarked that it meant you did not have to leave the building. Did that even enter your mind?'

'No.'

Scott realised he was beginning to tire. An unnecessary poke at Reid showed him that. He took a breath and for the first time changed the position in which he was standing. It was important to stand very still. He could never understand why trial lawyers in America walked about, or at least they did in the movies. Don't. Be very still.

'The money you won at the hotel was in the room upstairs when the attack occurred. What you say was an attack.'

'It was an attack.'

'I understand you say that. But the money was upstairs in the room?'

'Yes.'

'Downstairs my client gambled with his own money, and then he put some of his money in front of you to play with?'

Sally saw how weakly Scott had put it. But that was

235

obviously intentional. Now she could see what was coming. 'No', she said, 'he handed me six hundred pounds in chips to place.'

'Was this a gift?'

'I don't know what it was.'

'Whatever it was it was a lot of money.'

'Yes.'

'And you took it?'

'I played with it.'

'You played with it?'

'Yes.'

'Did you ever give it back?'

'I had no chance.'

'You mean he attacked you and after that you had no chance to repay it?'

'Yes.'

'Mrs Murray, as you left the casino did you repay the money?'

'No.'

'Why not?'

'I don't know. I was excited.'

'You were excited. As you went upstairs to your room, you were excited?'

'Yes.' She had asked for it and she could say nothing else.

'By this time did you know my client's name?'

'No.'

'By the time you took him to your room did you know his name?'

'You know I didn't, Mr Scott.'

'What I know is of no importance, madam. Did you know the name of the man you took to your room?'

'I didn't take him.'

'Did you know his name?'

The court was silent, breathless. They were watching someone slowly being destroyed. A woman being flayed about sex. One of the jury licked his lips nervously. He didn't really want to see this: It wasn't what he had expected.

'No.'

'We shall come to who took whom to the room later, Mrs Murray. First answer me this, did he advise you how to play?'

'Yes.'

'He had a system?

'Yes.'

'A thing people often laugh at?'

'I suppose so.'

'You won?'

'Yes.'

'And the money you won was on the bed upstairs when you had physical relations with this man?'

'Yes.'

'How much money?'

Sally had to say it, and as she did so she felt her face again being pushed into the notes, as he put his hands between her legs to open her up to him. She swallowed. 'Thirty – ' She coughed. It was not possible to control it, her reactions were visceral. 'Thirty-three thousand pounds.'

There was an audible gasp. Scott kept his head rigidly down towards his papers.

'What does thirty thousand pounds look like on a bed, Mrs Murray? Does it cover it completely?'

237

'Do you really want me to answer that?'

'Yes.'

'I won't.'

'Why was it on the bed?'

'He had put it there.'

'You are saying it was his fault?'

'Yes.'

'He did it without your consent?'

'Yes.'

'Just as he discussed the picture without your consent?'

'This is different.'

'What does that amount of money look like?'

'It was everywhere.'

'Like a sheet, like a carpet of leaves?'

'Yes.'

'A bed of money.'

Sally said nothing. She remembered the story of the anonymous couple in a hotel who filled the bath with champagne and then went to dinner, only for the cleaner to pull the bath plug. What other tangled, complicated pleasures did the readers of the evening paper immediately assume they were going to indulge in after they came back from dinner?

Scott carried on. He had to deal with all the events, although he knew he could almost stop there.

'When you left the casino you were so dazed by what had happened that you stumbled and nearly fell.'

'I don't remember.'

'Can you not remember it because you were in a daze?'

'I don't know.'

'You mean that might be the reason?'

Sweat was beginning to gather under Scott's wig. He

238

looked at the clock. An hour and a quarter had passed. It seemed like a moment.

'It might be.'

'You wanted to stop and look at the money.'

'Yes, I did that.'

'You had taken it in cash?'

'He had advised me to do so.'

'And you wanted to look at it again?'

'Yes.'

'Where were you going?'

'He said just get away from the table.'

'You had said, "Let's do it again"?'

She remembered the phrase. God, that must have sounded like a young girl begging a man to do it again, and sulking on the bed when he did not, or could not. Scott had seen the connection too, that's why he repeated the exact words. Heavens, he had been well instructed.

'You were excited, Mrs Murray?'

'Of course.'

'Large amounts of money engender powerful emotions?'

'I was excited by it.'

'In fact he made a quiet joke. He said, "Never drive a car or work dangerous machinery after winning a lot of money"?'

'I remember.'

'He had just caught you from falling when he said that?'

She thought back. 'I don't remember.'

'But that's why he said it, Mrs Murray, because in the heat of the moment you had fallen.'

'I don't remember.'

'After he said that, he moved his hand to your shoulder?'

'I remember that. I remember his hand on my shoulder.'

'Did you object?'

'Why should I?'

'Where were you going when you left the table?'

'I didn't decide. I don't know. We went to my room.'

'You said you didn't take him. Did he take you?'

Again Sally saw that, whatever her reply, she would come off worse. Anyway, it wasn't a real question. Who decides how these things happen?

'Are you saying this man took you to your room?'

'No.'

'Earlier you said you didn't take him.'

'Yes.'

'So you just went. It was agreed without even talking about it?'

'Yes.'

'But what I am concerned to ask about is this. There was no discussion about it? He didn't say' – Scott allowed a long pause – 'your place or mine?' One of the advantages of sex cases was the large number of double meanings available.

'No.'

'Both of you just went to your bedroom.'

'Yes.'

Sally noticed that now her room had become a bedroom.

'He had ordered some wine to be brought there.'

'He must have done so, there was wine there. I saw it the next morning.'

240

'Have you no memory of that?'

'I remember wine waiting at the room.'

'He had ordered it?'

'I didn't.'

Scott flashed back to the other case he had done. 'The one who orders the drinks is the dominant personality', was that it?

'On the way upstairs you dropped your key.'

'I do not remember that.'

'And the door was opened by my client using your key.'

Sally said nothing, she could not remember this.

'The waiter was standing there, he could not help but see. You don't remember?'

Sally shook her head.

'Then perhaps you would recognise him?' Scott turned to the judge. 'Might Martin Ancona step into the court, please?' The judge nodded.

The case had not only been fearsomely well prepared, but it was running like clockwork. There was no annoying wait, destroying the tension. Instantly a man stepped into the back of the court, where both the jury and the witness could see him.

'Do you recognise that man?'

'No.'

Scott said, 'He is the floor waiter at the Ritz for your room. He was standing holding a bottle of wine on a tray as you entered your room.'

Sally tried to remember. She could not.

'Thank you, Mr Ancona,' Scott said.

In the small pause as the waiter left, Scott remembered. It was the case where the woman had ordered the champagne.

'You don't remember? May I go back a moment? You left the casino in a daze. You stumbled and fell against the banister.'

It suddenly became important for Sally to remember. She was beginning to look as though she had lost all control at the hotel. And her failure to reply seemed to mean that whatever he suggested was what had happened.

'Yes. I think I did stumble. I certainly remember the banisters.' She put her arm up and rubbed her shoulder.

'He was walking on your right-hand side.'

She visualised it. 'Yes, that would be right.'

'And he grasped your arm to stop you falling?'

'He might have done so.'

'And where you just rubbed your arm was where he grasped you.'

'It could have been.'

'And that is precisely where the injuries are shown on the photograph?'

Sally paused and then said, 'Yes.'

Scott left it there. He had destroyed the evidence of bruising.

'As you entered the bedroom, you said, "I don't think I can eat anything. After that I just want to go to bed."'

'I doubt that I said that.'

'You said it in the waiter's presence, Mrs Murray.'

'If I did, it meant nothing.'

This was the important part; the jury would hear about those words again. Scott said, 'It may have meant nothing to you, Mrs Murray, but—'

'Is this a question, Mr Scott?' the judge intervened immediately.

'No, milord.'

'Well, at least you admit it, Mr Scott,' the judge said.

'Did you feel guilty about winning the money?'

'No,' she said.

'You did, Mrs Murray. You said, "Do you think the hotel mind?" And my client replied, "It's not the hotel who lost it but the couple opposite." You remember them, don't you, Mrs Murray, the curtain manufacturer and the thin lady with pink nails.'

The curtain manufacturer and the woman who earned her living painting her nails. She remembered it now with astonishing vividness. She couldn't deny it.

Scott saw it working. Always make the question as vivid as possible; the witness doesn't stand a chance. Who could have denied that image even if they had wanted to?

'Yes. I remember them.'

'You said you felt guilty, and he said, we won it from them not the hotel?'

'Yes. I remember now.'

'And you felt guilty because you had done nothing to earn the money?'

'Yes.'

Scott thought of saying, 'You hadn't earned it yet,' but thought better of it. Was even the impulse to ask the question discreditable?

He continued, 'When you got to the bedroom, you took some of your clothes off.'

Sally said, 'Mr Scott, I went to the bathroom to freshen up.'

'Did you telephone anyone?'

'No.'

'Not your husband?'

'No.'

'To tell him that you were suddenly thirty-three thousand pounds richer?'

Sally remembered thinking in the bathroom about how
she might conceal the money from him, and how she had
felt worried about what she had done.

'No. He was away, at a constituency . . .' She broke off
the word, no sense in telling the court her husband was an
MP. 'He had an appointment.'

Scott hadn't even known Sally's husband was an MP.

'Has he no mobile?'

'Yes.'

'Then you could have rung him wherever he was.'

'He doesn't like it.'

Scott thought to himself, He doesn't like this woman
ringing him?

He said, 'He doesn't like you ringing?'

'No, he doesn't like just chatting on the phone.'

'But for important news, Mrs Murray?'

She could not reply. Had she mentioned at the hotel
being worried where to deposit the money? She was sure
she had not. Did she have to volunteer her thoughts about
the subject?

'Perhaps you did not want him to know?'

Sally found herself jumping ahead. Scott obviously
knew or guessed about her marriage, but what had that
to do with being raped? She replied, 'Whether I did or did
not want my husband to know does not mean I consented
to having sex with your client, Mr Scott.' How the hell did
Scott know anyway? She hardly knew herself. He was right
of course. Then she realised that what she had just
admitted out loud she might just as well have said out
loud, 'My husband and I do not love each other any

more.' How often she herself had been pleased when witnesses spoke out unnecesarily.

Scott was restrained. 'But it helps develop the picture of what was happening, Mrs Murray, and what you might have wanted.'

Sally did not reply.

'Doesn't it, Mrs Murray?'

Then she said, 'I am sorry, I didn't hear your question.' But that sounded like she was avoiding it. 'I didn't hear what you said,' she repeated. She knew the jury must think she was trying to avoid something.

'I said that knowing whether you wanted your husband to know what was happening helps us appreciate the picture.'

'Did I say that?'

'I think you did, Mrs Murray.'

'Oh,' she said. She did, didn't she. The picture had become clear despite her protests.

'But if you did not say it in so many words, Mrs Murray, I'll ask you again so you can tell us the position. Did you want him to know?'

'That is not relevant, Mr Scott.'

'That's for me to say, Mrs Murray,' said the judge.

Scott switched the subject.

'Why did you later say to the young lady who worked for you, "This man got into my room somehow"?'

'I didn't.'

'Again, I think you will find that you did, Mrs Murray.'

Scott picked up Anne Timms's statement. Of course her evidence would come later but he read out the passage. '"She told me that the man had got into her room somehow."' He turned to the judge. 'Page ten, milord.'

245

Speaking to the judge directly always assisted counsel, putting them apart from the witness. 'Lord Denman's Act obliges me, if I wish to contradict you on something you said, to make clear the time and place you said it, Mrs Murray.' Again for a moment the mumbo-jumbo of the law would set him apart from the argument, giving him a slightly different position, an impersonal force, rather than being a particular person. 'You said to Anne Timms in your house the next day, "Somehow he got in my room." Now do you deny that?'

Sally had never seen Anne Timms's statement. Had she said that? She replied, 'I don't remember saying that. I remember saying a man was in my room and he raped me.'

'But it wouldn't be correct to say that 'he got in somehow", would it? Because you let him in.'

'I don't remember letting him in. All I remember is having the key in my bag the next day. I gave it to the police.'

This was the evidence that had resulted in Scott's client being locked up while waiting for trial.

'Did you intend to give the impression that this man had got into your room without your permission?'

'Mrs Murray hasn't accepted yet that she said it at all,' said the judge. 'You'll either have to accept what she says, Mr Scott, or contradict it in another way.'

Again Scott was pleased to be given a reason to leave it, and now he was able to set off on the most difficult part of his questioning with a good wind.

'When you got home the next day, were you feeling guilty about leaving the children?'

Sally looked up sharply. What was this? 'No,' she said.

What did he know about this? She hadn't told anyone of her worries about the children.

'You said in your evidence, "The children love Anne." '

'Yes.' So he had noticed it.

'When you got home you cried about the children.'

Sally could remember the confusion of emotions and the absurdity of not being able to go to the school to pick up the children seeming more important than what had happened at the hotel. Perhaps it was?

'I did,' she said.

'Would you have reported this incident at the hotel if Anne had not seen the injuries?'

Would she? She didn't know. Her indecision showed. 'I think so,' she said, then she tried to strengthen it: 'Yes, I would.'

'You think so? All the time you were driving home down the M2 to Kent . . .'

Scott took his time with the question. It was good sometimes to slow up. He had gone down the M2 to see a body. That was the case against Sally. Why had he not remembered?

'All the time you were driving down to Kent, weren't you thinking about it?' he said.

'Yes.'

Sally wanted to say, 'Jeremy, stop it. Don't do this to me.'

Scott thought, What was the date of that trial against Sally? He said to the judge, 'If I may take a moment.'

'Of course, Mr Scott, you have wasted no time at all.'

He had received payment for that case only two days before and still had the bill in his pocket. He looked at it for the date of that trial. Yes, it was the same day.

'Do you mean that you were thinking about whether to report this all the way down?'

Sally had to say, 'Yes.'

Scott remembered she had arrived late at court, and after the hearing had asked him to come for coffee. Something had upset her. It was this, this had upset her.

'So it wasn't an easy decision?'

'No.'

'Why not?'

'Because – because . . .' She hadn't thought this through. She had known it would come up, but had avoided thinking about it. Why? She had no real answer.

'But you are sure that this man raped you? "Got into your room somehow" and raped you?'

'Yes.'

'So you do say he got in your room somehow?'

Sally was transfixed. She could say nothing.

'Yes.'

'And yet thinking that in the car you are not sure you are going to report it?'

'I had to be sure . . .'

'Sure he raped you?'

'No. Sure I wanted this.'

'But how could there be any doubt?'

'I was hurt.'

'All the more reason, Mrs Murray, to report it.'

'No.'

Scott moved in. Now he was going to hurt her as well. 'You wouldn't have reported it at all, would you, had it not been that Anne saw marks on your body?' He had let her down once before. At that party all those years ago he

248

had gone off with some journalist; he could remember her looking after him.

'Yes, I would,' she said.

Sally looked at Scott. He looked distressed. Was he? Or was it the light?

'And you had to produce an explanation for the marks.'

'I didn't have to.'

'But you did, and this is the explanation, fuelled by your distress about your not being with your children.'

'No.'

'You even set off down the road of accusing him of coming into your room against your will.'

'No, I didn't say . . .'

'We shall see, Mrs Murray. Anne Timms will give evidence of what you said, won't she?'

Sally said nothing.

'Because it would have been a complete untruth to say he got in the room without your permission, wouldn't it?'

'I didn't want him there.'

'You may have decided eventually that you didn't want him, but did you or did you not let him in?'

Sally stood looking at Scott. How could she have underestimated this man so? He stood below her, able to do with her anything he wished.

'I let him in.'

'Of course you did.' Scott risked it. 'It's not your fault, Mrs Murray, that the defendant was remanded in custody because it was believed he had tricked his way into your room, is it?'

Sally immediately understood what must have happened. She herself had been the cause of his being locked

249

up. She looked up at the man in the dock for the first real time and saw prison marked on him.

'Of course it isn't, Mrs Murray.' Scott left it. 'But you had to provide a reason for the marks on your body. Were you ashamed that your nanny had discovered you were staying in a hotel in London instead of being at home with the children?'

'No, I wasn't. Not at all.' She was shocked at the idea that that was what people were thinking.

'Mrs Murray, please don't think I am saying you should have been ashamed. I was only asking if you were.'

'Of course it would be wrong to do that,' she said. By saying what she felt, Sally had just accepted Scott's allegation.

'Is that why you cried, Mrs Murray? You weren't crying for your rape. It was your children that you wept for.'

'Tis not Goldengrove you weep
  for . . .
But Margaret you mourn for.

Scott wished he could quote the poem. Sally said nothing.

'While you were talking to Anne, why did you start crying about the children? Had you betrayed them?'

Sally knew he blamed her for using her skill to destroy Nichols. Now he was doing it to her.

'No.'

'You agreed to sleep with this man.'

The court was utterly silent.

'The heat, the money, the wine, the excitement. You lost your head. Your body betrayed you. You betrayed yourself.'

'No, I did not.'

Sally gave way to her tears.

Scott sat down and said no more. No one had heard his voice cracking. He had allowed the sound to be drowned out by Sally's desperate reply.

'I did not. He was too strong.'

13

Trials swallow up emotion and move on as though nothing has happened.

The Crown called Anne Timms.

All Scott had to do was stand up and read out parts of her witness statement to her. He could do this cross-examination in his sleep.

'You made your witness statement the morning after the events which it describes?'

'I don't remember.'

'Well, look at the date and the first words, Miss Timms. You said, "Yesterday I was at Mrs Murray's house . . ." '

'Yes.'

'So you made the statement the next day?'

'Yes.'

'And given that you made it only the next day, your memory of what happened would have been better than it is now?'

There was a pause. Witnesses always paused when asked this question, because it did not always seem the case. But then they considered and realised it must be so.

'Yes,' she said.

'In the statement you said, "Mrs Murray was in tears. It was about her children. She said she wanted to collect the children."'

'Yes.' Anne had the statement in her hand and was stuck with what it said.

Scott read out more: 'I spoke to her about bruises which I saw on her arm. She obviously did not realise they were there. I said, "You have to report this." She said, "Anne, I will."'

'Yes.'

'She also said, "The man got into my room somehow."'

'Yes, she said that.'

Scott risked an open question. 'She didn't tell you that she invited this man into her room, then?'

'No.'

'But one thing is clear from what you told the police the next day. Please look at it. "She didn't start crying until the subject of her children came up."'

'Yes, I said that.' Anne wanted to add how it was obvious that when a woman is hurt she will cry for the things close to her. She'd seen it before. But the man who was asking her questions wasn't even looking at her. He clearly did not want her to add anything. She wanted to go home now.

Once Scott might have tried to improve on the evidence, maybe ask about her relationship with the children, but he had learnt better; if he even looked at her she might start adding things. 'Thank you, Miss Timms,' he said.

Anne's evidence had been like a moment of calm after the storm. Although their heads were turned in her direction he doubted if the jury listened very carefully

253

either; he could see that they were reorganising their feelings after the cross-examination of Sally. All that this evidence was doing was confirming the doubts that must have arisen about Sally's motives.

People didn't usually see such intense emotion close up. Either they themselves were involved or it was being shown on television or in the cinema, which was not so real, nor so draining.

The judge rose. As he did so he said, 'I shall be unable to sit tomorrow afternoon,' and he left. The afternoon session was over. Scott relaxed on counsel's bench and took his wig off. His hair was wet.

'I need a drink.' Scott ordered a glass of Velvin.

When he was a pupil barrister, wondering what on earth he was doing, Scott was told by his pupil master, in the joky male way that was normal then, about barrister's droop. He had given Scott other advice as well, but it was barrister's droop which Scott remembered. If it did exist it had to be caused by the regular sudden release of tension at the end of the day, and then again by the need to recreate the tension the next day. He had never heard anyone else talk about it, and now his pupil master, dead of alcohol at fifty-five, couldn't tell him any more. Did it really exist?

Scott leaned on the mahogany bar and stared at a small spillage of wine. As he did so a cloth appeared, mopped up the puddle and disappeared. The trouble was that if you asked a doctor then he would immediately assume that you were enquiring about yourself. The tension, off and on – it must affect you. Certainly it made some people drink too much. Scott looked around El Vino and saw the regulars. He waved at someone he knew and found himself beckoned over to the group.

'Are you doing that Sally Donne rape case?' Henry asked. News travels.

'Yes, Henry. Yes.'

'Trouble, I would have thought.'

'Well, it's tiring.'

'That too. You know she's in line for Treasury counsel?'

'Is she? Is she that good?' Scott said.

'How good do you have to be?'

'Well, I would have thought you'd have to be pretty good.' It was another of those fatuous conversations.

'She's got it on looks,' someone said. As if that was relevant. Maybe it was. If charm helped a man why should not beauty help a woman? Each was equally useless.

Scott wondered if one of the others was going to confirm the opinion and say, 'She's a looker.' No one did, so he did. 'Yes. She's an attractive woman. I gathered from some evidence that she was married,' he continued. 'I didn't know that.'

'Yes. A man called Murray in civil chambers. He does general common law, running down, medical negligence, that sort of thing. He also plays ferociously ambitious golf, so now he's a Member of Parliament. If you play golf in this job you have to end up as something.'

Henry had a way of talking that involved a circular movement on the heels of his feet, so that everyone was included. At the end of each remark, whoever he was facing had to say something. He ended up looking at Scott. 'Oh?' Scott said. He only had to sound vaguely interested and this could run on for ever.

'It isn't a great marriage.'

Scott realised that all along this was what he had been waiting to hear said out loud. It was the answer that showed him what the question was about. 'Is that so?' he said. He remembered Sally's answer, her hand at her throat: 'No. Not for a long time.'

'No,' said Henry. 'Her husband has arrived at the stage where bed is the place for a good book. There's nothing there except the kids. And they've been – how long? – about six years?'

'Yes?' said Scott.

'She probably hasn't had a good seeing to for years.'

'Oh.'

'Except by the defendant in your case of course, but that hardly counts.'

'Of course not.'

'Though sometimes it does.'

'Yes?'

'I came across a witness,' Henry said, 'who married the guy who raped her. She sent a letter to the judge asking him to be lenient.'

'Good heavens. Was he?'

'I don't remember now. But it's not the kind of thing you're allowed to say out loud now, even in a book. You'd be lynched.'

Everybody laughed.

'Well, Sally's no surrendered wife. She works like a demon. Leaves the house every day before six.'

'Gracious.'

Henry's glass was empty.

'Another drink, Henry?' Scott bought drinks for the group. They were poured out with great panache, helped by the fact that they were all doubles and all

256

extremely expensive. A round was the cost of a small meal.

'But those chambers are like that,' Henry said.

'What chambers?' Someone else took up the role of questioner and Scott's thoughts drifted away.

How do people get this sort of information? Scott had been in a group the other day when someone produced a run-down of the appointment of the Old Bailey's new top judge. The person talking had known everything – who had applied, even why the Lord Chief Justice had told some people they could not apply, and what had happened when one of those people did apply. He knew why some people were not considered suitable even though they obviously were the best choice, and finally why the one who was appointed was appointed. Amazing. He seemed to know everything. How do these people get to know these things?

Perhaps if Scott asked Henry, he'd be told in detail what his own chances with Sally were: 'Well, you'd be the third person who has tried this year. Your difficulty is you're not successful enough for what she wants. She likes people who are something. No chance, son, someone like you is not even in the running.'

Sally went to her chambers. She was not dressed in her court suit and felt out of place. At least that was her explanation for how she felt.

Her clerk said, 'That big set of papers I sent you, they need another conference. They still haven't given us the name of someone to do the case with you. So treat it that you will have to do it yourself.' Paul went on, 'We'll hear at the end of the week who the new treasury appointments are going to be. If you get it then this will certainly be your first case as Treasury counsel.' Sally found she was completely indifferent.

'You've got the extradition hearing tomorrow.' Paul watched her. She was obviously upset, but looking at her he didn't think what had happened would affect her; she was tough, this one. 'How did you get on today?' he asked. Paul was the only person she'd met who had mentioned the trial.

'OK.' Sally wasn't interested in talking about it. It was over now, perhaps life could get back to normal, but there still seemed to be unfinished things. How did Scott know what he did about her?

She walked back to Blackfriars to make the connection for the train. She took the right turn off Tudor Street, underneath the happy housewife, and came out directly opposite the Blackfriar's pub. She risked crossing the main road rather than go down the tunnel, where the homeless man sat with his dog. She didn't want to face any homeless men.

The garden outside the pub was full of men drinking beer out of pint glasses. They stared at her. She crossed underneath the bridge, past the site of the old Henry Moore sundial, the one all the fuss was about. Some lawyer selling the property had made a monumental mistake, not defining whether the statue was part of the fixtures and fittings. Or had he been badly instructed? It was probably that. Scott had been well instructed. He seemed to know everything that had happened, every word, and what was worse he seemed to know the meaning of everything that had happened. Sometimes he knew better than she did. Defence lawyers have to guess what people are thinking, but not like that. This was spooky: how did he know so much about her?

And anyway, why had she been so upset about the children that evening? Had she betrayed them? Not just that night, but always, by never being there. They seemed to have more fun in Granny Timms's kitchen than they ever had in hers. But why cry at that moment for the children?

What had the events in the hotel shown her? That her marriage and her family were a sham? Was it the events in the hotel that had shown her that, or was it Scott? In a way it was he who had done it, who had opened her eyes to what she was. Was she a bolter like her mother?

14

James Reid felt he had not been putting a sufficient mark on the case, so he ordered the doctor who examined Sally to attend the Old Bailey at nine-thirty the next day.

'There might be difficulty,' said Angela Deakin. 'We have trouble enough getting her to Maidstone when she's needed, let alone getting her up to London.'

'Tomorrow at nine-thirty,' said James Reid.

Unaccountably, doctors, however discourteously they are treated by the courts, are still nervous of them, and Dr Thomas turned up on time.

'There are two matters which I want to take up with you,' Reid said. 'Each is about the victim's injuries.'

Dr Thomas looked at the man. She did not approve of men prosecuting rape cases, nor of women defending them, nor of doctors who gave evidence for the defence, nor of juries who acquitted rapists, rapists who would, no doubt, walk free to rape again. There was an epidemic of rape in Dr Thomas's clinic which appalled her, and she dealt with it by adopting a breezy and indifferent efficiency.

'First, these injuries to the victim's arm. You have said they are fingermarks.'

'Yes, Mr Reid.'

James Reid found her pleasingly formal. He thought that the maintenance of a proper distance while discussing these subjects was desirable. 'Could they have been caused by someone grabbing the victim's arm as she fell, to prevent her, perhaps, from falling?'

Dr Thomas smiled. She had heard a multitude of excuses for everything, including the most grotesque injuries. Nevertheless she considered the possibility seriously. She was, after all, a good doctor.

'Yes, it is possible. But remember, the bruises thin out in the direction the fingers are likely to have been pointing. It would therefore depend how he says he grabbed her. If she is lying on a bed so, and he held her down . . .' She took hold of Reid's arms. He found the close contact a little distressing. 'Then the fingers are going to be pointing that way, as the photograph demonstrates. Look.'

She let go of Reid's arms. He adjusted his rumpled suit discreetly and reorganised his sleeves. Every morning he dressed for court with particular care; indeed he chose his health club for the quality of the changing-room facilities, for the way he was able to hang up his clothes without marking them. In the back of his Jaguar coupé he had a coat hanger.

'So, need I call you to say that in evidence?' he said.

'I wouldn't have thought so, it's obvious. Look.' She held the photograph against her own arm to demonstrate, and it was.

'Good.' Reid made a note in his book. He then cross-referenced it.

He had a series of cross-referenced notebooks recording his every case at the bar. He was proud of his notebooks. Once he had handed one up to the Court of Appeal to demonstrate the correctness of some evidence. 'Mr Reid, you keep a neat book,' the Lord Justice had said. James Reid had felt good.

'The second point,' Reid said. 'The injury to the posterior fourchette.'

'Yes.' Dr Thomas looked brightly at him. She enjoyed talking about injuries to the posterior fourchette. She had thought of making a special investigation of them.

'What I want to know . . .'

'Do you know where the posterior fourchette is?'

'I do,' said Reid. He cleared his throat. He felt a little hemmed in by women. Angela the detective sat, looking interested, just behind Dr Thomas's shoulder. 'Certainly I do,' he repeated and then wondered whether that sounded odd. Why should he know it certainly? Perhaps it should be something he ought only reluctantly admit to knowing about.

He said, 'This injury. You call it an injury, and then in your statement you move on to another subject. I was hoping you could expand a little. Why do you call it an injury?'

'I can show you the photographs.' Dr Thomas went through her file. At the back there was a brown envelope clipped to the cover. Dr Thomas came round to James Reid's side of the table, preparing to show them to him. Angela came to the other side. Each leaned over him. He could feel their presence. He thought he could feel their breath on his shoulders through his suit.

262

'Here we are. Here are the labia. Here is the opening to the vagina, and here are the folds and lips.'

James Reid always found the idea of a vagina having lips slightly disturbing, as though he might be eaten up. He wanted to move around inside his clothes, to free himself from what seemed a kind of stickiness, but could not because of the women being so near him.

'And here is a close-up. I call it a close-up, although truth to tell it's all pretty close up, isn't it?'

Angela laughed, a clear bell-like laugh.

'Now you see this smudge?' the doctor said.

Reid braced himself and looked closely. All three heads approached the grainy photograph. Reid could make out nothing at all.

'Oh yes,' said Angela. 'Oh yes indeed.' For her this was pleasing. This was evidence in its purest form.

'That's an injury?' Reid said.

'It's damage to the surface of the fourchette. Very slight of course, but put it the other way, it is not undamaged. It wasn't that way before he raped her. Since rape her he did.'

Reid wished it was so simple. He still couldn't get to the point he wanted.

'But damage caused by . . . ?'

'Oh, bucking about a bit.' Dr Thomas leaned backwards and rotated her groin and stomach in an enthusiastic way. Reid nearly put his hands over his face. He closed his eyes for a moment. He imagined Angela might join in the movement any second and he would then be trapped in this very small room with two women enthusiastically re-enacting sexual intercourse.

'You did say "bucking about a bit"?' he said.

263

'Yes', said Dr Thomas. She was sitting down now, looking at him with pleasure. She had got her point across. 'Often happens,' she said.

'I don't think I need you then,' said Reid. 'Thank you for coming,' he added, and escaped.

' "Just bucking about a bit." Give him credit, at least he told me what the doctor said. He needn't have done, he might just have said, I'll read the witness statement, I needn't call her after all. "Just bucking about a bit" – so Reid's great rape injury disappears, poof!' Scott kissed the ends of his fingers goodbye.

Tim Spencer grinned at him and leant forward and dropped his voice in reply, though there was no need to be discreet since there was no one within hearing distance. Lots of conversations in the bar mess were about other members of the bar and how to prevent them guessing the weak point in your defence, so voices were often lowered.

He said, 'I was chatting to a fellow who was in a case against Reid and he said the best bit is his complete lack of imagination. In that case the ex-partner was meant to have raped the woman after they separated. The defence was that she had started it, in order to get him to come back to her, so the evidence was that one moment they were fighting, the next,' Tim looked around and laughed, 'they were bucking about a bit. This was a state of affairs completely beyond Reid's imagination and he kept saying to the jury, "Can you believe it? Why should a woman who hates a man one moment be sleeping with him the next?" Since that seemed perfectly normal to the jury, they weren't hugely impressed. Mind you, Jeremy,' Tim said, fishing for a cigarette, 'he cross-examines like a tidal wave. Don't underestimate him.'

'You've already got one alight, Tim,' Scott said, pointing at the ashtray.

'Oh, so I have,' Tim said.

Scott thought he knew what Tim meant by a lack of imagination, and he was right. Reid was unable to envisage any alternative version than his own for what had happened at the hotel.

Scott had sat with his client in the cells and reminded him of the points Reid would use in cross-examination. 'The way you were dressed, no underwear. It's of no probative value, I mean it doesn't prove anything at all, but it will appeal to him, he'll think it shows you are odd. Second-rate prosecutors think that if they can show the defendant is odd then the case is half over.'

His client smiled and said nothing. Scott was becoming used to the arrogance of the man. He only hoped it would not show too much.

Scott said, 'Another thing. You left the bedroom after the event, no goodbye, nothing. Why? And the key, how did you get into the room? He thinks it was by a trick. Remember he won't have understood the full implication of the waiter yet. And then of course the ordinary things: you had only just met her and minutes later there you are in bed together. The injuries, the tear to her skirt, sorry, the button off her skirt.'

Usually this sort of analysis of the case against the defendant was completely beyond Scott's clients. Their desperate insistence that they were innocent prevented them from seeing both the strengths and the weaknesses

265

of the case against them. 'Yeah, but I didn't do it, Mr Scott,' was the normal reply. This man was different. He sat listening to him. Clearly he already knew most of what Scott was saying, but he wasn't impatient, he was listening in case he heard something he had not already taken account of. Scott went on, 'Some things you should never say. If you are asked, "Why did you not say that before?", for God's sake don't say, "I wasn't asked." It sounds awful. As far as the jury is concerned, merely being accused is being asked the question. And that's what's going to make the interview so difficult for you. You made no attempt to explain yourself.'

Scott had understood from the first why, beyond saying he was innocent and confirming the basic facts, his client had refused to answer any of the woman detective's questions. He had found it demeaning.

Scott could see what had happened: the sudden arrest, his clothes taken from him, sitting in a paper suit, being put in a cell with no indication of any sort as to why things were taking so long, and, oddly enough a very small thing, the over-familiarity with which he was treated. He had said to Scott, 'Right from the start she called me by my first name. I know nobody, save my very oldest contacts, who does that. Who does she think she is?' But for the jury all that, just like his being locked up before the trial, would be irrelevant. Indeed they might even regard it as perfectly proper treatment for someone suspected of rape. They only had to convict to justify it.

And even if they said 'Not guilty', who would care how he was treated? By then he'd got away with it.

*   *   *

266

Scott's forecasts of what Reid would choose to ask were fairly simple, and mainly right. But he needn't have bothered. His client was completely equipped to deal with them.

He said to prosecuting counsel, 'Mr Reid, I have been in custody for two months now because of speculation about this key and how I got hold of it. I picked it up when Mrs Murray dropped it. I used it in full view of the waiter, and I put it on the dressing table. I ordered wine to be taken to the room, and went there with the occupant. Why should I need a key? If your detective had made the slightest enquiry she could have worked that out.'

Reid took slightly too long to respond; after all he wasn't used to people who were so articulate; most prosecutions involved bullying the unintelligent. In the pause the defendant carried on, 'Had your officer lifted a finger to enquire about it, I wouldn't have been locked up for those months.'

Reid tried another tack.

The defendant answered, 'You ask why I left so quickly. Mr Reid, sleeping with a woman you don't know and waking up in the morning with a woman you don't know are two entirely different things. In the morning one may regret what one has done in haste the night before. Which I guess is what Mrs Murray herself has done. The second is therefore much more likely to be embarrassing than the first. She fell asleep, so I left. I did not do so quickly.'

Reid would have done well to stay away from questions about the defendant's underwear.

'Mr Reid,' the defendant said, 'I want to be clear what you are saying to me, so I can answer you properly.'

Scott watched with growing amusement. Normally a

witness is prevented from asking counsel questions, but this remark neatly got round the problem. 'Are you suggesting I do not wear underwear, in order that I can rape women more efficiently?' That was so obviously the purpose of Reid's question that he was forced either to say yes or just not reply. He didn't reply. The defendants' response was crushing. 'Mr Reid, I have never worn underwear. Many people don't. That is why clothing is lined. If you don't accept that it's common, ask any ambulanceman.'

Scott did not have a clue whether ambulancemen would agree nor obviously did Reid. He should have seen that coming too. The police had asked the defendant about his clothes during the interviews after arrest, and it was one of the questions he had answered. 'I have never worn underwear,' he had said simply. 'I regard it as unnecessary.'

Who knows about these things? Habits vary. Scott had been to see a judge for coffee once during a trial, and the judge said that his uncle had never washed his hair. 'He scrubs it thoroughly every night with a large silk handkerchief. Gets it much cleaner; it also preserves the natural oils.' Apparently this was perfectly common until shampoo manufacturers changed people's perceptions. 'In fact it used to be one of the reasons for owning a silk handkerchief,' the judge had said.

Reid was getting nowhere at all. He expressed surprise about how quickly the defendant had got Sally into bed. The defendant answered, 'Mr Reid, consensual sex on a first meeting is not unusual. In America it's called "getting lucky". Presumably that means getting lucky for both people, though that is never said out loud as far as the woman is concerned. Please do not try to suggest that

268

women, even married women, never do such things. That is wrong and you know it.'

Scott's client was doing what Scott himself had often wanted to do – challenge the smug assumptions on which prosecutions like these were based. Scott remembered Sally's question to Nichols: 'Are you really suggesting that minutes after she met you this woman was willing to have sexual intercourse?' That was the question that had done for Mr Nichols. He hadn't been able to do what this man was doing.

Reid turned to the interview. Why had he not answered all the questions?

The defendant replied, 'Mr Reid, I didn't answer the detective at length, but don't forget I said quite clearly I did not rape her. I admitted sexual intercourse, so taking my clothes from me at the police station was quite unnecessary. I repeated at the beginning of the interview what I had said when I was arrested. I did not rape her. I said it when I was charged. What I did do was to refuse to go into detail.'

'But why not answer the questions?'

'There was only one question. Did I rape her? I was clear. I did not. If I had not been with her at all, or if we had only had dinner together, do you not think I would have protested and described my movements? Of course I would.'

Reid said, 'An innocent man—'

'Ah, Mr Reid, how can you say what an innocent man would do? It is only your speculation. In this case the innocent man is denying he raped her – what more do you want?'

'Some detail.'

'How can I give you detail of something I didn't do?'
'The detective was asking about specific things.'

Then came the answer Scott had been waiting for for years. 'Mr Reid, it was clear that the detective did not believe me, and that she was not going to. From the start, as far as she was concerned, I was guilty. Now, what you believe about this case, Mr Reid, is quite irrelevant and will not be allowed to affect your questions. That is not so in a police station. Every question she asked me was the expression of what she believed. Unfortunately she was not able to divorce her feelings from her work. I am on trial in this court, not in that detective's office.'

This answer was greeted with silence.

Scott wondered if his client had gone too far. Juries liked defendants to play the game. Policemen were, after all, entitled to be full of righteous anger about the evil they combated, why otherwise were they allowed to stand on the steps of the court and talk to television cameras about the wickedness of defendants? The rules were that defendants ought to be respectful of policemen. Prosecution counsel properly ought to be contemptuously arrogant towards defendants. Juries expected it; normally they got it. Would this jury be able to deal with the difference?

In the cells after the evidence was over, Scott said, 'He's made his speech, I'll speak tomorrow. The judge will sum up. My guess is that will take us till after lunch or thereabouts, then the jury will go out to decide. They will be allowed to discuss it till about five, and if they haven't decided by then, they'll go home for the night.' Scott nearly added, 'That used not to be allowed,' before he remembered that no one other than a lawyer was in the

270

slightest interested in what the law used to be. Old law was even staler than yesterday's newspapers.

Scott and his client were sitting together. The judge had reminded the court that they were going to rise early and had asked Scott if he wanted to make his closing speech immediately, or wait until the case resumed. Scott chose to leave it.

The decision was made easier for him by the judge, who turned to the jury and said, 'Ladies and gentlemen, you have just heard a rousing address from Mr Reid, but you mustn't make your minds up before you have heard Mr Scott. You must wait. I expect Mr Scott has answers to the questions Mr Reid has asked you. So don't think it is finished yet.

'Tomorrow then, please. Remember, don't discuss this case with anyone at all.' The court rose.

Of course it meant Scott had an empty afternoon before his speech. He knew what would happen. Gobbets of argument would keep surfacing in his mind; he would suddenly find sentences forming, and would not be able to relax completely. But in the end it would improve it, the speech would settle down and would be the better for waiting.

Scott had gone down to the cells and his client was brought in to sit opposite him at the plastic table. He seemed totally relaxed. He asked about the likely times of the trial and Scott told him. 'The jury will have about four hours on the first day.'

Scott waited to be asked – they all asked this – how long it would take for the jury to come to its verdict. But he was not. There was no doubt that this man was unusual; he seemed completely unaffected by the pressure – not once during the whole proceedings had he asked a nervous question, nor sought reassurance. It was intriguing. Usually this form of indifference was related to psychopathy. In America they called them icemen – people who have no awareness of the rhythms of ordinary contact and communication, but who are paradoxically utterly charming. This man wasn't that – he was utterly charming, sure, but surely too balanced to be ill. But then maybe that was the problem: he was too balanced, too balanced to be normal. People ought to show weaknesses, particularly under this pressure; perfection was itself wrong.

'What do you feel?' Scott said. 'Do you think everything has come out that ought to have come out?' Scott watched him. Was there a flicker?

Scott's client said, 'May I have cigarette?' Scott pulled out the packet.

Even the man's use of cigarettes had been extraordinary. Early on in the case the solicitors had handed Scott a hundred cigarettes, Sweet Afton. Scott hadn't seen that brand since he used to run out to buy them for Jimmy Comyn at Weingott's. He thought they'd gone – along with Weingott's. 'Could you keep them for him?' Archie said. 'He doesn't want to smoke in the prison.' Here was a man who was utterly particular about his tobacco, and yet sufficiently in control to use it only when he wanted.

Scott handed him the packet and said, 'Yes,' when he himself was offered one.

Normally he refused cigarettes, except when borrowing one off Emma, but now he sensed he might be able to talk to this guy. He joined him in a cigarette.

Scott said, 'Why did you let me defend you? You must know people at the bar?'

'I do. I meet some at opera occasions.'

Scott said nothing, making it easier for him to continue.

His client said, 'Do you know Johnny Marriott? I asked him about you, or at least I asked someone to ask him about you.' He lit his cigarette and handed the matches back to Scott. 'Apparently he doesn't like you.'

'Oh,' Scott said. This was slightly disconcerting.

'He thinks you don't count.' The comment sounded strange on the man's lips since he had hardly ventured an opinion about anything during the time Scott had known him. 'That's all he said. He certainly didn't say you don't know what you are doing. And knowing Marriott that's something he would have considered. So I reckoned that if Johnny only dislikes you for not counting, you can't be all bad.' His cigarette glowed. They burned differently from modern cigarettes. Scott thought of a time when a cigarette must have been something one chose because of its particular tobacco. An old-fashioned world in which discrimination was a word of approval.

His client went on, 'In fact from him that counts as a compliment. Marriott's got his head so far up the establishment's arse that he gives them heartburn – and yet at the same time he thinks of himself as a free spirit. I didn't want someone as deluded as that looking out for me. I like people who have a reasonable estimate of themselves.'

Scott remembered Marriott coming over to him in the bar mess upstairs and he said, 'Marriott's a friend of yours then?'

'Who has friends? I only have acquaintances, people I know.' The man looked at Scott. 'Do you know him?'

'Yes, I know him. But he's no friend.'

'When did you see him last?'

'This week.'

'Did he speak to you about this case?'

Scott wondered, How did this man guess that? 'Yes,' he said.

'What did he say?'

'He warned me.'

'Warned you what?'

'I don't know, he just warned me.'

'What did he say?'

'He said, "None of your tricks."'

'That's a warning?'

'Yes.'

'Why?'

'I suppose he was telling me what the people who count think. And how I should behave.'

'But you don't care about that?'

Scott was about to say no, but then he stopped. Of course he cared. It would be pleasant not to be an outsider, it would be pleasant to be one of the group, someone who effortlessly fitted in.

His client laughed at the hesitation. 'So it does matter? At least you think it does.'

Scott brought himself to deny it. 'No, it doesn't matter to me.' But he didn't convince even himself.

'I believe you, though you don't believe yourself. Why? It's like this. If you changed the way you behaved to fit in, then one could reasonably say fitting in was important to you. But you don't, so how can it be important? The real test of what you are is what you do. All you have is a touch of anxiety. All outsiders, even the strong ones, have that. Listen, Marriott lies awake at night worrying about being one of the crowd. He always has.'

'How do you know?'

'He told me.'

'Really?'

'He was drunk. He didn't know what he was admitting. I gave him dinner one night. I paid for him. At my table in the Ritz, the famous table.'

They sat for a moment in silence. Scott's effort to get the man to say something about himself had not worked very well.

Then his client said, 'I paid for that woman too.' Scott looked up.

'Oh?'

'For God's sake, how much money did she win? Thirty-three thousand, and she's never even given me the stake money back. Most women only cost a couple of hundred. Who does she think she is?'

'Thirty-three thousand. That's a lot of money.'

'So how do you think she said thank you? It wasn't even as if she was very good in bed. Lay there like a plank.'

'Well . . .' said Scott.

'You didn't ever put that to her.'

'What, put to her that she lay there like a plank?'

'No. Put to her that she was extremely well paid for what she did.'

'That wouldn't have been wise,' Scott said.

His client grunted and went silent. Then he said, 'I don't see why not. You'll say it to the jury?'

'That she's been well paid?' Scott repeated it.

'Of course.'

'I'd be a fool to do that.'

'Why not? She was well paid.'

Scott realised what it was that caused the detachment he

275

had observed. It was vanity. The man was suffused with a vanity made even more intense by his money. His "fuck you" money. He was so vain that at first it didn't show, he seemed instead charming and poised, perfectly able to see right into other people's motives. But when it came to anything he wanted, or anything that affected his opinion of himself, then nothing was allowed to get in the way. His elegance, his manners, were not a reflection of good taste but only a continual cry of 'Look at me'. His whole life was one long gaze in the mirror.

'Why not say that?' the man repeated.

'Because on the whole juries don't like the idea of people thinking they can buy other people.'

'I'm not saying that.'

'You are, you know.' Then Scott softened it, there was no need to get into an argument. 'Mr Clarke, you must believe me, that's what the jury would think.'

'She took my money. I've had dozens of girls from the bird table. Each saying thank you. It was the least she could do.'

'The bird table?'

'Yes, the table she sat at. It's where women on their own are put. Why do you think I ask for the table next to it?'

For the first time Scott began to feel angry on Sally's behalf. He had better stop this now. 'I tell you, if I try that argument then it will immediately seem as though we are saying, "Only spend enough on a woman and you can act as if you bought her."'

He had obviously said exactly what the man had been thinking. It was not a good note to end on. Poor Sally. Scott understood what had happened now.

*   *   *

276

The walk back to chambers was cold and the wind whipped up towards Ludgate Circus from the river. The case had turned bitter in his mouth, but still he had to fight it. He wasn't paid to do the judging.

Another coffee shop had opened at the bottom of Fleet Street opposite the big jewellers' clock; this time it was Turkish. How many could the street take before saturation was reached? The old journalists who had been here only ten years ago would have scoffed. The whole place had become a paradise for merchant bankers who had swarmed into the old Telegraph building, selling money to each other.

He trudged up the hill past the opera restaurant. The spot where the old boy in the black bowler hat and suit had declaimed the gospels had been overshadowed by a hoarding where the Express building was coming down. More room for bankers no doubt.

At least banking was an honourable thing to do, as long as you made a profit. There was no need to pretend. His speciality was selling lies, and he had to go on doing it.

15

The day after she had given evidence, Sally went to argue Gaynor's case. Because it was not starting until later in the morning she would be able to drive the children.

There was shrieking in the bathroom. 'Mummy's taking us to school!'

'Can we have the roof down?'

'No, it's far too cold.'

'Will you stay for line-up?'

'Yes, of course.'

'Will you tell them I can't do Minims today?'

'But why should I?'

'Oh, but Mummy, Anne said she would take us to Toby's today, and I can't go if I go to Minims.'

'Toby's mother said it was all right.'

'Anne has it all arranged.'

'Please, Mummy. Tell them.'

'Who's Toby?' Sally said, feeling a little out of it.

'Toby's come to live near the school.'

'Mummy, I can't find my shoe.'

'It's under the table where you left it.'

'Anne, Anne, you are taking us to Toby's today, aren't you?'

Anne looked at Sally apprehensively. 'I said I would take them, Miss Donne. Toby has invited them, he lives down the road. The children have been there twice now.'

The feeling that their lives were going on without her was overwhelming. Every remark she made had to begin with a question: What's that? Who's he?

Harriet said, 'Anne, Anne, you take us, you speak to Miss Sharples. She'll understand if Anne speaks to her. Mummy, let Anne take us to school, she'll persuade Miss Sharples.'

The children didn't wait for an answer but dashed out of the kitchen. Sally could hear them whooping across the gravel at the back of the house to the cottage where the little car was kept. There was a crash and Sally knew that the dog had jumped from the stable and was galumphing after them. She stood and looked at Anne. 'Sometimes, I think they get on better without me,' she said, softening the remark with a smile. Anne clearly did not know what to say and Sally made it easier for her. 'I'll see you this evening then, after you come back from Toby's – whoever he is.' They both laughed. Anne left the kitchen, picking up the children's satchels at the same time.

Silence. They were gone. It had all happened so quickly: one moment the children had been calling and laughing at the idea of Mummy taking them to school, and the next they had transferred their affections completely. Children weren't meant to be promiscuous with their feelings. What was it called? She remembered the phrases she had seen in psychiatric reports – 'socially disinhibited', that was it. Reports were full of this language scattered like leaves in child abuse cases: 'attachment theory', 'reactive attachment disorder of childhood', 'disinhibition', 'no fear of strangers'. It was what happened to children who had no firm primary carer, who were farmed out to anybody passing. This wasn't guff, it was as clearly demonstrable as the fact that germs cause colds.

She switched on the coffee machine. It ground some coffee, dumped it into the container and geared itself up to squirt steam through it. In a moment a soft beeping said it was ready.

'Dysfunctional,' Sally said out loud, as she pressed the button. The machine hissed at her and a thick trickle of coffee poured into the hot milk waiting in the cup below.

She remembered the pop festivals where children had so charmingly clung to her skirts, and not just to hers, but to anybody's skirts, children who held one's gaze and answered directly back, children who seemed completely free, it was all so attractive. But now she realised they ought to have been frightened, ought to have been unwilling to talk to any old adult. What looked like a vivid life for them was in fact no life at all.

Had she done this to her children? Nonsense, of course not, she was just being morbid. She was completely unsettled. It had been more awful than she could have imagined in court. That was Scott's fault – of course it wasn't, he was just doing his job. She thought about him. He was good company in his way, although certainly not promiscuous with his friendships – God, no. He could hardly bring himself to talk to her. He seemed cut off. Like she was from the children sometimes. The children. Perhaps she didn't love them? Perhaps they were better off without her.

The idea brought her up short.

It was thinking of this sort that was a sign of real disturbance. But you can always trust what jumps into your mind unbidden, can't you? She took the coffee and sat at the kitchen table. It was absurd. If she loved them then her presence could never harm them. Obviously she did love them, she couldn't wait to get home to them. But then, the real test of what you want is what you actually do, not what you think you ought to do. And what was it she did? She spent most of her time away from them. Why didn't she stay at home with them? There was no need for her to stay away. And if she accepted appointment as Treasury counsel she would be away even more. Why do it? He earned enough to keep the whole family.

'He.' She had said 'he'. She rubbed her finger in a small pool of coffee spilt on the surface of the table. She noticed the way she was thinking. Her husband had become 'he' now. Perhaps he was even on the way to becoming 'it', just as she had seen in the woman's diary produced in that kidnapping case, the silly one with the hysterical police-woman. No, that wasn't going to happen. What was wrong with Brian wasn't that she disliked him. She didn't even dislike him. He was too boring for that. She couldn't talk to him. She couldn't talk to anyone. The last time she had really talked to anyone was with Scott.

He had challenged her in the mess during that case. And later. Later they had talked about Monty Bach. What was it he said? Become a person again? What was he saying? Was he saying she wasn't a real person? Is that how he was able to attack her like that in the witness box? He must know all about her.

She sat at the kitchen table and knew that she would

281

never, never, be glad again. The cups and saucers grinned at her, hanging from their hooks, and the clean, clean floor mocked her. She got up from where she was sitting and stood at the window that looked out from the back of the house. In the distance, blue hills marked the beginning of London. It was a view she normally only saw when heading, determined and organised, towards her work, but watching it now with no need to rush, free of the urgent need to be on time, a feeling of futility filled her. She followed the idea through. Was the reason she didn't stop work and stay at home because her husband was boring? It was an unavoidable conclusion. She should be quite happy to give up her work for the children, but giving up her work would be to submit to the role . . . She stopped. It was inescapable. She needed the intense hurry of escape to the city to stop her thinking.

And what was that doing to the children? A child's affection wasn't something that you could share out, or ask someone to hold on to for a moment like the loose end of a piece of rope. She tried to formulate an image. A child's affection was malleable, and retained the form into which it was shaped. It was almost a physical thing. How children were dealt with affected what they would become in the future. What have I done? she thought, and started gathering her things to leave.

Sally waited for Gaynor in a cell next to the court. She stared at the wall pockmarked with messages, names and dates picked out of the peeling plasterboard. Opposite the table at which she sat was a green bottle-end glass panel forming one wall of the cell. Through it she could pick out shapes and movements outside. Doing this job enabled one to become a connoisseur of prison architecture. Each generation had its own approach and when these courts were built, in the fifties she imagined, the ability totally to exclude prisoners from the outside world had not yet been perfected. Such a wall would not be considered now. She pictured how the court must have looked when it opened, a fat morning-coated attorney-general sent down to cut the ribbon, accompanied by his sharp-faced wife in a fox stole.

The security staff were taking a long time to get Gaynor, but that was all right. Just sitting, doing what she knew was a release.

The moment the idea entered her mind, the thoughts she had been avoiding all the way up to London flooded back and the tension gripped her again. For a moment she turned and faced them. This thing was utterly absurd, there was not the slightest reason to think that the children were turning against her, nor that Anne Timms was taking them from her. But underneath there was an abyss. Feelings swept up from it with a power that made what her good sense told her irrelevant. She clung to what she knew was true – she knew these feelings were absurd, but there was no solidity any more, the whole basis of her certainty was being swept away. Not just once, but every time she turned to face the problem, despair rose up to meet her. She could shut it down, and she did so now, click, the lid was on, using the same discipline that got her out of bed in the morning, get up and get on, but now she knew that that solution was only temporary. It would not be long before she had to open the lid again, before maybe it opened on its own and she couldn't shut it down.

Gaynor appeared at the door. Today she was dressed in a suit, a silk shirt. Her hair was tied back.

'You're looking good,' Sally said. In that moment she found herself transformed back into a lawyer, in control, able to take decisions, professional.

What happened was Gaynor said to Sally, 'I'm here because I couldn't take it any more. Everything that seemed so solid and important turned out overnight to be worth nothing. Do you remember that Dr Hook song, *She knew that she would never?* Well, that was me. And there was no one to talk to about it. People didn't want to hear, instead they insisted that I should be grateful, having a home and family. That's when I really began to understand those daytime TV programmes, you know, the programmes where people come out and talk so openly about themselves?' Her voice rose at the end of the sentence, so annoying normally, but here it seemed only to emphasise the despair.

'In real life there's no one listens to anyone else any more. But those people do, on television they do. There you can say how you feel, and there's someone to say you're wrong or you're right. But above all someone's listening.

'Through them I found John Lorne, he shows how you can change. But you have to change all the way, inside as well. Then anything you want, you can do it, there is nothing stopping you.' She fished about in the property she had brought to court and produced the thin paperback, *Reborn in America*, published by Loompanics. 'I got you a copy of his book.' Sally looked at it.

'You can have it,' Gaynor said. 'I brought it for you. I won't be seeing you again.'

'Why not?' said Sally.

'Well, they're going to take me back, aren't they? If they decide against me, I'm not going to argue about it any more. What happens, happens.'

Sally remembered. The real acts of bravery in the courts were those of the defendants – the young black kids, up on charges of assaulting a police officer perhaps, willing to complain about their treatment, even though they knew that it would increase their sentence. Those cases held in front of magistrates, or some bored judge in an empty courtroom: sometimes at those trials – she didn't do them now – she had been more frightened than the defendant, had found herself standing up on behalf of people braver than she was, and their courage had infected her. That was a kind of reality. What she did now was nothing, trotting out evidence and arguments from the detachment of a prosecutor's bench at the Old Bailey. Where had it gone, that edge? She had lost touch with that reality.

'You've spoken to Monty about not appealing?'

'Yes.'

'What did he say?'

'What did you expect him to say?'

'I should imagine he said it's your choice?'

'Yes.'

'Why didn't he tell me?'

'I wanted to tell you myself.'

'Why?'

'Because you are trying to help me, and you deserve to be told by me.' Gaynor paused and looked at Sally. 'Are you upset?'

Sally said, 'No, not yet.'

'Why?'

'Because I think I can win this for you.'

But of course she couldn't. Sally could tell by the very manner in which the magistrate entered the court that she was not going to win the case. He walked straight to his seat, not even acknowledging the presence of the people standing at his entry. When Gaynor's name was read out, he raised his eyes for a moment and inspected her. Like a piece of meat. That was that. He looked down again, and he didn't look up, not during the introductions, as Sally's name was given him, and not during the short opening of the case, when the allegation was outlined. 'I know that, thank you,' he said, when the terms of the extradition treaty were referred to. 'Get on with it.'

The sheer, concentrated vindictiveness took Sally aback. This was utterly different from the courtesy with which the courts treated her nowadays, and again she remembered her days at Snaresbrook and Sessions when the same thing had occurred to her daily, the days when addressing the court had seemed like pleading with an oyster shell, fast shut until the moment when the judge's face snapped open to dismiss her arguments. It shook her. She had left this all behind for a politer, more detached version of justice, but of course it had been going on all along, and the people to whom it was done were being chewed up and spat out every day of the week.

'The only point in the case with which I am concerned is the question of identity.' Sally stopped. She was determined this man was going to have to raise his head to meet her eye, to acknowledge her presence, and after a long moment, forced to react by the silence, the magistrate did so. 'Yes,' he said, immediately looking away again. But for a moment Sally had seen his yellow eyes.

286

'I have set out the argument in a short written submission.' This time she finished with a direct question: 'Have you seen it?'

'I received it twenty minutes ago.'

It was extraordinary how the man transformed everything into a complaint, as though somehow the people before him were to blame for his being there at all. As if, had they not been there, he could have sat and done his job in peace, unprovoked by interruption.

Sally was direct. 'Well, since the document was sent to this court some days ago that certainly seems unfortunate.'

'I was only given these case papers twenty minutes ago.'

'So when you remarked that you saw my submission only twenty minutes ago, I was wrong to think you were referring only to that?'

'Get on,' he said.

Sally took a deep breath. 'In that case you will no doubt wish me to take the next point very slowly.' She stopped, again forcing him to raise his head. Against this behaviour there was no appeal. A magistrate or a Crown Court judge could behave exactly as he wished, as long as he did not give reasons for the decision that could be reversed: all that remained was a bad taste in the mouth. There was no peer pressure on him, no public judgement passed, save in the end the loneliness of what he was doing. Sally noticed that it often got them in the end.

'As I understand it, the applicant, in order to obtain extradition, must demonstrate there is a case to answer. Evidence which, if it were uncontradicted, would be sufficient to prove the charge.'

'Yes.'

'We argue that in these papers there is no proper

evidence of identity, no proper evidence to link this woman with the person who stole the money in Las Vegas. There are no fingerprints. There is no recognition evidence. There are no admissions, there is no connecting documentation, or continuity of pursuit. Nothing properly to connect Frechette Wallace with Gaynor Beeline. Nothing of any sort to say she is the same person. There can therefore be no case against her.'

'What about the evidence of Agent Pisarski?'

So the magistrate had read the papers.

'That is not proper evidence, not even admissible to prove what it purports to prove. The agent has been sent a photograph of the detained person. He has a photograph of the wanted woman Frechette Wallace. It is not even a good photograph, indeed the evidence that purports to say the photograph is of Frechette Wallace is inadequate, only a name written on the bottom of it. By whom? We don't know. Agent Pisarski has compared these two photographs and has said that in his opinion they are of the same person. What value has this evidence? I might as well call someone in from the street to say the same thing.'

The magistrate sat silent. The point seemed so clear to Sally that even repeating it seemed to reduce it. If it wasn't understood immediately then it was not going to be.

'This is no evidence of identity. It proves nothing. It is merely the officer's opinion. The codes concerning—'

'The codes do not apply here, Miss Donne.'

'Even if they don't apply they illustrate good practice. It is quite clear we are dealing with mere opinion evidence, made more unreliable by the quality of the prints.'

'Why do you say that?'

This was astonishing.

288

'This federal agent did not even know the fugitive—'

The magistrate suddenly changed tack. 'Identification evidence in these courts doesn't have to be complicated,' he said. Sally knew she was about to be treated to a prime piece of intellectual dishonesty. Such remarks as this always seemed to precede an attempt to evade the obvious. He went on, 'Nowadays of course in motoring cases there is no need for identification evidence at all.'

That was true. It had been a staggering change in the law, made for the convenience of overworked magistrates, wholly unnoticed by the press.

'This is not a driving case.'

'No, it is not, Miss Donne. But in any case a police officer may study a video tape and say that the person in it is in his opinion the defendant.'

It was a point Sally thought might be used. 'In those cases the officer normally has a videotape of some length and he can compare the people filmed on it with the defendant, someone whom he has the opportunity of seeing in the flesh. Anyway, such evidence would certainly not be sufficient on its own. This case is not that.'

'But it is admissible, Miss Donne?'

'Yes.'

'It is the same. And I say it is sufficient.'

The magistrate raised his face and looked at her. Again it was a movement she recalled from her early days at the bar, the act of a man getting rid of a troublesome case, a man imitating decisiveness, and in the act saying that a decision is enough, even if it's wrong. He was also saying 'I am not going to listen any more' and he didn't. 'There is a case to answer here,' he said and wiped it from his mind. Gaynor was going to be sent back to America by an unsuccessful lawyer in a salaried job, who either would not or could not listen to an argument. Sally had been bounced back to the reality of the courts, and the feeling of complete hopelessness she remembered from those days when she first came into contact with the law swept over her again. She had forgotten this. She had erected a barrier between herself and this: it was the same barrier Jeremy Scott had been complaining about.

The court rose. Sally could not go straight down to the cells because her clerk, determined to keep her busy, had given her another case and straight away, as though determined to be difficult, it was called on in the court next door. Gaynor would be taken away without her seeing her again.

The magistrates, unpaid lay magistrates this time, filed in and Sally stood up to open the facts. Somewhere below in the same building Gaynor was sitting waiting. Sally's attention began to wander but she jerked herself back to her notes and the story she was telling. 'The children's mother was at that time living on her own in a flat in Thamesmead.' Sally produced photographs.

The bench would see that it was a newish flat, remarkable for an almost complete lack of furniture. There was, Sally pointed out, a table and a chair, a cot and a bed. That was all. Equally unusually, on the cot there were no bedclothes at all, so when the police arrived they found the baby quite naked, lying on the plastic covering of the mattress. 'There had been no attempt to wrap her, to keep her warm at all,' Sally said. Sally remembered the sweet heat that a small baby emits, an elemental force, so that when you wrapped or rewrapped them, the blanket was warm to the touch, with a soft evanescent warmth.

Hugging a small baby, wrapping it, rewrapping it, letting it lie, protected and snug, seemed such a basic thing that it was difficult even to imagine how someone might not do it. She carried on. 'Tied to the leg of the table was another child who, it seems, had survived for some time by tearing at scraps of paper and sucking the gum off the back of a roll of Sellotape. Certainly nothing else was found in the child's stomach.

'The baby itself had not been fed for, it is estimated, some thirty-six hours and had been dead for perhaps six hours when the police arrived.'

Sally ran her fingertip down the pathologist's report, to confirm the figures.

Here were the photographs of the children. She handed up another set. 'May I invite you to go to the first few only, please. You may find the others distressing, so perhaps we can leave them for a moment.'

She paused and looked at the three magistrates. There were two older women, the one in the centre the wife of a once-famous politician, and with them, sitting on Sally's right, a black man. She remembered meeting him once. He wasn't a person you'd immediately think of as a magistrate; he was a well-known painter of startling, highly coloured pictures. The usher carried the photographs round to them. As she had anticipated, they were taken aback by the image of the wrinkled little body.

She pressed on. 'In the photograph you can see a bottle, empty now of course. It is the Crown's contention that this bottle contained the last meal supplied to this child and that it was given by a neighbour. Her fingerprints were found on it. She had apparently been telephoned by the defendant, and was asked to go in and give the child

291

the bottle. Whether on that occasion the neighbour saw, and if she did whether she cared that the other child had been tied to the table, we don't know. She herself has now disappeared. It is in fact irrelevant since there was no duty in law for that neighbour to do anything to help these children. There is no duty on someone who is not a parent to help, only not to harm.

'There was no other food in the house. The floor and the cot, as you can see, were stained with faeces. At some stage a rodent, probably a rat, or more than one, seems to have got in and disturbed the situation. It, or they, had not yet got into the cot. The remaining photographs are of what the police found in greater detail. I do not invite you to look at those photographs at all. They are stapled shut in your bundle. Counsel for the defence has agreed to this.

'What is clear is that this defendant deserted her children.' Sally coughed. 'I am sorry, madam.' She stopped and coughed again. She turned to the back of the court to speak to the usher who had sat down and was reading *Reader's Digest*. 'May I have some water please.' The usher got up and poured the water. While she waited, Sally glanced back at the defendant, whom she had last seen sitting crumpled in the dock. She noticed that she had now put on Anne Timms's face.

'Thank you. The allegation of course is that these children were abandoned. Abandonment is cruelty in law. To abandon is positively to do harm.'

Again Sally was interrupted by a cough, though this time deep down in her throat, but it wasn't that which stopped her, it was the cry of a child which floated in quite clearly through the half-open metal window of the court. She looked up at the magistrates, who stared impassively back at her. They hadn't heard anything. She turned. The woman with Anne Timms's face had heard it, she could tell. She was looking at the window.

'We know that at some time on the Thursday afternoon a taxi had been called to the defendant's address and the defendant' – Sally nearly said Miss Timms – 'asked the cab driver to take her to the West End. The fare was twenty-eight pounds, the fare was paid in cash, with a five-pound tip.

'The Crown says it was then that the child was tied to the table. There are marks on its wrist. Please turn to the second unstapled photograph.' Sally sobbed deeply. She looked up. Nobody had noticed. She turned to look at the defendant, who smiled broadly at her. 'All right?' the woman said. It wasn't Anne Timms's voice, but it was certainly her face.

'A child of three must have food, at the least every six or seven hours. It is necessary that he or she receives a calorific intake of . . .' She looked at the figures she had prepared. They swam before her. 'The child needs a sufficient calorific intake,' she said, abandoning the figures. 'The effect of lack of food is a sharp drop in the physical activity of which the child will be capable after about twenty hours. So we can say that the marks on the furniture and on the roll of Sellotape – if you turn the page you will see the toothmarks on the Sellotape – must have taken place in the hours of Friday night and Saturday morning.

'We think that when the animal mark was inflicted to the child's right leg, which is the next photograph and the only one unstapled, she was probably already dead. We put the death in the early hours of the Monday morning.

At that time the defendant was in a club in north London. She was drugged and probably by that time unaware of where she was.'

She turned and saw that Anne Timms was sneering at her.

'I shall have to break off now,' Sally said. 'Perhaps the court could rise for half an hour.'

'Why certainly,' said the sensible elderly magistrate, who for a little time had been concerned at the tears running down counsel's face. 'These matters can be very disturbing.'

Sally left the court and walked south towards Oxford Street. The crowds were just beginning to thicken as people started to go home.

A large white prison van manoeuvred into the narrow street, coming away from the court. Its windows were black so nothing could be seen inside, but Sally knew that Gaynor might be looking out. She waved just in case; it felt odd because there couldn't be a response. She felt as though she had lost a friend. Of course she could have been waving at the woman who had abandoned her children to die, she couldn't be sure.

Scott had been buying coffee in Rathbone Place, and was stepping out of the shop when he saw Sally walk past. He didn't know how to react at first. She looked tired, or at least older. He found himself on the pavement only feet behind where she was walking. He wondered whether to turn away. She would never notice, nor would she ever know. Then she stopped and waved at a large white van. Scott recognised it as a prison van. It had slowed near them. Scott could see nothing in the blacked-off windows, he could see nobody to wave at.

294

'Hallo, Sally,' he said on impulse. 'Are you still talking to me?'

He was nervous. Maybe she would just lash out at him. She would after all be perfectly entitled to. But she did not. She said, 'Oh, Jeremy, what are you doing here?' Her voice was flat.

'Buying coffee,' he said.

'You come all the way here? Just to buy coffee? How odd.' Scott noticed she was speaking quite tonelessly. 'Without affect', it was called.

'It's the best coffee,' he said, lamely. Suddenly buying coffee seemed a rather sad thing to do, and he stood holding the package. 'Where are you going?'

'Nowhere,' she said. 'I just came out of Wells Street Magistrates, and I suppose I should go home. But what's the point? There'll be no one there. They'll all be at Toby's.' She felt like crying. The experiences in the court, the behaviour of the magistrate and then the strange vision of Anne Timms had filled her head. Was this what a breakdown was like?

Scott said, 'Well, if you're going nowhere, let's sit down for a moment.' He tried to make his remark sound indifferent, just ordinary, but it wasn't. Something bad was happening to Sally. Her face was drawn, her mouth hard and grim.

'I've just met the most extraordinary woman,' Sally said. 'Not that she has done anything remarkable, except steal from her employers.' She laughed. It was shrill. 'I don't know when I met someone who disturbed me more.'

Maybe the woman with Anne Timms's face was just as disturbing, Sally thought, but that was too difficult to explain. Was it even real? She still could not understand what had happened. She said, 'I had a strange experience in there, you know. I'm not sure I feel very well.'

She was intent on talking. Scott knew enough not to interrupt her.

'This woman. I've just represented her. She was living an ordinary life, I think, husband, children and, well . . .' She stopped and then said, 'Do you remember the song, the Dr Hook song? *She knew that she would never, never drive through Paris in a sports car* . . .' Sally said it with a beat and then added, 'It's a song about a nervous break-down. She quoted it to me. This woman changed herself. Not just changed. Everybody thinks they want to change in some way, but she changed completely. She walked out, changed her name, took on a new identity, everything. She got hold of this book.' Sally scrabbled in her bag and pulled out the thin brown paperback and gave it to Scott. On the cover it said, *Reborn in the U.S.A.* She waited for him to say something, clearly thinking that the title had made what she was saying immediately clear.

Scott had almost no idea what she was talking about. 'Americans are keen on being reborn,' he said. He looked at the book. ' "Chapter 3: Proof of identity. How to get a new social security number." The chapter headings are direct enough,' he said.

'That's it exactly,' Sally said, 'it is. Although it pretends only to be a primer on how to escape the law and create a new identity, in fact it's a mystical book. Look.' She took the book from Scott. 'Here it is. It's in question and answer form.' She found the place and started reading.

Scott was standing on the busy pavement, pedestrians swirling around him, listening to this distraught woman reading from a book.

' "Question: Can I contact my old friends? Answer: No. Your asking this question raises doubts about your motivation. Do you really want to start anew; are you sufficiently committed to go through with this?" Isn't that exactly like St Paul? Rather simpler maybe, but then St Paul is pretty simple.' She read from the book. ' "You must clear your mind entirely of those things that have until now preoccupied you. Everything must be thought of as exciting, appearing now in a new light. Everything is now possible since there is nothing in your past that can hold you back. Being reborn means being given a second chance." Pretty powerful stuff. He's a lawyer. Look, John Lorne LL B, he's a lawyer on the west coast. But it's just like St Paul's letter to the – who were they? – the Ephesians. But you can see the author was a lawyer. Look, here's a flow chart for building a British identity: "Open a bank account. Apply for a Visitor's Passport. Obtain a driver's licence. Obtain credit cards." He's quite right, listen: "Surprisingly in the UK the idea of an original birth certificate does not exist. All birth certificates are copies of an entry somewhere else. Despite this a birth certificate is regarded as proof of identity." He sets out the procedure for getting one. And then he goes mystical again. "Identity in the past was always based on what you did, not on what documents you produced. Modern bureaucracy has attempted to change that, suggesting that unless you have the right documentation you do not exist. We must now attempt to turn that on its head and say that since documentation has no value, since it is meaningless, a . . ." wait for it, this is where the change of tone catches you, "a mere carapace within which you can be anything you wish, then it can also be a chrysalis for your rebirth.

When you shed the skin of your old identity you can emerge new and glistening." Pretty strong stuff – no wonder it attracts. After all, it's unusual to find someone who doesn't define himself by his achievements, his house, or his money, or like the people in my chambers, by what car they own.'

Scott could see that she was totally engrossed in what she was saying, trapped by it. Suddenly she looked up at him and he could see her eyes were full of tears. She said, 'Not like you, Jeremy. You don't care. You're free already.'

He saw that she wasn't talking to him, but was just talking because he was there, he was there to listen. He said nothing.

Sally said, 'I mean, you don't care what people think of you, or whether you succeed or not. I know. I can see that. You only care whether what you are doing is right at the time.'

This was extraordinary. Where did she get these ideas from?

'It seems to me that's the right way to be. I shouldn't think you've got many friends, have you? I'm meant to have lots of friends, but of course most of them are not friends at all. Not really. They are just people I have to dinner.'

Scott followed her down into the whirlpool. She was right, and she was wrong, both. No, he didn't have many friends, but that was hardly an achievement, was it? But he stopped this line of thought. She wasn't talking about him, she was talking about herself and using her idea of him to hurt herself.

'Don't talk like that, Sally,' he said. He tried to find the right words. 'You're only angry. If it's what I said in court to you—'

'Angry?' She raised her head and looked at him. Scott was shocked to see the tears soaking her cheeks. 'Angry? Of course I'm angry. I've sold myself. I've sold myself for nothing. What's it called, for God's sake? My womanhood. What am I? I should be a mother, not a bloody machine. A cash cow. And what do I get out of it? My children prefer the nanny's company to my own. And my husband, Brian or whatever his stupid name is, what does he do? He talks about how free I have to be. Freedom. I should have been free to stay at home and love the children.'

She stopped talking and Scott watched her squeeze herself tight. Her shoulders trembled, and she pressed her arms hard against her body. Her vulnerability twisted into Scott's chest. He suddenly became aware of where they were, standing on a pavement in Oxford Street. He looked around. Nobody was paying them the slightest attention. Sally was leaning slightly towards him, she was inviting him to touch her. He felt a lightness in his body. He wanted to protect her, but Sally wasn't the kind of woman who needed protection. But of course that was just what she was complaining about, wasn't it?

He put his arm out and touched her shoulder. She leaned towards him more, and then, when he touched her, she sank into the crook of his arm, and what was amazing was, she fitted into the crook of his arm so well.

She said nothing more. She wouldn't speak. She moved when he led her away from the corner, but seemed to take no part in what she was doing. What should he do? It wasn't a case for taking her to hospital, and he wasn't going to take her to her chambers to become an object of curiosity. Anyway what would he say? There seems to be something wrong with Sally?

He took her to his flat in a taxi and managed to get her to lie down. She still didn't speak. She was neither willing nor unwilling, doing what he told her to do as though she were in a dream. He took her jacket off and loosened her collar. He took her shoes off and covered her with a duvet. He pulled it down from her face, since she must be so hot in her clothes, mustn't she?

She said nothing to him, just watching him. Sometimes she cried.

He said, 'You shouldn't hurt yourself by thinking other people are special. Often we imagine other people are everything we are not.' She closed her eyes. She had stopped taking part.

He left her in the bedroom to sleep and he sat and read a book. In it Huxley said exactly the right thing. 'On such merely carnal sins as gluttony and lust, the body imposes by its very nature and constitution, certain limits. But however weak the flesh, the spirit is indefinitely willing. To the sins of the will and imagination, kind nature sets no limits.' There was no limit to the pain Sally might inflict on herself. She might lacerate herself indefinitely. Kind nature would not intervene to prevent it. She might even transfer the energy of her self-hatred on to him in a flash and instantly loathe him with the same ferocity. After all she had good reason.

But this thinking didn't deal with the living fact that this woman was sleeping in his bed. The evening wore on. Tomorrow he was going to have to make a speech, but he

300

was having difficulty preparing it – other things kept intruding.

Of course what intruded was that the speech was going to be an attack on someone whom he had befriended, and whom he was helping. That wouldn't matter though would it? All his cases were artificial arguments. There was no feeling. He could be against counsel and then they could walk away and laugh together. He was just an arguer, an advocate; everything he had learned had enabled him to distance himself from the argument. Of course it had become more than that: what he did in his work reflected a divide in himself, the divide that came from suppressing his feelings. What he had taught himself to think of as admirable, to be able one moment to argue on one side and the next to argue on the other, most people would regard as odd, even sick. How could you? How could you attack someone whom you liked, maybe even whom you loved?

Love? Nonsense, he had a job to do – it was nothing to do with what he felt. Feelings were irrelevant.

He slept in a chair.

The next morning Scott woke to go to court. Sally slept on through the time Scott got dressed and made coffee. Neither the coffee machine's screeching nor the knife he dropped woke her up, but she did wake when he softly closed the front door.

She lay on the bed wondering where she was.

As he left the flat – it was just seven-thirty – he turned his mind again to his speech, shutting everything else out. He had three hours to prepare it. He knew what he wanted to say. The points he had to make rose directly out of the structure of the case, so there was no danger of

301

leaving anything out. But he had to find a way into the speech. That was going to be the difficult part – getting started was always the problem.

He sat on the top of a number 11 bus and read his notes from the beginning, as though he had never seen the case before. The best way of finding the opening was not to try to think of it directly, but merely to go through the notes of the case again and see what happened. He just had to trust that it would come; it always had in the past.

The central London roads were still relatively clear and by the time they reached the Aldwych he was still reading the notes from his cross-examination of the complainant. The complainant. That was Sally. He had successfully pushed her to the back of his mind. This case wasn't about Sally any more, and it certainly wasn't about his own feelings, it was an argument involving a series of events that existed for him on paper and in evidence. He was just one of the voices arguing.

He continued reading, on the lookout for something particular, something specific, something which the jury would instantly remember when reminded of it, which started the argument off. It may not even have been particularly noticeable at the time it happened.

He looked up: the bus was just passing the entrance to Middle Temple Lane. He could see Bernard Eaton's special rocking chair in the window of their room above the gateway. Scott always told lost tourists who accosted him that the gateway had been built by Christopher Wren. Was it? Where did he get that information from? The bus lumbered on.

Memorable but not too noticeable – that seemed to be a contradiction, but it was not. Some events which during the trial seemed to scream out as being explanations were, paradoxically, not of much use when the main argument was reached. They were too obvious.

He passed the clock above Ludgate Circus. It always reminded him of the clock from which Buster Keaton hung.

Of course, the clock. The watch. The woman in the hotel had taken her watch off, and had left it on the bedside table – why had she done that?

16

Sally walked into the court while Scott was making his speech. Scott looked around and saw her, but he didn't miss a beat. He said, 'We say that Mrs Murray was not raped. We say that what happened, happened with her consent. The circumstances of the evening, the excitement, the alcohol, the money, all these things, all conspired towards her doing something that she regretted.' He spoke slowly and very carefully. 'Regret then matured into shame, and shame turned naturally towards self-justification and denial. Self-justification has become this allegation.'

It had to be said. You had to say the defence out loud. Not because it wasn't obvious, but because once it had been said, all arguments led to it. Scott had put his central proposition down on paper. He had written it out because, though a speech couldn't be prepared word for word, a sentence like that had to be carefully constructed, all the unnecessary bits cut out. If you were going to sum it up in a sentence, you had to get the sentence right.

By the time he had arrived at court the place was still quiet, and he had sat in the empty bar mess library upstairs. The room overlooked the roof of the old building, and a few feet from where Scott sat there was a ladder with a notice saying, 'Use Crawling Boards'. The slates were white with pigeon droppings. Scott's eye followed upwards to the place from which the droppings must have fallen, up towards the dome where the golden, blindfolded lady stood remorselessly with the scales. It was odd how domestic this international image of the law seemed to him, and presumably also to the pigeons sitting balancing each other on either end of the scales. Above the desk there was a line of red books, the *Notable Trials* series. He looked at the titles, and his mind slipped away and he thought about Sally.

He tried not to think of her as the woman in the trial, but of her sleeping figure in his flat. When he had last seen her face, her eyes were still smudged. She had still looked tired, even in sleep. He had got nothing much out of her about why she was upset, though once or twice while he was helping her she had said, 'Now I'm with you, I feel better,' so it was difficult to think that it was entirely the trial that was affecting her. He had said, 'I'm sorry for what I did,' and she had replied, 'Don't worry, of course you were only doing the job'.

He stood by the bed next to her. He could hear her breathing quicken: she was disturbed. Once during the night she called out, though he couldn't make out what she said. He had put his hand on her temple and stroked her hair, feeling a light film of perspiration. Men perspire, women glow. She had glowed with anxiety, and twice at least she had said, 'Jeremy.' Once she said, 'I didn't mean it.'

What didn't she mean? What was the matter?

He snapped back to the present.

People were arriving in the bar mess. He looked at the clock: he had another hour and a half or so, but now his speech had taken shape, he could begin to relax. He ran his pen down the notes of his client's cross-examination again. When he read the answers he was reminded of the arrogance of the man, and realised he was beginning to dislike him more and more. In response he consciously turned off his feelings, underlining yet again the replies which helped him.

Then he came to his witnesses. They had given perfect evidence: the floor waiter, the waiter at the restaurant who saw Scott's client most days, the maid who had cleared the empty champagne bottle away in the morning. Empty bottle. Empty. Scott underlined it. It all slotted in easily.

He could hear voices and he looked up. At the other end of the mess coffee was being put out, and one or two people were waiting to take a cup from the jug. He got up and walked over, picking up a copy of the *Sun* on the way. On the first day of the trial the case had featured as a small article, 'Top Lawyer Raped in Hotel', but then the story had not reappeared.

'How did Sally take it?' a voice asked him.

Scott looked up from the newspaper. He said, 'Oh hallo, Valerie. All right, she was all right. I don't think I was too nasty to her.'

'She's not a happy woman.'

'I don't really know.'

'She works too hard, they all do in those chambers. She

306

rarely gets home before nine. Never sees her husband – you won't catch me doing that.'

'I'd wait at home for you, Valerie.'

'Well, my husband doesn't have to, I'm home in good time, and soon I'm going to stay at home all the time. None of this Treasury counsel stuff for me.'

'Who's Treasury counsel?' He wanted it said again.

'Well, Sally's in the running. The new list should be published fairly soon, maybe today.'

Scott remembered what had been said in El Vino that night. He had known she was doing well, but until this trial he had not appreciated just how well. He said, 'Well, good luck to her. It's not what I would want either.' He was surprised to realise he really meant it.

'I can't see this is going to hurt her, is it?'

'No,' Scott said, 'no. I don't suppose they'll hold being raped against her.'

'Don't be so sure,' said Valerie. 'Men are odd creatures, as you probably know yourself, being one.' She stirred her coffee and looked at him as though she knew precisely what was going on. 'They certainly do the oddest things.'

Scott thought about Sally lying at home in his bed. Was that one of those odd things that men do? But what else could he have done? He could have organised it so she went somewhere else, but where and how would he have done that? And anyway he didn't want to. The only thing he had to do now was admit to himself just how much he wanted her to stay.

The jury listened to him intently. By now at least they knew what he was setting out to prove. 'We say Mrs Murray agreed to sexual intercourse.'

307

He paused a long moment, and then he said, 'Why else would she have taken her watch off before going to bed?' He let the question sink in, studying the faces of the listeners. It had its effect. One of the women even turned to her neighbour, put her hand on her arm and said something. 'I noticed that too, didn't I?' He knew what she was saying. He had hit the jackpot immediately.

He followed it up, but carefully – he mustn't overdo it, mustn't get it wrong. 'She can't have taken the watch off after this attack upon her, since she said she fell asleep or unconscious immediately. And if she did it before this "attack", what was she doing? Do you take your watch off before sitting on a bed to take a drink? Or perhaps, do you take your watch off before you go to bed? Before you go to bed for the night.' He repeated it.

It was a good question, the best so far. Leave it there.

'Let's go back to the beginning. We know a little about Mrs Murray's life. We know she left home very early: she told us that she does so every day, before six o'clock. She leaves home well before her children wake up. Some people work very hard indeed, perhaps to the detriment of other parts of their lives, and that can have its effect, ladies and gentlemen.'

Don't spell it out. Leave it to them.

'Mrs Murray did not have a good day that day. She left work before her usual time, but did not go home. She went to the West End, apparently on impulse. She bought the picture on impulse. She stayed at the hotel on impulse. I think, to be fair to her, we can disregard the idea that she stayed only because the hotel porter invited her in.

'And she took something to drink.

'It may be remarked that she is fortunate – after all, she

308

works hard enough, and is presumably well enough rewarded to be able to indulge her impulses.'

Indulge. It was going to have to be a crucial word. Indulge. Luxury. Money.

'She did not tell us what had upset her that day that created this need for indulgence, and it is of course irrelevant. All that is relevant is that she was upset. But there is no doubt that a life such as the one she leads is a strain. She works long hours. It clearly demands discipline, and energy. We know that some of that self-discipline, some of that self-control slipped away from her that evening. Indeed, might that be why we are here now?'

Scott half turned, still aware of Sally watching him from the back of the court. She was sitting where only he could see her, concealed by the wooden panelling of the dock from both the judge and the jury. The courtroom had seemed to darken as he spoke and the only natural light fell from a skylight high above them. The shadows at the back of the court almost hid her from him in the darkness.

'She met my client.' Scott paused for so long that there was nearly a moment of embarrassment, so when he started to speak again the tension had been ratcheted up another notch.

'Ladies and gentlemen, consider this. This meeting was not of my client's making. He did not manipulate the situation so that it should occur, nor did he attempt to prolong it. He left after speaking to Mrs Murray. He did not know, he could not know that he would ever see her again. That is a continually recurring comment that can be made upon his behaviour. He did not press his company upon Mrs Murray.'

He paused. This slightly old-fashioned language was

useful. It slowed the story down and gave him room to say what he wished, uncluttered by associations. Modern language always carries more baggage with it.

'It may be said, either in the jury room or after I have finished addressing you, that he was an opportunist. But remember, if that is said, it is said only because the Crown has not proved what it said it would set out to prove – that this was a carefully calculated approach.

'Again it must be repeated: Mr Clarke could not have known that Mrs Murray would be dining at the Ritz. He could not have known she was staying at the hotel. He could not have known that she would consent to gamble with him. Nor could he have known that she would win such an astonishing . . . no, not right, what word should I use?' Scott paused to think. '. . . such an unsettlingly large sum of money. Yes, unsettling. Large amounts of money unsettle your arrangements, they disturb your normal approach.

'If any one of those things had not occurred then we would not be here. Does the Crown say the defendant could have manipulated Mrs Murray's choice of hotel? Or that he had some control over the spinning wheel? Of course not. Far from Mr Clarke introducing the note of disturbance into this story it is Mrs Murray who does that.

'The next point I have to make is unavoidable. Mrs Murray took too much wine. I am not saying that she was drunk, that would be nonsense. But she had drunk, you may think, more than was usual for her. We all know what happens when we have taken too much to drink, even a little too much. We tend to say things we regret. We tend to do things we regret, and we have already noted there is a thin line between regret and shame.

'I say this point is unavoidable since it is not the defence which has foisted an image upon Mrs Murray against the evidence, or in spite of her protestations. The reason she stayed in London that night was that she had drunk too much to drive home, and she herself admits that even after that she had more to drink. We point to that fact when we consider what happened, and why, that evening.

'And there is a third point. I make this remark because it may be of interest when dealing with Mrs Murray's circumstances. You will remember that she bought a picture which, she said to my client, was not her husband's taste. It was a picture that she herself agreed might well have reflected what she felt that night.'

This was difficult to say and Scott doubted that the jury were going to follow him. At any moment he might have to throw it away.

'The picture is of a woman who is not afflicted by the pressures that Mrs Murray is. A woman who, as Mr Clarke remarked to her, was different from her. Did she want to change? Was she unsatisfied with her life? I have to leave that question, because it is imponderable; a court is not equipped to lay bare the bones of motive when they lie that deep.'

Sally sat at the back of the court. She knew exactly what Scott meant and was surprised he didn't continue with it. The picture she had bought was still in the boot of her car; she had not dared even to unwrap it. Until Scott said what he did, she had not realised how much she needed to keep it stored away, to keep it hidden. The image was still clear in her memory, the woman sitting on the bed, completely calm, completely composed. The object of Henri Le-Basque's indifferent gaze.

311

How did Scott know how important that was, that in a way the picture was the cause of this whole thing? How could he know that? Again she felt apprehensive. She had come to listen to him, to be near him, but now she realised that of course she was going to listen to him dismantling the life of this other woman, this Mrs Murray. She was not sure she wanted to hear that. She was frightened.

'At that point Mrs Murray herself realised that she had been affected by alcohol. She was tired, she was upset. In those circumstances what more natural than to seek comfort, and you may think there are few places better to do that than the Ritz hotel.'

Scott was rewarded with smiles from some of the jury. His speech was slipping down easily. So far it was uncomplicated: he was posing questions without even asking them, and implying answers without giving them. Gradually the jury were being drawn in.

Sally remembered the warmth and the light of the dining room, the soothing colours. She had sat in an armchair and watched the other guests go by. He was right. It was comfort that made people drop their guard.

'When Mrs Murray decided to stay at the hotel, rather than travel home that night, it must have lifted the weight of responsibility from her. Once she was there, too late to get home, she was able to relax. There was no longer any responsibility.'

Sally noticed that he did not say what the responsibility was, but of course it was clear and need not be said. Responsibility for the children. Responsibility for getting home to them. It was, if anything, clearer for not being said.

'What followed, ladies and gentlemen, can only be viewed in the light of what I have just said. Remember this is not a case where the ordinary rhythms of daily life have been invaded by violence, but a situation where it was Mrs Murray who changed her normal routine, where already things out of the ordinary were happening to her. Or rather she was doing things which for her were out of the ordinary. We must not diminish the fact that she was choosing to do them, especially since this case is about choice. It is about whether she chose to sleep with my client. The final change perhaps.'

Scott watched the jury. He was beginning to control their attention completely. He had seen that detached look of interest before; it wouldn't take much more of a push to start convincing them. They had begun by merely following his recitation of events, but now they were beginning to be involved in the slow unfolding, the inevitability of his argument.

'It is quite clear that Mrs Murray was happy to have my client's company. Of course that in itself is no answer to this charge, but the events in the dining room show she was perfectly willing to enjoy the company of someone other than her husband.' Again he used old-fashioned, rather stiff language, so the meaning would not come too quickly.

'And why not? This is a perfectly normal event. Mrs Murray's being apart from her husband is perfectly normal. A single woman meets a man in a hotel where she is staying on her own and they spend time together. There is nothing odd about that. He suggested a visit to the casino and she agreed. That is not odd. What happened in the casino you may think was odd, in the sense that it was

313

unusual. You will remember that when my learned friend for the Crown' – the archaic expression gave Scott time to balance and select his exact words – 'when he opened the case he spoke of the extraordinary nature of the events. Of course he did not tell you to begin with of the most extraordinary event that night' – long pause – 'not the fact that a man and a woman found themselves in the same bed – after all that does happen – but that Mrs Murray suddenly found herself thirty-three thousand pounds richer. In cash.'

Now he could take his time and change his tone. He could make it slightly more aggressive.

'Is it any wonder that she stumbled when she left the casino? You will remember that is the evidence of the waiter, of my client, and eventually agreed by Mrs Murray. That because of that stumble my client had to hold her arm and cause her the bruising that is now so conveniently relied upon to prove something else. I do not suggest that it was drink that nearly caused her to fall. What was it? Was it the same tension that had her saying "Let's do it again", while the cool behaviour of my client saved her going on and perhaps losing all the money she had won?

'What was it that made her forget that she had dropped her key, and forget also that my client had picked it up for her? Was it the excitement of winning?

'Of course the tension that made her forget those things has already put my client in prison to await his trial – on the basis that he must have obtained this key from somewhere else, and that he was therefore, as far as the police were concerned, a dangerous man. That particular injustice does not concern you save for this: that the whole sorry episode is indicative of the central mistake that the

314

Crown has made, for it was Mrs Murray's key with which the door to her hotel room was opened – done you will remember in full view of the waiter. It was with Mrs Murray's agreement that the champagne was drunk in the bedroom.'

Not for the first time Scott wondered how reliable the evidence was from the staff. But that was not his problem now; it had hardly been challenged at all.

'It was Mrs Murray who said while waiting at the door, "I don't think I can eat anything. After that I am ready for bed." What did that mean, ladies and gentlemen? Clearly she was able to eat something, clearly she was able to drink something, because we know she did. You will remember the evidence of the young lady who cleared the room the next morning. The sandwiches were gone, save I think for one, and the wine bottle contained only dregs of champagne. It had all been drunk, all eaten. And yet Mrs Murray spoke of an almost immediate assault upon her. An assault that would have given no time for food and drink at all.'

This description of the bedroom in the morning had been evidence that the Crown did not prepare itself for. But it directly contradicted Sally's story. When Scott had put it to Sally the Crown had either not noticed it or thought it irrelevant, so when he called the witnesses the Crown had no chance of accusing his client of throwing the stuff away, to make it look as though he stayed longer.

'It was on Mrs Murray's suggestion that the bed was covered with money. The defence say that it was with Mrs Murray's agreement that there was sexual intercourse. I suggest to you that it is the only sensible conclusion to be drawn from the turbulent events of Mrs Murray's evening.'

Now Scott was able to return to his beginning.

'And that is why Mrs Murray took her watch off and laid it on the bedside table. She was preparing herself for bed. A thing anyone who wears a watch does.'

It was coming more easily than he had hoped. Now Scott could afford to relax and allow the effect of the argument to unfold on its own. It was during the strongest parts of the argument that his attention was free to roam and watch what was happening. The judge was sitting quite still. He had stopped making notes, his complete attention was on Scott. Scott had sat there himself, he had sat as a judge watching as counsel carved an argument in the air, so strong that it was impossible to get away from it.

Reid was slumped in his seat. Scott had been there too, had sat feeling the case being taken from him.

'Picture the scene. Thirty-three thousand pounds laid out on the bed in fifty-pound notes. A bed of course that had been turned back. The heady effect of the wine. No wonder Mrs Murray needed to freshen up – did she use that expression? I don't remember the evidence. But she didn't say that she was "going to slip into something a little more comfortable", did she? People only say that in films. Well, perhaps not in modern films.'

He had to be careful not to stray too far. 'What do we know? We know already that Mrs Murray forgot vital moments that led up to this central event. What else has she forgotten?

'Do I say forgotten? How can one forget agreeing to sleep with someone? Of course one can't. But do we sometimes deny things? What is the relationship between regret and denial? Between shame and putting the blame on others? If it is someone else's fault, does one sometimes blame that person for what has happened, even though one agreed to go along with what they suggested?

'For an answer to those questions, and those are the questions you have to answer in order to give a verdict in this case, I suggest you look to see what happened afterwards. What did Mrs Murray do afterwards?

'First, what she did not do. She did not telephone the hotel switchboard and ask to see security. She did not telephone the police. She did not, first thing next morning, telephone the police. She did not telephone a friend and ask advice, telling her what had happened. All, or rather, each, of these things would have been admissible in this trial to prove that she did not consent. But there was no such complaint.

'Instead Mrs Murray went to work.'

Of course now Scott knew where she went, though the jury didn't. He could picture her, asking him to stop and sit with her, and he heard again his curt refusal. He was almost a witness to the damn thing he was now condemning. If he had known this at the beginning of the case he would have had a reason to refuse to do it, but now it was far too late.

'There was no complaint of any sort until she got home that evening.'

Was it this which she had wanted to talk about? Had she wanted to confide in him? Of course not, there was no reason why she should have wanted to. She hardly knew him. But on the other hand that is what had happened last night. She had said, 'I feel safe with you.' He pushed on, Sally sitting in the gloom behind him.

'You will remember what occurred. Anne, Mrs Murray's nanny, happened to see the bruise on her shoulder.

317

She drew it to Mrs Murray's attention. Obviously Mrs Murray was not aware of it. Can it really be suggested that what the prosecution describe as an aggressive injury during a rape would have remained unnoticed by the person who was assaulted? Does the Crown suggest for instance that "women bruise easily", the excuse of the wife beater, and that therefore she might not have noticed it? Would she not remember being held?'

He turned and looked at her, and of course saw what was happening. He was tearing their friendship apart. I can't do this. I'm going to stop, now. But he didn't. Always do your job.

'What we suggest did happen was this: Mrs Murray found herself admitting what she had done, that she had stayed in the hotel. She found herself admitting it to the woman to whom she had entrusted her children. The woman her "children loved". The children she had let down. Why else when she cried did she call out for her children, rather than in complaint about the attack upon her?'

There was a quietness in the jury that he had seen before in other juries, other cases. He could say what he liked now. He knew the case was won. He had got over the rise, pulling the jury with him, and everything he said now was merely further demonstration of something proved already.

'Of course it was for her children she cried. She hadn't been there to collect the children. And this case. It's about that, isn't it?'

Sally couldn't remember now. Had she said all this in the witness box, or had Scott guessed it? She remembered

318

what she had said to Anne at home as she wept, and she wondered why it was that she had cried. He was right. Perhaps she had not been raped and was only crying over what she had done to herself and her children over the years.

She didn't hold the speech against him – he had to make it. She was used to arguing with an opponent in court, even attacking him, and then walking out of the room and acting as though nothing had happened. But what was certain was that he had seen right through her. He understood her totally. What contempt he must feel for her! He had refused to speak to her that day, and during all these years he had known her, he had kept his distance, even though she knew others found her attractive. Even though she knew he found her attractive. She hadn't reached him, because he was a free man, not driven by the stupid things she wanted. He didn't need to be anyone. He didn't want to be around people who needed to be someone. It was the contempt of the free for the enslaved. And the worst thing of all: last night she had forced her way into his flat, and all the time he knew she was a fraud.

She got up and left the court.

Scott heard the doors slapping against each other as they closed, but he didn't look round. He knew what the sound meant. He knew what he had done.

17

Archie, Scott's solicitor, turned up too late for the verdict and only met Scott as he was leaving the courtroom.

'How did it go then?' he asked. He was breathless as usual: he had been running or cycling – which, Scott couldn't tell. He was dressed in his normal combat clothes, wound around and over his dark grey suit. On other occasions Scott had watched as he had untangled himself from his webbing and scarves. Archie was a member of the TA.

'Acquitted,' said Scott.

'Great. Well done, Jeremy,' Archie said. 'Where is he?'

'In the cells being processed.'

'I'll go and see him, or will that delay his release?'

'No. They have to get confirmation that he is not being held for some other reason, and that can take half an hour.'

'Righto, I'll see you later.' He moved to go and stopped. 'Oh, what about costs?'

'Defendant's costs order. He gets all his costs.'

'Great stuff, Jeremy,' said Archie and he bustled off.

Scott turned away and promptly dropped his books.

The papers scattered on the marble floor. He always marvelled at those people who never seemed to carry anything. He assumed it was their skill at concealment rather than any other reason – everyone has to carry papers, don't they? He gathered his things up, and noticed while he was doing so that he was still watching out for Sally. Surely she had gone by now. While they were waiting the half-hour for the jury to return he hadn't seen her in the court building. He had knocked on the women's robing room door, only to discover Jane, wreathed in cigarette smoke, there on her own.

'No, I haven't seen her. Everyone's looking for her though. The clerks were looking for her last time I rang.'

She wasn't in the library, nor in the public canteen. That wasn't unreasonable. Scott reflected on what he had said in his speech, but then, he was only putting his case. It wasn't what he really believed. Surely if she could understand his doing the cross-examination then she could understand that? After all, she did this for a living too. Then he thought, Is it possible to be that deluded? You tore someone's life apart and expected them to accept that it was all in a day's work?

He packed his things away in his bag, went down to the main entrance and rang chambers from the phone by the main hall. 'I've finished,' he said into the silence that followed the phone being picked up. Scott wondered whether he had got the right number: the clerks' room never said who they were when they answered the phone; obviously the thought had never occurred to them.

'OK,' a cheery voice said at the other end.

'It's me,' Scott said.

'Who's that?'

'Jeremy Scott.'

'Finished for the day, or finished completely, sir?'

'Finished completely,' Scott said.

He heard the voice say to someone else, 'Mr Scott's available.'

'Back on the taxi rank,' Scott said. The young clerk on the other end of the phone obviously had no idea what that meant. Scott said, 'Can you put me through to voice mail?'

'OK, sir.'

There was a pause and Tony Bennett started singing to him. Scott listened for a few moments and then, when it looked as though nothing else was going to happen, he rang off. He redialled straight through to voice mail. There were the usual messages which he had failed properly to delete and a message from the bank. The bank? What did they want? He was still wondering when he heard another message come through, Sally's voice, which said, 'Jeremy, two things. There's a package for you in my chambers, and I'll be in Timoney's later, about seven-thirty.'

Scott noticed that there was a slight movement in his chest when he heard her voice and he knew he was in trouble. He immediately played the message again, listening to her voice, hearing the slight catch in her throat. He allowed his feelings for her to flood into him and he did not reject them this time as he should have done, and as he knew would have been a better thing to do. Because if you don't allow yourself to feel, you don't get hurt.

Archie appeared and interrupted him again. 'I've seen Alan. He's coming out now. He asked you to wait. He wants to say thank you again, I think.'

'I doubt it,' said Scott. His dislike of his client suddenly

322

grew into loathing. 'I've been downstairs to see him once. That's all I need do. I'm going now.'

'What's the matter?' Archie was astonished: Scott was normally so good with the clients.

Scott apologised. 'Nothing, Archie. I'm sorry I was so abrupt. Look, I don't think he's a very nice man and I can do without any more of him today.'

'But you'll come and have a drink with me to celebrate?' Archie looked at him, hurt.

Scott couldn't refuse. 'Of course, Archie.'

'I'll be at the TA mess at seven then. I'll see Alan out of the cells. See you at seven, Jeremy.'

Scott watched him go. Seven would be all right. Timoney's was only a step from Archie's mess room.

He went to the Temple. He avoided going into his clerks' room and instead left his papers in a pile downstairs in Natasha's room. John Plumstead was there. 'How did you get on?' he said, rolling a cigarette. Scott could talk to him; John's world-weariness always struck the right note.

'Right result, wrong case,' Scott said.

'Oh, one of those.' The cigarette John was rolling became fat in the middle, like a stuffed vine leaf. He picked at the bits he had left sticking out and then lit it with a flame thrower, cocking an eyebrow to avoid being burnt.

'She's a nice girl – why didn't they believe her?'

Scott said nothing.

'You worked your magic?' John said.

'Something like that,' Scott said.

'And now you're thinking about all the ones who didn't get acquitted, but who should have been.'

'Yes. Can I take one of Emma's cigarettes?' Scott indicated a pack of Marlboro lying on the table.

'Well, since she's left them in my care, I can give you permission. Here you are.' John pushed them across. 'You know what you need?'

'No?'

'You need to be with some really nice people for a while.' Then he laughed, a chuckle that travelled from deep down inside him and released itself into the Temple air. 'Get away from all these people. Be normal for a while.'

Of course, John Plumstead, the sanest man at the bar, was right.

Scott went straight to Sally's chambers. There was a party going on.

'Hallo, Jeremy, what do you want?'

The clerks' room was full, and in the background a cork was popping. Scott was careful. He could hardly ask for Sally outright after what had happened; he wasn't very likely to be welcome.

'I came to collect a package,' he said. 'It's been left for me.'

'Paul will have it. He's over there by the wine. He always stands by the wine.' Scott looked and could see the clerk standing near where some bottles of champagne were set out on a table. 'You've got to have his permission to open one.'

'What are you celebrating?' Scott said.

'Treasury list has been announced. We've got two on it.'

'Good for you,' Scott said.

'Sally's one of them. Bit ironic, isn't it?'

Scott looked at the man who was talking to him. What was he saying? 'Well, that's good,' Scott said.

'Hallo, Jeremy!' another voice interrupted. 'What are you doing here? Come to congratulate Sally after all you did to her?' Scott saw some faces turn towards him. He'd better be positive.

'No, I'm meeting her later, she told me she left something here for me to collect.'

He started moving towards where the clerk was standing. Behind him he heard someone say, 'What's he doing here?'

Ahead of him he saw Victoria. 'I'm going to a house in Scotland, reeling,' she said, then she looked at Jeremy and said, 'Hallo, Jeremy. I'm surprised you showed up here.'

'Victoria, I'm only here because Sally left me a package. To be honest, I've got no wish to be here at all. Spoiling your party.'

Victoria threw her head back and laughed. 'Oh, you can't do that.' Then she said, 'Paul, Paul, have you got a package Miss Donne left for Mr Scott?' She didn't wait for a reply. 'Can you get it, please.'

Scott noticed that treating the clerk like the head gardener worked rather well. The parcel was produced. He took it and pushed his way out of the crowd. The less time he spent in that company the better. 'He knew precisely what he was doing, the shit,' were the last words he heard as he left, and he looked round, though there was no reason to think the remark was about him. He could see who had said it – the same man who had congratulated the Lord Chief Justice on his party-going. Scott realised that 'knowing precisely what you were doing' was probably the highest compliment available, but whether that made you a shit depended on circumstances.

He found himself out on the steps clutching a square packet. He felt it. It was obviously a picture.

'Mr Scott, Mr Scott?' He turned round: he was being followed by one of the junior clerks. 'Are you seeing Miss Donne?'

'Yes.' He was wary of what would come next.

'We've got a message for her, and we can't deliver it. It may be important.'

'I'll try,' said Scott.

'It's not clear. The young chap who took the message didn't get all of it, and we think he got it mixed up. Could you ask her to ring home, please? He got that all right, but then there was something else. They mentioned Topham Cross, and this is the worrying bit, something about her car. Her car at Topham Cross. Something's happened to her car at Topham Cross.'

'What's Topham Cross?'

'We don't know, sir. That's the point. We've rung her home – all we know is she wasn't there last night. We haven't heard from her since yesterday.'

Scott stood still for a moment, then he said, 'Tell me. Does Miss Donne know that she has been appointed?'

'We don't know, sir. The only contact we've had was a message this morning saying she's not coming in and that parcel arriving for you.'

Scott realised he was standing by Sally's car. 'But her car is here,' he said.

'We know. But that's what the message said. Something about her car, and the children. Something's happened.' He said it again.

'Her children?' said Scott.

'Yes. We're always getting messages about her children. Paul says we're like a clearing house for a crèche.'

'You want me to ask her to ring home.'

'Yes. But of course she may ring us before you see her.'

'Yes, well if she does, that's OK.' Scott put the parcel under his arm and set off to Archie's Territorial Army mess.

There was no one there.

Scott had climbed the stone stairs meeting no one and then pushed his way into the large bare room. It looked like a set in a fifties film. There were one or two tables with check tablecloths on them. On the wall there were instructions to help the reader resuscitate people who had variously been electrocuted, drowned, and shocked by bomb blast. There was an announcement about what the TA intended to do after a hydrogen bomb had been dropped, and a notice setting out the times during which the bar would be open. It was open now, a counter set in a wall with a shutter pushed up. On the counter there was a small artificial barrel partly covered with a tea towel.

Scott stood reading the notices. He looked at the clock. It was five past. If Archie didn't come in soon then he would be able to slip away and get to Timoney's in good time. No one came. There was a noise from the room behind the bar, but again no one came out. Scott stood still. Topham Cross? He thought about it. Topham Cross – to do with Sally. He had been there once. Then he heard the sound of people coming up the stairs, and Archie's laugh. Damn, now he would have to stay another twenty minutes or so.

He suddenly remembered the police in the Land-Rover, but was forced to leave the idea as Archie came in. He had two men with him; both wore cavalry twill trousers and tweed jackets. 'Here he is.' Archie exuded companionship and his friends responded. 'Here's Jeremy. I've been telling them all about you, Jeremy.'

Scott grinned and shook hands. This was just what he didn't want.

'So it went well?'

Scott realised he would have to move really quickly if he was going to get away from this, but he wasn't quick enough. Archie was already at the bar. 'Drinks please, Jim,' he was shouting to the back room, while the others looked expectantly at Scott for an answer.

'Obviously they know all about it,' Archie called. 'They know Alan, and he won't mind your talking about it. He told me that.' He turned. 'Jim!' he called. 'Service.'

'Archie, I can't stay long.'

'No, don't worry, just a drink, we've got to be off too.'

Any chance of getting away was being effectively ditched. Scott thought of just getting up and walking out. But he couldn't do that.

'I hear the jury were hardly out any time. Good old Alan, I knew he would get out of it.'

'He always does.'

'But to spend time in the chokey.'

'The longest I ever did was two days in close confinement when that smart alec Trotter shot Dickie.'

Scott wondered whether Trotter was a rank or a position, or was it a name?

'They said it was my fault for allowing live ammunition out, but of course it was nothing to do with me. That was only two days. I never read so much in my life, and if there is one thing I don't enjoy it's reading.' There was a shout of laughter. Scott joined in.

'Now come on, what was it? What got him off?'

Archie joined them. He had gin in glasses and unopened bottles of tonic. Jim the barman followed him with ice. Scott took a bottle of tonic, though he noticed that the two men with Archie added only water to their gin, something he hadn't seen for years. Actually he didn't think he had ever seen it.

'What was it, Jeremy?'

'What got him off?'

He was going to have to talk about the case. 'Well, he was very good in the witness box. He stood up for himself.' But that didn't satisfy them.

'My old boss used to say that was no good. I'm a solicitor, conveyancing, not the same line of work as you. But my old principal used to say about criminal cases, it doesn't matter how good you are unless there is one little thing that turns it in your favour. Now what was it?'

This was a relatively sophisticated question and Scott was going to have to answer it.

He remembered the police car had gone through Topham Cross. It was where the roundabout was.

One thing got him off? They were probably right. He remembered thinking much the same: you have to have one thing to start with, to work with. That was when he was starting to build his speech up, that morning on the bus. That morning? Was it only that morning?

The police car had hung back from the roundabout at Topham Cross because of the huge lorry sweeping down on top of them.

'Well, there was one thing which was inexplicable in

329

terms of rape. I mean, if it was rape, then it was inexplicable. The woman took her wristwatch off, before going to bed. At least before she ended up in bed.' He looked at the two men leaning forward at him over the small round table. 'Taking your watch off seems to me to indicate some sort of consent.'

'Consent to what?' They were completely flummoxed.

Scott tried again. 'What was meant to have happened was that she had come out of the bathroom where she had been washing her face, and was about to sit down and have a drink, when he was meant to have jumped on her.' They watched him talking and he wished he could stop. 'Now if that was right she wouldn't have been taking her watch off just to have a glass of wine, would she? And it seemed to me anyway that taking your watch off is something you do before going to bed, like taking your earrings off. So I said it was taking her watch off that showed what had happened.'

'Oh.' One of the men leaned backwards slowly. 'Clever. That's very clever. I wouldn't have noticed that.'

There had been a small car at Topham Cross, the little Mini with the children, and that must have been Sally's house the car had gone to. Those were her children in the back of the car.

'Do you think that affected it?' Archie asked.

'I don't know, but it enabled me to start the speech well.' Scott hated talking about cases in detail with people who weren't trial lawyers.

'Unless of course she had taken the watch off to wash her hands and face.'

'What?' Scott said.

'Perhaps she took her watch off to wash her face, then

carried it in with her. Lots of people do that, that's why I don't wear one, I leave them on washbasins. I lost one here.'

There was silence.

'There is that, yes,' Archie said after a while. 'But you got him off, Jeremy, that's what's important. The jury were only out for half an hour and I only just got there in time to see him. That's as good as the jury coming straight back. Not guilty. Cheers.' He lifted his glass. 'I wonder how it will affect her?' he said.

'What do you mean?' said Scott.

'Well, what with her being disbelieved by a jury, and all. She's a lawyer, isn't she?'

'She wasn't disbelieved, it was just that they didn't disbelieve him.'

'They didn't disbelieve him when he said she was making it up.'

Scott didn't argue. Of course that's how people would talk about it.

'Didn't want her husband to know. That's what it was, so she had to make it up.'

'I've got to go,' Scott said. 'I'm sorry Archie, but I've got to deliver something to someone at seven-thirty.' He picked up and showed the package. 'I'm late already,' he said, looking at the clock. My God, it was nearly eight.

Lincoln's Inn was deserted. Perhaps Chancery lawyers go home earlier than they claim? That seemed unlikely. Scott hurried down the pavement towards the Wildy's arch, to find it was closed, scaffolding blocking it. He doubled back to Lincoln's Inn Fields, now beginning to trot in his distress at being late. He had said to himself it wasn't far, but of course it was. He had to decide between turning left and then cutting down Bell Yard past Tozer's chambers, or going right down toward the LSE. He swung over to the right and, looking quickly to his left, ran across the road, dropping the packet. He had to stop to pick it up and then wait for a passing line of cars which had appeared from nowhere.

What was he going to say when he met her? 'You've got to ring home, something may have happened to your children, by the way I'm sorry I said what I did.' Should he leave out the bit about her being appointed Treasury counsel?

By the time he arrived at Timoney's it was ten past eight.

It was heaving. The chatter was decibels high. He couldn't see Sally in the benches at the side, and pushed his way round the back. Still no Sally. There didn't seem to be anyone to ask, and then he saw Marriott sitting with two people he had seen before with Sally. Marriott was leaning forward listening to the person opposite him, his hand on his chin, his fingers fanned out in front of him. Scott could see that the buttons on his sleeve were undone, and a gold bracelet hung from his wrist. He disliked him intensely. He didn't want to speak to him, but he was going to have to ask them where Sally was. At least he could say she had told him she was going to be there. As Scott approached, Marriott saw him and leaned back.

'Well, look who it is. Mr Defence Counsel himself. And what do you think of your result? Spiffing, eh?'

Scott didn't reply. He said, 'I've been given a message for Sally Donne by her clerk, and she told me she'd be here at seven-thirty.'

Marriott continued, 'And why did you do the case without leading counsel? Was it because you wanted the chance of attacking Sally yourself?'

This was enough. Scott now disliked Marriott as much as he disliked his client. Amazingly he discovered he was ice cold. He said, 'I did it myself because he asked me to. After all, he knew you well enough, so why didn't he ask you?'

'I wouldn't have done it.'

'Well, you didn't get the chance, did you? Do your friends know that the man who raped Sally Donne is a good friend of yours? Or at least someone who buys you dinner – which is probably the same thing.' It was in him at that moment to hit Marriott in his silly, pursed little face, but he didn't, he turned and left. Again he was followed. It was one of the women sitting opposite Marriott. She said, 'Take no notice of him, he's a shit. She was here. She was sitting with us, hardly talking. Very upset. She was obviously waiting for someone, and then she said, "He's not coming," and went. We asked her where she was going when she left, and she said she was going to look at some pictures. I think I know where she is – she left this on the table.'

She handed Scott a card. It was an invitation to a private view. Paintings by Lachaise: the Connaught Gallery, Albemarle Street. That night.

Timoney's stands a little way back from the Aldwych and Fleet Street, so Scott had to cut up through Essex Street to get to where he might find a cab. It had started to rain. When he reached Fleet Street he could see knots of people standing on either side of him, obviously waiting for cabs as well. He was not going to be able to get one, so he turned and jogged towards the Strand. By now the rain was beginning to soak his suit, and he was sweating. There was a bus stop opposite the church. A number 15 would take him to Piccadilly, wouldn't it?

The rain beat down. He joined the crowd under the shelter. They were all going to Waterloo and the buses seemed to know it. One after another came for Waterloo. He looked at his watch. He'd be lucky to get there by nine. Eventually a bus came and he climbed to the top floor. It was crowded, surprising for so late, and the sweet damp smell of wet clothes filled the air. He found a seat near the front and sat with the parcel on his lap.

Slowly, with sudden and unpredictable lurches, the bus beat its way along the Strand. On either side the shops shone out with light while blanketed shapes settled down under them for the night. What he was going through, what Sally was suffering was nothing compared with them, but then the image of the little Mini trembling at the edge of Topham Cross roundabout intruded, and he saw a lorry hurtling down off the motorway.

Scott tore at the brown paper on the package to take his mind off the image which was gathering. He knew what was in the package: it would be the picture of the woman sitting on the iron bedstead. Her eyes peered out at him in the dark London night. Water dripped from the window next to Scott on to the picture frame. Scott tried to brush it away.

'She was here,' said Anthony Brown. 'Yes, Miss Donne. I know who you mean. We've sent her invitations to private views, but this is the first to which she has responded. I remember selling her that picture. It was a really good buy.

The kind of thing that, once you have bought it, makes it impossible to imagine what your life would have been like without it. Does that sound pretentious? What I meant was that some things become part of your life and you can't imagine not having bought them, and some things don't — and that's in the first category.'

Scott held his wine and listened, though what he wanted to do was to run into the street.

Anthony Brown continued, 'It's stunning. Of course if I wasn't in the business of selling these things I would have to keep them all.'

The gallery was being tidied and wine bottles were being stacked away. The door into the street was open and the room was getting cold. At last he answered the question. 'She only left a few minutes ago. She wasn't here long. Didn't speak much and didn't have a drink. No, I don't know where she went, but I do know she turned left, because I thought to myself that she must be trying to get a taxi. Please come again. Can I put you on our list?'

Scott walked out into the night and turned left. Ahead of him he saw the hotel. He suddenly knew where she had gone. He walked down the road and waited to cross Piccadilly. Traffic eventually became dammed up by the lights and he walked across. By the time he reached the main entrance of the Ritz he was completely soaked. He walked up the steps, ignoring the doorman. The hallway opened up to him and the warm soft air started to dry him immediately. He walked straight ahead with the picture under his arm. On his left a group of women sat at a table with drinks, smoking through long cigarette holders. They looked down on Scott, bedraggled, as he passed, the wrapping from his parcel hanging down.

He approached the entrance to the dining room where a tailcoated man was standing with his back to the door. The man looked up expectantly. Scott didn't stop but walked past towards the large window straight ahead. Under the window he saw a dark-suited man sitting at a table. It was Clarke. He was holding a handkerchief to his face, and on his shoulder was a red stain. There were two waiters standing over him. 'No,' he was saying. 'I want nothing done.'

Then he saw Scott. 'You too?' he said. 'I wondered whose side you were on.'

'That didn't matter,' said Scott. 'My feelings about you are irrelevant.'

'The old, old lie all lawyers use.'

'Where is she?' Scott said. One of the waiters turned and Scott saw a group of staff standing over a chair set the other side of the restaurant. For the first time he noticed that the dining room was completely silent, all the diners looking at where Sally was sitting. He turned and walked over to her.

'It's finished now,' he said, and he took her hand, slowly, gently. She got up and walked with him out of the dining room, and down the passage. He was still clutching the parcel.

'You have to go now,' he said.

She didn't reply. Scott wasn't sure she could even hear him.

They walked out of the hotel. The taxi that would have prevented all this happening was outside waiting. It drove off, and sitting in the corner of the back seat she remembered the bucketing journey to the picture gallery and the cabbie who had said how sad the Old Bailey was.

They eventually reached his car and then she sat cold in the passenger's seat beside him. South London drifted by, orange and cold. She watched it disinterestedly. At the Sun in Sands roundabout, he dropped on to the motorway, and the road uncurled ahead of them. He said, 'We have to go to your home. They've been phoning for you.' For a moment she wanted to ask how he knew this, but it didn't matter.

'I think there's a problem there.' Scott was frightened of speaking, but he had to try. When he got no response he was pleased that he did not have to say what was clattering in his head. He stopped trying.

The car sped on, occasionally coughing; the dashboard lights were too dim to show how much fuel they had. He pulled into a service station, a bright, cold pool of light in the night. He filled the tank, and walked over to pay the cashier. 'Cold night,' the man said. Scott watched Sally sitting silently, not moving. She hated herself.

'Bloody cold,' Scott agreed. He didn't turn his head until he realised he was being rude, then he collected his change and smiled a bright smile before walking out into the night.

Fog appeared as they reached the countryside, drifting up occasionally from the fields lying below the road. It licked at the car as it sped past. Down below it bred in the drainage ditches where Roger Nichols had blown his skull apart. Fog, fog everywhere. Scott swung off the road at Topham Cross. His car flew down the slipway to the junction where Sally's tiny school-run car lay, battered by the side of the road.

Scott stopped his car and got out. The whole side of the car was bashed in, all the windows broken. On the bonnet

337

of the car – there was no windscreen to put it on – there was a sticker saying 'Police Aware'. As Scott looked at the back seat of the car, undamaged, he realised he was looking for blood. There was a school book lying on the floor. He leant in and picked it up. He walked unsteadily back to his car. Realising what he had done he held the book behind him. Sally was sitting with her hand at her throat, rigid.

'What did you get?' she said. He had to hand her the book. She held it for a moment then handed it back. She turned away from him. 'Hurry,' she said.

Scott followed the lane towards Sally's house, able to see by the darkness that came rushing towards them that there was nothing coming. 'Are we going home?' she said.

'Yes,' said Scott, 'that's where they said to go.' What he was doing pressed in on him.

Sally gazed out of the window. Her body felt light. Colours and shapes flashed past her, as the hedges at the side of the road dissolved into a dizzying screen, lifting suddenly out of the darkness and receding into it, eternally present, insisting on the direction. When they arrived Scott was almost moving too fast to take the corner, and he skidded on the gravel as they turned into the driveway of Sally's house. 'Sorry,' he said.

Outside the front door a huge white LandCruiser was parked, the blue police light on the top swinging like a lighthouse. The front door of the house was open and light from inside spilled out, splashing on the ground. They ran to the front door. Inside, the scene frozen as they burst in, they saw two policemen, vast in yellow plastic, one holding Anne Timms by the arm. At the other side of the hall Mrs Hicks was clutching the two children to her legs. They saw Sally and were the first to break the silence.

338

'Mummy.' They ran across the hall and threw themselves at her. Scott breathed out. Sally held them hard, a shudder running through her body.

She looked up eventually and said, 'Are you all right, Anne?'

'Yes,' said Anne. 'I'm all right.'

'Were they with you?'

'No.'

The police officer did not let go of Anne Timms's arm, and with his question he set the tone. 'And who might you be?'

No doubt the way he acted sprang from experience, from the many occasions when he was forced to do it, but because he expected that everyone he dealt with had to be bullied he now had no other language, and it came out all wrong. Scott saw Sally stiffen. She shepherded her children towards the kitchen door, pushed Mrs Hicks through it with them, and then turned towards the officer. She said nothing but walked over to him where he still held Anne Timms's arm. There was fury in her face.

Scott stood on another planet by the front door.

She reached the policeman who, though a foot taller than her, took half a step backwards as she approached. 'I would have thought that completely obvious,' she said. 'Now listen. First you take your hand from that girl's arm, and then tell me what you are doing in my house.'

The distance in all her movements, the vacancy in her eyes and voice had disappeared. For a moment he did nothing, then the policeman dropped his hand.

Sally instantly responded. 'Sit down, Anne, and stay still.' Then she said, 'I am not interested in explanations for a moment. What do you want to do?'

339

It was a simple question. Scott had seen it in police training manuals. What do you do next? It is the question a policeman is always able to answer.

The second officer spoke. 'We want to administer a breath test.'

'That of course you are entitled to do if you have grounds. What are your grounds?'

'We believe she was driving when she had an accident.'

'And were you, Anne?'

Anne Timms was crying in the chair. 'Yes, Miss Donne.'

Sally noticed an instant's pause, or was it a catch in the breath? The officers had not noticed. One was assembling the kit, the other was watching her. 'And have you been drinking?'

Anne did not reply.

'And have you been drinking?'

'No, Miss Donne.'

'But there was an accident?' Sally was not going to risk asking the question in a way that might result in that pause again.

'Yes, Miss Donne.'

'Have you drunk anything since?' Anne wouldn't have done so. Sally had never seen her drink any alcohol. Something was going on here.

'When was this accident?'

The first policeman looked at his watch. 'About four hours ago.'

'All right,' Sally said. 'Go ahead.' The second policeman stepped forward. 'And you,' Sally turned to the first officer, 'please go and turn the light on your car off.' He did as he was told.

The silence stretched out. Sally could hear the policeman's boots crunching on the gravel and looked towards the door. Scott was standing by the door holding the child's book.

Anne blew a long breath into the plastic tube. 'Nothing registering at all,' the officer said, 'no problems.'

'All right,' Sally said. 'Sit down, Anne.'

Anne crumpled into the seat.

'Has this accident been correctly reported?'

'Yes.'

'Do you want Miss Timms to produce her driving papers?' she said to the police.

'Yes.' The first policeman tried to re-establish some control and stepped forward and said, 'You weren't driving, were you? It was that Darren. It was he who rang us.'

'He was with me.'

The officer was moving as though he was about to take hold of her arm again.

'Stop that,' Sally said. 'If you have questions to ask, ask them. But you'll not bully this girl in my house.' It was a direct challenge and was what the officer had been waiting for.

'And what makes you think you are entitled to interfere with me?' he said.

Sally found the despair that had been dragging at her dropping entirely away. After all, this is what she did. What had she been playing at all these weeks with all that maudlin self-examination? She answered the policeman's question directly. 'I can interfere because bullying a young woman at any time, anywhere, let alone in my house, is offensive. And if you continue to do so I shall lodge an immediate complaint with your Chief Inspector.' She

341

turned, showing the way to the door, and continued speaking, not even looking at the policeman. 'I know his name, I have his telephone number. I also have his home number. I suggest you leave now before you do anything you have cause to regret.'

The policeman, like Roger Nichols ahead of him, had met strong women before, but not in this league. Sally watched him back down: she knew he was going to do so before he did himself. 'We shall expect those documents,' he said.

His colleague, who had been standing in the doorway, turned without comment and they left. Scott could hear the gravel kicking up in the drive, heard the car slow as it reached the road and then speed away.

Sally turned to Anne. 'Darren was with you?'

'Yes.' Anne was crying now. Scott watched. The door to the kitchen opened a crack.

'Why did you let him?'

'He said no one would know. He was angry with me for refusing. He threatened me.'

'Mummy . . .' A small voice trickled into the room. Sally stepped forward, took Anne in her arms, and said, 'It's all right now.' She held Anne still for a moment and then said, 'Come in, children. Anne is upset about the crash.' The children came slowly into the room, nervous at the distress. Sally could feel the thin shoulders of the girl shaking gently. How young she was.

'It doesn't matter, Anne. Perhaps now you can get rid of him. He's not worth it.'

Her children came over to her and took hold of her skirt. For a moment all four stood together, held up by Sally.

'But the car, Miss Donne,' Anne said.

'Now don't worry. It's nothing that can't be replaced. These things don't matter in the end.'

They stood together. Sally looked over the head of the crying girl: she was little more than a child really. Sally thought of Sharma, slim in the chambers kitchen, holding the document. Perhaps she was also holding the world at bay. Sally thought of the Temple security guard's daughter, at Oxford taking her degree. She thought of her growing children.

Each of these young girls was edging forward into danger.

But she had managed it. She had survived; she needed to make sure that they could. And she would do so.

Her husband walked in the door. He seemed not to notice what was happening. 'Well done, Sally. Well done.' He was brandishing a list. 'You got it. Treasury counsel, children, your mother's been appointed Treasury counsel. Well done.'

Scott went out to his car. He dropped the school book on the front passenger seat, where it joined the swirl of old newspapers, sandwich wrappers and rubbish that cluttered the footwells, and he leaned over and lifted the torn parcel, still damp from the rain of the bus journey, from the back seat. He went back into the house. 'Sally, I've got the picture you left in London.' He spoke cheerily, as though addressing a meeting. 'Why, hallo,' he said to Sally's husband, seeming to notice him for the first time. 'We've never met. Well, congratulations on her achievement.'

Sally looked at the picture, sat down and put it on her knee. She tore the brown paper slowly away. The innocent, self-assured face of the woman on the iron bedstead stared up at her. Her daughters looked at the picture.

'Who is she, Mummy?' said Jenny.

'What's her name?'

'I don't know,' said Sally, 'but I think she's very beautiful, don't you?'

'There's water on it, there's a drop of water on it.'

'Someone's been crying on it, like Jenny cried on my picture,' Harriet said.

Sally laughed. 'Have you been crying on my picture, Jeremy?'

She brushed the drop away with her hand and looked round, but Scott was gone.